CW01238626

The Wolf of Whindale

Also by Jacob Kerr and available from *Serpent's Tail*:

The Green Man of Eshwood Hall

The Wolf
of Whindale

A Tale of Northalbion

Jacob Kerr

First published in Great Britain in 2025 by
Serpent's Tail,
an imprint of Profile Books Ltd
29 Cloth Fair
London
EC1A 7JQ
www.serpentstail.com

Copyright © Jacob Kerr, 2025

Text design by Crow Books

1 3 5 7 9 10 8 6 4 2

Printed and bound in Great Britain by
CPI Group (UK) Ltd, Croydon, CR0 4YY

The moral right of the author has been asserted.

All rights reserved. Without limiting the rights under copyright reserved above, no part of this publication may be reproduced, stored or introduced into a retrieval system, or transmitted, in any form or by any means (electronic, mechanical, photocopying, recording or otherwise), without the prior written permission of both the copyright owner and the publisher of this book.

A CIP catalogue record for this book is available from the British Library.

We make every effort to make sure our products are safe for the purpose for which they are intended. For more information check our website or contact Authorised Rep Compliance Ltd., Ground Floor, 71 Lower Baggot Street, Dublin, D02 P593, Ireland, www.arccompliance.com

ISBN 978 1 80081 1522
eISBN 978 1 80081 1546

The Wolf of Whindale

For Jeff

O, ye immortal gods! what is theogony?
O, thou too, mortal man! what is philanthropy?
O, world! which was and is, what is cosmogony?
Some people have accused me of misanthropy;
And yet I know no more than the mahogany
That forms this desk, of what they mean; *lykanthropy*
I comprehend; for, without transformation
Men become wolves on any slight occasion.

> Byron, *Don Juan*, Canto IX

If I forget thee, O Jerusalem, let my right hand forget her cunning.

> Psalm 137:5

Contents

Prologue: an extract from a lecture,

    'Mithras Sol Invictus: Mysteries Old and New' [. . .]   1

At Whindale Top   4

The Combination   27

The Scab and the Iron Devil   45

an extract: *op. cit.*   68

The Wolf of Whindale   71

The Pariah   86

At the Sill   106

At Brink House   143

The Tour   167

La Ghoul   187

The Prince and Poor Thomas   218

an extract: *op. cit.*   239

The Knack and the Shift   243

The Plan   262

an extract: *op. cit.*   291

The Prodigal   293

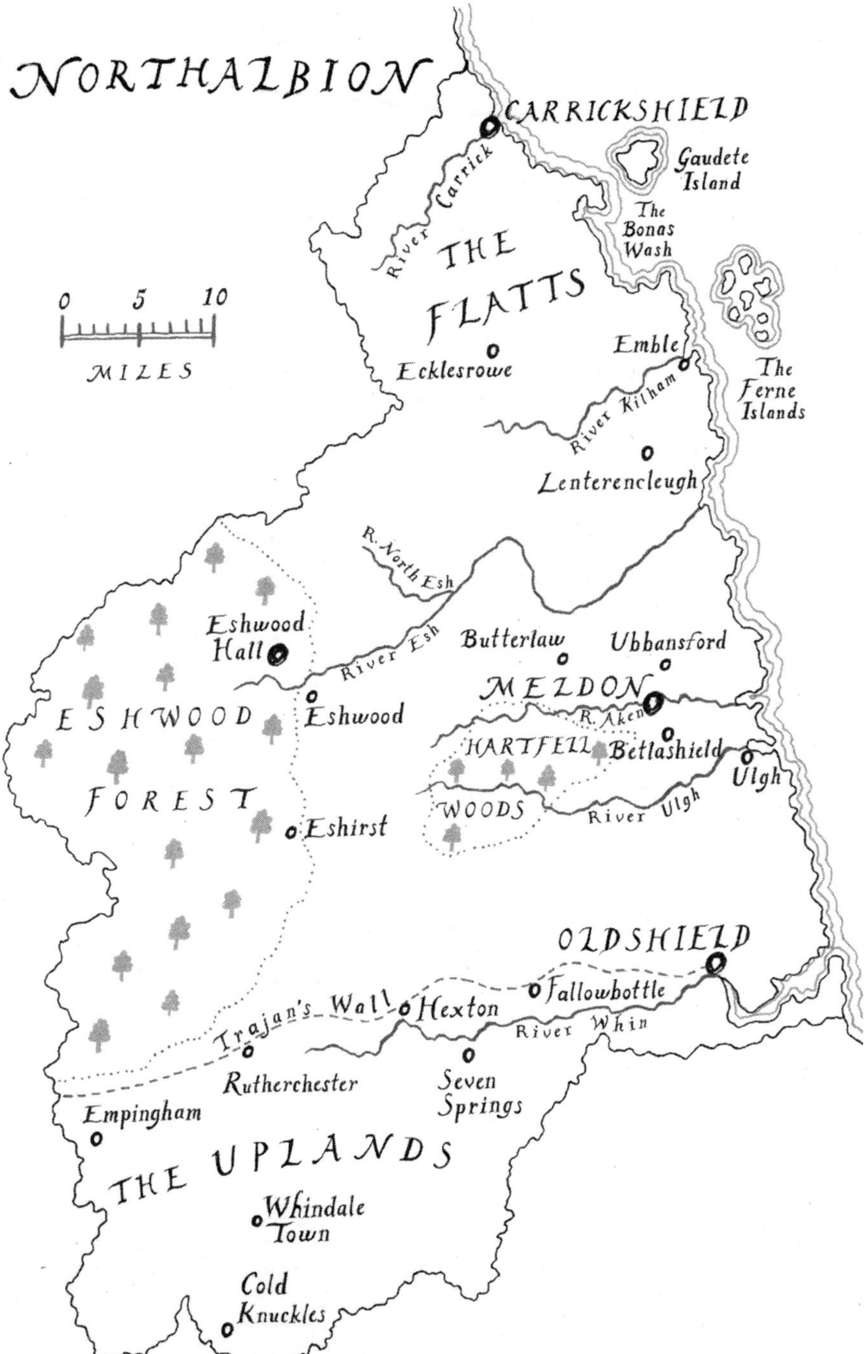
NORTHALBION
0 5 10
MILES
CARRICKSHIELD
Gaudete Island
The Bonas Wash
River Carrick
THE FLATTS
Emble
Ecklesrowe
The Ferne Islands
River Kilham
Lenterencleugh
R. North Esh
Eshwood Hall
River Esh
Butterlaw
Ubbansford
MELDON
Eshwood
R. Aken
ESHWOOD
HARTFELL
Betlashield
Ulgh
FOREST
WOODS
River Ulgh
Eshirst
OLDSHIELD
Fallowbottle
Trajan's Wall
Hexton
River Whin
Rutherchester
Seven Springs
Empingham
THE UPLANDS
Whindale Town
Cold Knuckles

Prologue

an extract from a lecture,
'Mithras Sol Invictus: Mysteries Old and New',
delivered by Dr Erasmus Wintergreen at the Hermetic
Philosophy Library, Oldshield, 18 December 1916

Ladies and gentlemen, I was honoured to be asked here this evening to speak to you all about the mythology and folklore peculiar to Northalbion, and I was delighted when the librarian, Mr Thorne, asked if I might pay especial attention to the lore pertaining to Mithras, the Roman sun-god who was once – long ago, and not since the fourth century, so we have been told – worshipped here, in dedicated temples all along Trajan's Wall. I accepted Mr Thorne's invitation with eagerness and gratitude, and that I encountered a most unexpected difficulty in obliging him is no fault of his. But I am running ahead of myself, so let me begin by introducing our subject.

By the time the cult of Mithras took root in Northalbion, the Roman Empire had spread over much of the known world, from the Nile to the Rhine, from the Black Sea to the ground on which we meet today. As usual, the Romans had set about syncretically absorbing the gods of the local population into their own capacious system, and this is how they came to know of an entity that had inhabited the region known as Northalbion for as long as anyone remembered. What the local population called it has not been recorded, but the Romans called it Mithras, borrowing the name of a Persian god, 𐎷𐎰𐎼 – 'Mitra'. Now, in the Avestan dialect of Old Iranian, 𐎷𐎰𐎼 means contract, agreement, treaty, oath, bargain. Terms would be agreed by shaking hands and swearing on Mitra's name. In one tradition, Mitra was Ba'al's twin brother, and just as Ba'al was the god of darkness and secrets, Mitra was sunlight and truth. The Roman Mithras, it was to be hoped, would retain the qualities associated with the good brother. But twins can be so difficult to tell apart! One twin may even pose as the other, if they have a mind to . . .

In any case, the Romans manufactured new rituals to worship this entity. Now, ladies and gentlemen, in my experience supernatural beings are rather like stray cats: so long as you keep feeding them, they will keep coming back. Soon enough, the entity answered to the name Mithras, or Sol Invictus Mithras, or variants thereof – though, as I say, none of these were its true name. The Romans declared the entity to be a mediator of the divine, sidereal and earthly realms, as well as a god of the intellect, and much else besides. They described it as having a body like a lion, wings like a bat and the face of a beautiful young man.

They depicted it standing, with its right hand raised and its left hand lowered, for its first lesson was the first lesson of all occult systems: *as above, so below*. Mithras, they said, had one hand in the divine realm and one hand in the earthly realm. Mithras, they said, was the one who had shaken hands with the sun – and, like the sun, he saw all things and knew all things. Indeed, his followers believed that the sun had knelt before him, hence his title Sol Invictus. Mithras was the one who spun the great wheel of the zodiac.

But I find myself in a rather awkward position today, for I fear I have come here under a false pretence. When our illustrious librarian, Mr Thorne, so kindly invited me, it was to speak to you all about the mythology associated with Mithras – and yet it has come to my attention that Mithraic worship is not, in actuality, a matter of *mythology* or *folklore* at all. Rather, it is a matter of *religion*. You see, as I plan to demonstrate, Mithras has, in living memory, retained at least some of his worshippers. And, for all I know, he has them yet . . .

I
At Whindale Top

1845

Mr Playfair was dead – his body, found two days afore, had been torn to rags, the head separated from the trunk, ripped right off, and placed on Windy Top, keeping toot, high on the law, a lookout all compassed about with his hands and his feet and his guts. The state of it, the sheer violence of it, led some folk to put two and two together. Even then but, there were others who said no, there was no such thing as the Whindale Wolf. Even then but, there were others who said aye, there *was* such a thing indeed, but that it had never been known to attack a person – as far as anybody knew or could remember, it had only et a sheep chancetimes; and, that being the case, a body – that is, a human body – had maybes killed Mr Playfair and made it *look* like the work of the wolf, with the turning of him inside-out almost, and the rending of his various parts.

Mr Playfair, or what was left of him, had been found by Stephen Myerscough while he was rounding up the sheep he had grazing on the law. He'd run to Whindale and told the parish constable, who, since he had experience in catching rats but none in catching murderers, sent for a constable from Oldshield. Word got round fast – but, still, we'd not have heard tell of Playfair's body being found if it hadn't been for Mr Jobsworth. By day, you see, we'd be at work down the mine, and by night we'd be sleeping in our lodging shop, ten miles south-west over the moors from Whindale Town. We mostly never saw a soul but each other from Monday morning to Saturday afternoon, when we'd head back home to our villages. But the night afore, Mr Jobsworth, who was the consulting engineer for the Whindale Mining Company, had stopped by the lodging shop for to give us the news. So we learned why Playfair hadn't turned up for work all week. Now we were back underground, but were getting nigh-on nowt done, for all we could think of was our old marra.

It was a terrible crime if murder it was, for Mr Playfair had a young boy of three – a bairn, really – young Thomas, and he'd be an orphan now, for his mam had died birthing him; and, besides that, Playfair was a well-liked man. Even I liked him, when it came to it. He was our steward, so to speak: our foreman in matters of combination, which is what you'd call union affairs, and his name was John Plover. I just called him Mr Playfair. And, while I'm at it, I should say, the consulting engineer's name was James Dobsworth. I just called him Mr Jobsworth.

My name's Caleb Malarkey. People have called me all manner of things.

There was six of us in our partnership, working this particular twenty-five-fathom stretch of the vein, and we usually worked in pairs: I was paired with Jack Roebuck (whom I called Mr Crow, because of the sound of his name, and also because of his jet black hair and beard: indeed, he was as hairy a fellow as ever I'd seen); and then George Henry (to whom I bequeathed no nickname) was paired with Zekiel Evans (whom I called Heavens-Evans, on account of his being such a staunch Primitive Methodist); and Mr Plover had been partnered with Lemuel Moughtin (whom I called Mr Muffin).

That day, as ever, we were at work, sixty fathoms deep, digging by candlelight. You cannot do that in a coal mine for the firedamp, but the fumes in a lead-mine are of a different nature and don't ignite, though they do for your lungs in the end. When I say fumes, I don't just mean the stench of tallow and the reek of the thunder-box, though that was bad enough – I also mean the dust, for it's five to one a lead-miner's apt to die of dust or the consumption afore he dies by accident or owt else. Still though but, it was pleasant and creaturely, much of the time, to be down there like a brock in his sett, or like rabbits in a warren, with the sobbing, flickering candle flames glistering off the spar so the walls seemed speckled with crumbs of light, all a-twinkle.

We were tight in our pairs, and in our partnership, and you might even say that we were tight with the agents and engineers and mine owners, for we shared a common dream: all the while we were digging, we were dreaming, you see, dreaming that we'd be lucky and fall in with rich ore. If that were to happen, we'd all be the richer for it, not just the mine owner, whoever that happened to be at the time, for our wages were tied to the value of the ore we dug. That was our bargain. We shared in the gamble, and we'd share in the rewards – or the misfortune, according to happenstance. But to work like that at keeping up a dream takes a toll on you. It breeds uncertainty and suspicion. The way we'd speak of the vein was testimony to this:

'She's frightened to climb yon hill, I tell you, and swins away to the sun side!'

'Aye, deek at how she throws the north cheek up!'

To hear us on, you'd think we were engaged in capturing a wily beast, or guessing at a lover's caprice, or rationalising the interventions of a moody god. The lead was like a force – a living thing, that is to say – and we'd call our waterfalls and waterways forces, too. We worked at the mercy of these forces, for we used waterwheels in our trade, so a drought could mean weeks off work, and torrential rain was just as bad. The water would 'quit us out', we'd say. But, really, everyone lives in a world of forces, regardless of whether they care to name them.

The grove – for that's what we'd tend to call a lead-mine, a grove – was on the eastern flank of Windy Top. All of this is by the by, but, still, you should know it, so I'll get you told afore I forget: a vein of lead runs vertical like a fluted curtain – as opposed to coal, which puddles horizontal – and this lead curtain is bottomless or, at the least, it's deeper than man can delve. She was a strong vein at Windy Top, running east and west. Against her north cheek was a soft dowk, partly shivery, and fornenst it a cawk or spar about a yard wide, joined on the south by a strong rider three or four yards wide, the southernmost portion being mostly pearl spar or calc spar, in which lay ribs of ore four or five or six inches across. Sometimes, instead of being ribbed, the spar was flowered with ore, and all mixed up in the matrix of the vein there'd be zinc blende, copper and iron pyrites, and various species of what-have-you. And here and there the vein would form a sort of flat, and the pearl spar would flutter in amongst the riders towards the north cheek. She was bonny to look at.

At four-and-twenty, I was the youngest of us; hardly a bairn, you may say – but sometimes it matters that all your peers are your elders, as it can be like being the last-born of many brothers, which is to say it's a condition you never altogether escape, howsoever long you live. To make the matter more apparent, it was the style then for a fellow to have long moustaches, and I could never grow mine. I affected a disdain for the fashion, which didn't fool anybody. As George Henry liked to say, I still had my milk face. Anyway, a man's youth is a strange quality that dies hard, and is apt to throw off freaks and flukes and sports long after it should have said its say. So it was with me, in any case, and in consequence I cannot speak with complete authority regarding my choices back then, for I was all but a different man entirely, having so little to regret and so much to dream of doing; whereas today those categories are transposed. And I can give you, besides that, another reason not to wholly believe what I have to tell you: to be young is often to be bored – you've no time for it later – and to be bored is to be capricious. Many's the choice I made for really no better reason than I was eager to see whether I could set an action in motion, or upset a thing from progressing in its natural course. It seems to me now that there was often no more accountability in my behaviour than that of a kitten left alone with a ball of wool. Though, had you asked me at the time, I'd have given you, no doubt, all manner of hifalutin reasonings.

Anyways, I was young, and many around me were doing their best to tolerate it. Principally there was my mam and my sister, Mary, whom I called Mop. Now, I've no memory of what Mam was like afore Dad, as Mam put it, 'buggered off back to Ireland', but I think she must have been very different – less severe in her religion anyway, for by the time I got to know her she was as good and bitter a churchwoman as you could hope to meet. Even as a child, it seemed to me that she'd tied all the loose ends Dad left behind to the church, so, if you followed any one of the threads of her life for any distance, you'd find yourself back there afore you knew it. When I was a bairn I had no choice but to get caught up in it, singing the hymns with all my might and crying myself to sleep with fears of my imaginary sinfulness, but as I got older the hellfire burnt out, and I began to suspect I'd been fed on ashes, and my childish heart deceived.

Mop was different, or – no: by the time of our story

she was as like Mam as a pea's like a pea, but at one time she could have been different. Yes, things could have been different for Mop. I mind how, as a child, she had a passion for pear drops, and to this day the smell of a sweetie shop brings her back to me, as she was when me and her was thick as thieves. I made it a policy always to keep a poke of pear drops handy, so as to be sure to have something to bribe her with if the need suddenly arose. I hid them in the cavity of the tall clock, which seems a very obvious hidey-hole now that I think of it, but she never jealoused them. When Mam was raging at the wicked world and at Dad for having buggered off, and Mop was in mortal need of a treat, I'd tap her on the shoulder and say 'Look what I found . . .' and so things wouldn't seem as bad for a spell. But I suppose there's only so long you can hold the world at bay that way, and when she got to be twelve years old or so, she took a turn. She disdained fancy-work, and read nowt but the Bible. More and more, she would keep to herself, or cleave to Mam, and she put away childish things and wouldn't play at marbles or jack-ball. In short, she came out against both pear drops and me, saying that I was tempting her, and that she would be good and reject them forthwith, for they were worldly things, and had a fulsome, vulgar smell, and so on and so forth, until I knew that she'd gone down the selfsame path as Mam, and had tied herself to the selfsame church, which only made me detest it all the more. As a consequence of Dad's having buggered off, I was stuck supporting them – and they were stuck being supported by me, for the only work they were qualified to do was pick stones out of rich men's land, which was hard labour and paid a pittance. In short, we were each other's gaolers and each other's prisoners, and there was no end to it in sight.

'What's the difference atween a wolf and a dog anyway?' someone asked, of no one in particular, back in the gloom of the grove. We'd been thinking of Mr Playfair all the while. For weeks now, the Whindale Wolf had slunk and skulked in the peripherals of our waking thoughts, but now it was front and centre. Mr Crow took it upon himself to frame an answer, for he fancied himself a natural philosopher.

'Well, first, there's the size, of course. This isn't such a great difference, speaking in general, but our particular wolf appears to be a creature of unusual proportions, a freak of nature. Mr Plover was no small man. Also, I'm told that the bite marks that our wolf leaves on the sheep it kills are bigger than those of any dog. So there's that: there's the size difference. And you cannot tame a wolf, neither: that's the second great difference. A dog likes to be trained, to know his place in the order of things, but with a wolf, the training won't take, and you'll never can trust him . . .'

We let Mr Crow blether on for a bit, for it was pleasant to have a body to listen to while we worked, if there wasn't a song being passed about, as often enough there was – though on no account is whistling allowed down a mine of any sort; it is with miners as it is with seamen, and for as mysterious a reason. Anyways, eventually, George Henry, who was an umbrageous and polrumptious sort, put it to Mr Crow that, for all his flannel, he knew no more about wolves than the rest of us, whereupon Crow fell to scratching his great black beard, as he did whenever he was put to the blush. Over bait we talked it out in the round, and this proved to be more effectual than any one of our attempts to speak authoritatively.

When was the last wolf killed and caught in England? According to Mr Muffin, it had been hunted down by Prince Edgar in fifteen-hundred-and-something-or-other, but there had been wolves in Scotland and in Ireland as recently as eighty years since, and Scotland was as nigh as damn-it, so owt was possible. Anyways, Heavens-Evans said, it was widely understood that the lonelier parts of Wales yet teemed with the beasts.

Wasn't there an English king killed by the wolves he was a-hunting? There was indeed: Bad King Memprys – and, though we couldn't agree on the year, we were sure it must have happened in January, which was of old called the wolf month, this being when the creatures were especially hungry and cruel. And hadn't Bad King Memprys come back from the dead, as a wolf? No, someone said, that was Bad King John, who had in life brought famine to the people.

We pooled a number of proverbs into the bargain: I repeated the old farmers' saying, 'Better a wolf in the field than a fair February.' 'Life to the wolf is death to the lamb,' said Mr Crow. And even Heavens-Evans made a contribution, somewhat reluctantly though but, for he didn't much want to encourage the discussion, 'Speak of the wolf and his tail appears, or so I have heard it bruited among the vulgar.' Mr Crow was minded of an old ballad, from the days of the reivers, which ran thus:

> *They spairit neither man nor wyfe,*
> *Young or old of mankind that bare lyfe,*
> *Like wilde wolfis in furiositie,*
> *Baith brint and slewe with greate crueltie . . .*

I thought this a very barbarous lay, and said so, and Heavens-Evans agreed, until I made plain that I spoke in reference to its rough numbers and not to its subject matter, which I entirely approved of. George Henry made no contribution, except to say that listing proverbs was a foolish enterprise, to which I could not resist replying '*lupus non timet canem latrantem.*'

All the while we worked, we'd be hearing the great wheel turn. It was an enormous thing, buried deep in the grove, a wooden wheel maybes twenty-five feet across, and, the whole time we were down there, it would be pulling down great tubs of water from on bank, and with the water came fresh air, and that's how we didn't suffocate from the chokedamp and the stithe. Wherever we happened to be, we'd hear the wheel going cluck-clunk, like the slow, steady heartbeat of the earth itself, sometimes up close and unignorable, sometimes faint and unthought of as the beat of our own pulses. It was a reassuring sound, and made a fellow feel less lonely down in the depths.

'What about you, Caleb?' says Mr Muffin to me on this particular day. 'You've been uncharacteristically quiet on the matter. Do you think Mr Plover was killed by the wolf?'

In truth, I was undecided on the matter, but since the talk was tending one way, I found myself arguing the other, as was and is my wont. So I says no, there's no such thing as the Whindale Wolf.

I might have left it at that, but Mr Muffin keeps on. 'So, what, you reckon it was murder, is that it?'

I says I supposed so, and that such seemed likeliest, unless Mr Playfair had tripped over a toadstool while taking the long way home.

'Likeliest, eh? And who's the *likeliest* suspect in this case of murder, Caleb, oh ye who are so wise?'

I could see that Mr Muffin was goading me, but I have ever found annoyance to be conducive to fluency, so I found myself saying that the party with most to gain was none other than the mine owner.

'Dobsworth? You think James Dobsworth was up on the law at yon time o' night tearing Mr Plover to bits and pieces?' Now, here Mr Muffin was being obtuse. Mr Jobsworth was no more the mine owner than I was; he was merely the consulting engineer, and he'd drop by once a month to make sure we were behaving ourselves. Even the company didn't exactly *own* the mine; they held the lease of it from the bishop of the diocese, but it was ultimately the property of the Crown.

'I say nowt of the sort. I say only that, with a strike about to begin, the party with most to gain from the death of our foreman is surely the mine owner. And Mr Jobsworth is Brinsley Siskin's man now, if what I've heard is true. I don't suppose Master Siskin does his own dirty work, but he's set to gain most from this, all the same.' What I was getting at was how, while Playfair was kicking around, there had been a chance of organising the men and us all combining with the one will, for Playfair had a way with him in such matters, though it pained me to admit it. I had, in fact, argued bitterly against the strike. He and I had rarely seen eye to eye, but now he was dead and the rest of us were in a new dispensation, like unto so many lost sheep, and we'd have to wait for the fog to clear and then see where we stood. We were going on strike because there'd been a move to change the bargain and put us all on fixed hours per week, and Playfair had persuaded us that our current state of affairs, in which we all shared in the dream together, kept the various parties from being conspicuously dishonest, in that anyone who tried to run a concern on skinflint principles would likely have no more success than he deserved.

'So once again you reckon yourself best informed, eh, Caleb? And what are the rest of us doing? Casting about in the dark?'

Mr Muffin was trying to wind me up, and I considered pointing out that casting about in the dark was very precisely what we were doing, but no, I let that cup pass and merely said, 'If fools went not to market, bad wares would never get sold, and then what?'

Mr Muffin had been behaving queerly all day. He was practically idle, not having his second, Mr Playfair, to work with. If you were digging shale you could work alone with a poll-pick, but with limestone you had to work in pairs, you see: one of you would hold a picker against the rock face, balancing it on your shoulder, and your workmate would whack the back of it with a hammer. And this was done by candlelight, so the back-man needed to have a good aim, and the foremost man needed to be the trusting sort. You gave the picker a twist just as it was struck, and that stopped it from getting jammed. Sometimes this split the rock clean away; at other times, you'd use this method to drill into the rock, after which you'd use a sort of long spoon to scrape out the hole, then you'd poke in some black powder wrapped in paper, and bung it with some thill and shale. Then you'd poke a tiny hole through to the black powder to lay your fuse. After that, you lit the fuse and scarpered, crying 'Put nowt down!', which was the warning signal. When a miner heard those words, he knew to stay stock still and look sharp, for a blast was on the way.

Anyway, Muffin was idle now, without Playfair. He'd nowt but time to loaf and offer his opinion on sundry matters. Maybes Muffin was upset at the loss of his marra, or maybes there was an absence where Playfair had once been, and Muffin was looking to fill it. I got to thinking how this was like a goaf, which is what we'd call the cavity left behind once we'd excavated a portion of the vein. A goaf was a big empty space, all held up with props and such, and it was apt to fill with water or else be filled more dramatically by gravity, collapsing under its own weight. I muttered 'Muffin's a goaf, Muffin's a goaf,' and had a bit giggle to think that these words had likely never been uttered together afore.

Mr Crow changed the subject then, and said that the answer was surely to buy some land of our own and to make sure aforehand it had the sugar under it. (That's what we called it: the sugar. I should have got you told that. Only them that's never dug for it call it lead. It's the same with coal: a pitman won't call it such, for he'll want to specify what variety of coal he's on about – band or brat, swad or dant, cannel or claggy, crow or parrot, and so forth. If he has to refer generally to the thing itself, he's apt to call it black diamonds.) Mr Crow recollected how his grandfather, Old Roebuck, had been able to find the sugar by means of a hazel rod, which, when he held it just so, balanced twixt finger and thumb, would twitch in the general direction of lead, for he had the gift.

The doctrine of *Virgula Divina*, to give it its grander airs, was largely disbelieved by our times, and Heavens-Evans was quick to say that such superstitions had no place in the life of a Christian.

George Henry scoffed at that, and said that if it truly pointed to where the sugar was, we'd every one of us be at it, Christian or no.

Crow said it was academical in any case, as his dad had also tried his hand at the hazel rod trick but never had any luck, so the gift was not a birthright, evidently.

This led to much talk of fathers, as often happened in our line of work, for you'd naturally follow your dad in whatsoever specialism he had. Only a fool would have asked a fellow why he'd decided to become, say, an enginewright: he'd've done so because his dad had been one, or else he'd been a wheelwright or some such related thing. Not having a dad, I held my tongue and let them blether.

When Dad buggered off back to Ireland, he left nowt behind but his shelf of books, and my abiding image of the man is of him sitting in his chair, which subsequently became my chair, reading in one of his books, all of which subsequently became my books. This was my treasure, and unlike the items a more usual child might revere, as of an abacus or a doll or conkers, it was precious indeed. Dad had me and Mop reading so soon as we were able, and it became a lifelong habit with me, and even now, whenever I hear a new word, I find that it sticks to me the way a burr sticks to a badger's arse, until, still a bairn, I fairly bristled with the things.

I'd be doing much of this reading on the sly, for Mam was a creature of flinty stricture and rigidity of habit, and she mistrusted free thinking of any variety. She might have loved me, I think, had I been born a dunce. Alas. Soon enough, I'd read through Dad's shelf, and had to return and exhaust it once again. Like Mr Montaigne, I might say that I'd a skipping wit when it came to the plodding occupation of books, and soon as one grew tedious I cast it aside and took up another; but in truth, though my appetite was precocious, I understood hardly a tenth of what my eyes passed over, as would have been evident had anyone enquired of my opinion, though none ever did. I was learning the words for things, you see, but not the things themselves. So it seems to me now.

At length, I became frustrated with this endless reading that seemed to avail so little, and so I began to develop a new, contrarian system of engagement, and it is to this I ascribe the growth of my mind. If I was feeling especially happy and zestful, I read from Mr Burton's *Anatomy of Melancholy*; if I was glum and fixed on a particular complaint, some of Mr Montaigne's essays would lift me and shake me; if I was feeling wrathful or prideful or lusty or fantastical, I read from Thomas Browne's Christian morals; if Mam succeeded in forcing me to read any of Mr Foxe's *Book of Martyrs*, I doused the flames of righteousness with the cool sense of Mr Hooker's *Ecclesiastical Polity*; and if I was ever bored, I turned to James Thomson's poetry, which was so monumentally dull that my everyday tedium seemed a cornucopia of incident in comparison. And always we read the Bible, and we also had books of hymns and sermons, as well as volumes of Shakespeare, Milton, Sterne, Godwin, Byron and others, and books by John Bunyan, of course, as every house has them, all of which I made sure to read, upon sound contrarian principles, whenever I felt least inclined to do so – and thus I conjured the spirit of contradiction that was and is the presiding genius of my life.

Now, maybes it happened because I was thinking on my dad and maybes it happened because it was due, but at this point I had a seizure. I should have got you told about that: I have seizures, now and then. It must be unsettling for them that's around me at the time, as I'm told that I look ghastly when it comes upon me: my face bloodless, and with my eyes var-nigh popping out my skull, and my mouth pulled in tight like a drawstring. Certainly, it's unsettling for *me*, because whenever I take a turn I have queer visions that I suppose are like dreams, but they feel more real than dreams. More real, I reckon, than reality itself.

In my vision, I was just working as usual, howking at some shale and clearing it out of the way, when along comes my father, easy as you like, as if he'd just fancied stopping by to pass the time with me all the same. He was dressed well, in country velveteen and pilot coat, and looked to be about the same age as myself, though whether this meant he'd died at that age, and therefore his spirit had aged no further, or if it was simply because he must have been about that age when my infant eyes last apprehended him, I cannot say. We fell into talk like we were old friends and, though most of it is now past my recall, I remember wanting very much to tell him something, but failing to do so, which frustrated me, and when I tried to bring to mind what it was I should be saying, I could not do it, which annoyed me the more. My marras worked on and never minded our visitor. Next thing after that, he was leading me down tunnels I hadn't known were there, and we seemed to be descending ever deeper into the earth, until we were fathoms deep in the gloom, just the two of us, and then we came to a stop and I realised that we was now stood in a crypt, not a mine, and my father was ganging to and fro lighting the candles that were arranged about the place. Now my father was pointing to the inscription on the side of one of the tombs. He didn't move, only waited for me to respond to his direction. I crept forward and squinnied at the letters cut into the slate. I understood them to read *ex homine commutatus nuper in lupus*. I'd enough Latin to ken what that meant. I glanced up at my dad, who was looking very grim now. And then I looked back to see whose grave this was – and, when I read the name, I awoke with a great cry, whereupon this detail instantly vanished from my memory.

I came to to find Mr Crow watching over me. He'd always make me as comfortable as was possible in such a place.

'Is he still away with the fairies?' asked George Henry, looking at me with suspicion, as if I might be putting it on. He did this every time I took a turn. He ran on fixed lines, as a wagon-tub on its rails. Habitual anger will do this to a fellow. Mr Crow ignored him.

Mr Muffin was talking of Walter Corlett, who had worked at a grove up towards Rutherchester, and who had disappeared three months since. Nobody had thought owt about it at the time, for none of us knew Mr Corlett especially well, and his vanishing seemed not worth gaping at. It had been generally assumed that he'd struck off on a hunt for metals more precious than lead in foreign mines. So I'd adjudged the matter, anyway.

'But wasn't Mr Corlett an associate of Mr Plover?' asked Mr Crow.

Mr Muffin confirmed that he was an associate and, more than that, a friend. Corlett and Playfair had attended the lectures over in Hexton concerning political economy, and they'd shared all sorts of theories on these and related matters.

There was a bit of quiet after Muffin said this, as we each chewed it over: two friends, one disappeared and tother torn to bits, inside three months . . .

George Henry broke the silence, and to no more effect than was his wont. 'I think he went to the Sill, like as not, and if he left behind a green girl with a green gown, well, he wasn't the first.'

That's how we'd talk about it, the Sill. We'd say, 'Well, there's always the Sill.' Or, 'Next thing, you'll be off to the Sill.' Or, say, at a hasty wedding, some wiseacre might observe that it had been a coin toss between this and a career at the Sill . . . It was a name that filled out a proverb, and hardly seemed connected to an actual place. But it was a real place all the same though but, and real bodies had gone there to work and die. It was away off to the northeast, somewhere by Trajan's Wall, var-nigh in Scotland. As to what it was like there, we could but guess, for no man had ever come back to tell of it.

'They are the *residuum*,' George Henry had said, once, of the fellows who had vanished thus. Ever since he'd attended a lecture by Samuel Smiles, George Henry held that the poor were poor because of idleness, and, in short, that what a body got was an unfailing index of what a body deserved. I found it very amusing that a doctrine of industriousness should so promote idleness of the intellect, for, after George Henry had accepted Sir Smiles's one idea, it seemed he would never be required – or, eventually, be able – to entertain another.

Sill means trouble, Sill means trap. That was another of our proverbials. What we meant was that the metalliferous limestone in that region was understood to give way to an exposed bed of trap – which was our name for any dark stone that broke in pieces of a rhomboidal figure, and consequently exhibited steps like a staircase. In the case of the Sill, the trap-bed was whinstone, which we'd sometimes refer to as 'trouble', it being a hard, volcanic substance, difficult to manage, and having queer properties: if it ran too close by a seam of coal, then it would turn the coal to coke, and so forth. Today, you'd call it dolerite, but back then we called it whinstone.

As for what was being mined at the Sill, nobody rightly knew, but it mustn't have been coal and it wasn't lead: no one had ever seen wagons coming or ganging out-by, and it was as far from a railway line as could be. Indeed, the Sill seemed to be a vast but entirely unproductive concern. Mind, this wasn't as strange as it might sound, for many's the grove that turned but little profit. Indeed, it seemed to us that those with money passed their leisure hours by buying up each other's debt, or else writing off a debt by handing over ownership of a mining concern, or else a body would get married and acquire a lead-mine and a debt into the bargain. It was all we could do to keep track of who the present owner was, and who we worked for.

Some thought they must be digging for jewels at the Sill, but the mineral field had never yielded owt more precious than a bit of silver all intermeddled with the lead – *argentiferous galena* to give it its scholarly name. You'd could only get at the silver if you knew the delivering process patented by Mr Pattinson, where you arrange nine iron pots and heat them, and then melt the ore in the middle pot, and then, as it cools, you skim off the lead into one set of pots and the silver into the tother. Eventually you've got your dab of silver all right, maybes two ounces of it in a ton of lead ore, but it's hardly worth the faff. It wasn't *wageable*, we'd say. Other folk believed that those at the Sill were simply digging in search of a new seam of lead, but they hadn't found it yet and so they dug on, and so it had been for decades. I found it hard to credit this idea – a mine owner like a gambler on a losing streak who refuses to cut his losses! – but I would live and learn more about the strange ways of wealthy folk.

Mr Muffin chirps up now, and says it might be that the wolf has claimed more victims than we realise. Mr Plover, Mr Corlett . . . and who knew when the beast found a taste for human flesh?

The illogic of it all overwhelmed me, and, though still light-headed from my seizure, I sat up and found myself holding forth on how the deaths of two such fellows, both leaders of combinations of miners, was an almighty coincidence, and that this wolf's palate was certainly a dainty one in preferring flavours that secured the interests of the status quo.

Nobody said owt for a moment or two, and it seemed a relief when Mr Crow said, 'Plover's death is a blow to us, but, I tell you, it's a worse blow to his laddie, Thomas. That's both of his parents in the bosom of the Lord. When he grows up, he'll inherit his father's name and his father's debt and nowt but.'

And someone says 'Debt? How's that?' And Mr Crow says Playfair had died owing thirteen pound in back-rent.

'And him the gaffer!' says George Henry, laughing, as he did when he was up a height or disgusted. 'This is no kind of work. Mark my words, the criminals have it easier, I swear to Christ they do. The criminals in Botany Bay are laughing at us, even now. They're pissing their moleskins laughing at the thought of us cavilled here picking for sugar in a frigid hill!'

And then Mr Crow, who was forever singing or – when we were above ground – whistling some tune or other, took up the ballad that had been doing the rounds.

> *Had I my time to live again*
> *Had I my soul to save*
> *I'd never see Van Diemen's land*
> *Nor sail the ocean's wave:*
> *I'd rather kill a judge and swing*
> *Upon the gallows high*
> *Than live to be a convict here*
> *And here a convict die!*

We sang it through and around again. *We toil in chains and die in shame and fill forgotten graves.*

And then Heavens-Evans says, 'What's to become of young Thomas Plover, then but?'

'There's nobody but Plover's mam left to raise him, and she's on the way out. She's as thin as a sheet. Next winter will see her in the churchyard, you mind.'

'And once that happens, Poor Thomas will be carted off to the orphanage,' says I.

'They're like to set him on as a washer-boy soon enough, are they not?' says Mr Crow, to which George Henry says darkly,

'He'd be better looked after down here in the bowels of the earth with the likes of us.'

There were murmurs of agreement all round at this, for we all knew a washer-boy had a hard life, whether he was hotching his chats or shaddering ore on the knockstone, all under the eye – and under the heavy stick – of the Washing Master, whose jacket was white but whose heart was as hard and as black as the bowler hat on his head. It was a rough cavil, to be a washer-boy.

'It's Master Siskin who owns that orphanage, is it not?' says Heavens-Evans.

I says aye, it was indeed, and that fate was a mistress with a cruel sense of humour, and when she found a poor man with a plan, the old bitch licked her teeth.

Heavens-Evans misliked such dark murmurings, and said I'd no grounds to say such things. Mr Plover, he reckoned, had died of natural causes, like as not, and then after that the buzzards and the foxes and what-have-you would have been at him, making everything look worse than really it was.

And so you see, even then but, there were some like me who said no, there was no such thing as the Whindale Wolf.

2

The Combination

So that was Friday – and we had agreed to strike on the Monday. This had been Mr Playfair's initiative. He said that the mine owner was changing the bargain by asking us to agree to work to fixed-hour shifts per week. This, Playfair had contended, was no halfpenny matter. We'd always worked our own bargain and set our own shifts till then, you see, and we'd usually work every hour we could anyway, but we were free to change our plans, if it came to it, and work less one day and more the next or what-have-you. Playfair's point was that the mine owner had no right to make us give our word to do what we were already doing in good faith, as it amounted to giving away our word altogether. We were all dreaming together, and it was in everybody's interests to work and to find the sugar. If it was there, then we'd look sharp and find it, and we'd all be the richer for it; and if it wasn't, then what advantage was it to have dug in vain by fixed working hours? Why change the bargain merely to make it the more inefficient?

The rest of us weren't so sure that this was so great a matter, but nobody else seemed willing to put up much of argument against Playfair, so I took it upon myself to say I saw no sin in writing up a bargain we had effectually already agreed upon. But Playfair reckoned that it was nowt of the sort, and that this alteration was as subtle as the serpent in Eden. Fellows coming together in good will to accomplish a task, and divvying up the jobs accordingly, was one thing; but for us to agree to work fixed hours, nor more nor less, regular as clockwork scarecrows, was another – we'd be putting ourselves in thrall to the job; we'd be at the mercy of any bailiff with a pocketwatch; we'd be reduced, at length, to mere automata.

Back and forth we went, with Playfair making much of the principle of the thing, and asking if I was a pig would I agree to be pork? To the which I said no, but once I'd been made into a sausage there was no point in denying the fact. And so forth. And, as we argued either side, I noticed a strange thing happening, and not for the first time, neither: the more stronglier I argued against Playfair, the more the other fellows seemed to agree with him. Well, they thought I was a bit touched, of course, on account of the seizures, so my recommendations carried little weight with them. At the finish, I felt like Playfair was herding them together like sheep, and using me as his collie. I'd unwittingly played this role again when I'd speculated about Playfair's death benefitting the mine owner; this had seemed to harden everyone's resolve to go through with the strike, though that hadn't been my intention. I was just putting my two-penneth in, for pity's sake.

We had to combine, Playfair was forever insisting. That was his favourite word, 'combine'. In our combining lay our strength, he said, and the proof of that was the way our employers were always trying to prevent us from doing it, and asking us to agree not to do it, as part of our bargain. And a further proof could be found in the fact that our employers would themselves combine, on occasion, if and when it suited them, so as to enforce this very stipulation, which was rank hypocrisy. The more of us combined, the stronger we'd be, so Playfair would say.

But the manner in which we were paid made it hard to organise the men into a combination. Some of the fellows in our line of work were paid a daily or a weekly rate – the blacksmiths, stonemasons, joiners and what-have-you – whereas us miners got thirty shillings a month, but that was in lent money, which meant at year's-end you had to settle your account, according to how far you'd dug or how much ore you'd extracted: if you'd been lucky you'd get what we called a Great Pay. Some fellows made sixty pounds a year that way, or so it was said. But if you'd been unlucky, then maybe you hadn't made as much as had been lent you, and that's you in debt to the company. In any case, it was difficult for Playfair to ask the fellows for dues when the money wasn't rightly theirs as yet – and, of course, the mine owner had us over a barrel, as he'd put a stop to the lent money the minute we went on strike.

But Playfair had a way about him, and I'd given matters a nudge and all, as I've said, and in the event all of us miners had thrown in our lot with the strike: the lads I worked with at Windy Top and also the other partnerships, from Seven Springs to Empingham and beyond. On the Saturday, word went round confirming the strike was on. This was accomplished in the usual style, with fellows parading through Whindale Town carrying tin baths and bashing and wellying them like drums, yelling that there'd be no work for the foreseeable, which was a canny spectacle and always drew a crowd.

So on Monday morning, rather than setting out at the crack of dawn on the ten-mile walk to the grove, we found ourselves at large in Whindale, the town we never usually got to see on weekdays, swaggering about like soldiers come home from a war. The weather being fair, we made the village green our camp, so to speak, as it was bordered on three sides by inns and taverns, making it very convenient. That's where the most of us was gathered when Dobsworth-the-Jobsworth traipsed into town. He knew the score, as we'd officially informed him of our intentions. Still, it was all very awkward for him, I think, given that, when all was said and done, he was in the pocket of the mine owner, however much he wanted to pretend we were all friends and neighbours. Very entertaining I found it, to lie on the grass and smoke a pipe and watch him try to navigate that narrow and thorny way; I felt as an angel must feel to witness our human wrassling while we endeavour to serve both God and Mammon.

I decided to get the skirmish started, and asked Jobsworth how Mr Gould and Mr Baring were doing – for these were the names of the previous mine owners, who had recently been bought out by Master Siskin, and I wanted to see if Jobsworth was prepared to tell a barefaced lie with regard to the identity of his employer; but he dodged the issue by neither saying aye nor no, and not looking me in the eye. So I pressed him further, and asked him directly if it wasn't the case that the grove at Windy Top was owned by Master Siskin now?

'I don't see that it makes a great deal of difference, Caleb. What's it to us, whoever owns the grove?'

'"Us" is good, Mr Jobsworth. *Us.* Very good. But I'm a fellow who likes to know who he's dealing with. And, furthermore, I'm a fellow who likes to deal with a fellow who likes to know who he's dealing with.'

Why I should be so predisposed to swing a sledgehammer merely to crack open a peanut is beyond me, but, anyways, Mr Jobsworth heaves a sigh and says that yes, he gathered that Master Siskin had bought out Messrs Gould and Baring, but what was that to anyone, whether or no? He said these words to me, but his bearing was towards my workmates; he was silently insinuating that my questions were of interest to no one but myself, and, indeed, since none of my workmates chimed in, he might have been right.

Having thus asserted a kind of grouping, with me on the one side and him and my workmates on tother, Mr Jobsworth held forth for a time with what seemed a rangy, rambling assortment of observations. First of all, he was in great sympathy with us; that seemed to be what he wished us to understand. Even so though but, and he said this by the by, he knew for a fact that, over in Mexico, there were miners working for a fraction of what we were paid. And they lived in miserable huts it would be no hard task to erect in a single day. To the which, someone asked, did he think we lived in pomp and finery? (I thought of the shieling I lived in with Mam and Mop, which, though it had walls of stone, was little better than a hut when all is told; to give the place the appearance of comfort, we'd put some paper over the walls, but the wind would get under it and, between that and the canvas we'd drawn over the rafters as our ceiling, the whole house appeared to wheeze and shiver continually.) To which he said no, but these fellows, over in Mexico, they lived crammed in a hut without so much as a bed to sleep in. (We'd two box-beds in our shieling, one for me and the tother for Mam and Mop, and, apart from that, nowt but a deal table where Mam would make bread and that.) And, he added, they subsided thus without even a knife or fork or spoon to convey the beans to their mouths. To the which, someone asked, did he think we should be grateful for our cutlery? To the which he said no, but these poor Mexican fellows, they wore the same clothes in the grove and at home, and on Sunday as on everyday. To the which nobody said owt for a moment, for it would indeed have been a blow not to have had a change of clothes on a Sunday at least, as we were all not a little proud of our waistcoats, which brought a splash of colour to our social occasions; indeed, several of us was wearing them at that very moment. And Jobsworth, thinking to secure the point, went on to reminisce that some of these fellows, over at the Valenciana Mine it was, now he minded on, they worked such long shifts that they even worshipped in a church that they had built underground – aye, imagine it, a church sixty fathoms down the Despache, in which the lamps and votives were forever lit, and where the fellows would stop an hour afore their shift and another hour after, singing their hymns . . . To the which, someone asked, could they not work and sing at the same time? To the which he said aye, but that these fellows put a great store by having a consecrated church down the grove, and that none of them passed it without bowing to the painted images. To the which, someone said, so they're Catholics? And Mr Jobsworth said aye, like as not, and laughed – and so the difficult talk was gotten over, and very adroitly on his part, I thought.

Jobsworth went on his way after that, carrying the word, or his interpretation of it, back to his master. I had no regard for the fellow. He was the sort who, if he saw you walking past his house in the rain, would rush out and offer to rent you his umbrella. And expect gratitude for doing so.

As I recall, those days passed very pleasantly, especially when compared to what came after. We took turns picketing the various mine-heads, and we spent the rest of the time in Whindale, where there was an entertaining speech by Mr Feargus O'Connor on the benefits of forming a Chartist Cooperative Land Company, which sounded to me like a fancied-up way of selling lottery tickets, and there were public readings of Bunyan and Byron, and songs of course, and impromptu lessons for the washer-boys . . . We waited for the response to our action, as you might wait for the first clap of thunder after seeing the lightning flash.

That Saturday, I was back at home, and Mam and Mop had the burlap stretched out on the table, and they were working from either end with their hooks and rags, poking and picking, making a proggy mat. If Mam wasn't out in the fields picking stones for some farmer or other, or reading her Bible, or washing clothes or making bread, then she'd be shredding up some ratty old underdrawers for strips and yanking them through the burlap. Mop was usually helping. Once the whole floor was covered with mats, they would start work on the second layer. Now, Cicero says that silence is one of the great arts of conversation, but today, alas, they were practising one of the others, and talking their usual swill. Mop would advance some bit of news, or a comment on a local personage, and Mam would slap it down with merciless efficiency.

Says Mop, 'Isn't it cheery about Betty's new bairn?'

Says Mam, 'It is very sorrowful, for her legs've been right swollen up since afore the birth, and now, they reckon, the black erysipelas has took hold. If Dr Braistick cannot see to it, it will mean mortification and death.'

After a minute of hooking in silence, Mop would try again. 'Do you think we'll have a bit of mutton and potatoes on Sunday?'

Says Mam, 'Oh aye, with Mr Hopper at ninepence a stone of potatoes and Mr Croft at sevenpence a pound of mutton, which Lord and Lady will we get to buy us those?'

Mop seemed finally to take her lesson and put her head down, keeping the hook a bare inch from her eyes. But Mam had struck a vein, and followed it as excitably as Mr Crow with his blasting kit.

'Hopper and Croft . . . If one's an usurer the tother's a thief! It's their kind what's brought this wolf to our door. They paved the road for it, all the way from Oldshield with their wickedness. Skipping sermons on Sundays, or nodding off in the pews, as if Reverend Wrather wasn't trying to save *their* souls. False promisers, Reverend Wrather says, are like a cloud without rain. You wonder who'll be next, torn to shreds up on the law. It might be any one of 'em, as far as I can tell. And all them saying "Oh, whisht, it's just a big dog!" – as if they'd never learned better. As if the Devil himself weren't battering at every window to find a way in!'

I assisted neither with the speculative theology nor with the proggy mat. I had my spar box to concentrate on. Spar boxes were glass-fronted cabinets varying in size from a foot square to three-feet high or more, and each one a congeries of the bonniest variety of refractive minerals the miner in question had chanced on and slipped in his pocket as he worked. Over time, the boxes tended to increase in size, as fathers passed their collections on to their sons, to be combined or divvied up or expanded upon. It was down to you how you decorated your spar box. Most fellows simply covered the walls with shards and gleanings, so as to create a sparkly grotto of minerals which brought to mind the loughs, which is to say the cavities, in which the minerals had been found. It regularly happened that, in pursuing a vein of lead, we'd break into such a lough – and a lough might be the width of your finger, or your arm, or it might be several feet across, so you might can crawl inside – and instantly we'd be met with a trove of aragonite, dolomite, iron pyrite, blende and what-have-you, all clustered together, scattering light from hundreds of prisms of every hue. So that was one way of organising your spar box. But other fellows designed free-standing arrangements of stones – a pyramid of purple fluorite, say, or a rotunda of galena with needle-crystal columns, or maybe a great tree made of green feldspar with fruit of white quartz.

Lead-mining was seasonal work, and if you'd got snowed in you'd bide at home and work on your spar box. Most of us kept a few sheep and all, or maybes a cow; if you're a miner, you'll never can afford to higgle a pig – and you'll not can grow much in the way of crops in the uplands either, as you're that high up and the soil's that poor and the winter's that long. Mind, some folk tried to make a go of it, all the same – but all of us would tinker with our spar boxes while we waited for the thaw. Some fellows would angle little mirrors inside to bounce the light about or trick the eye into believing impossible perspectives, while others would place birds' eggs here and there, or even stuffed birds or other curiosities. For instance, though I never saw it and cannot vouch for it, they reckon that, after Mr Muffin's daughter died, he put the clothes-peg figurines from her doll's house in his spar box.

Not having had the benefit of a donation from my dad, my own spar box consisted only of my own gleanings and the things I'd bought. Now, some fellows had opinions on whether a box should properly contain bought stones, but then some fellows hold opinions on every bit thing. My scheme was to have stones arranged around the floor and the walls and the ceiling of the box, not random as in nature, but organised so as to represent the passing year. The idea had come to me in one of my queer fits, but I never let on about that, and generally stayed tight-lipped about the vivid dreams I had when the fit was on me. I started the box with a piece of red sard, maybes because it put me in mind of holly berries; and then yellow chrysolite, for mistletoe berries, or else for the candle flames that were also in season; and then sea-green beryl, because the only time I've seen the sea was one time in spring when I was a bairn, and I thought, then, that it must have been frozen solid in the winter and only recently thawed; and after that a cluster of fire garnets; after that, I'd wanted a carbuncle, but never found one to my liking, so I placed a blood-alley marble at that point in the construction; and after that came a beautiful piece of lapis lazuli, deep blue as the sky in summer can be; and then white carnelian, which must have been for the clouds; and yellow cairngorm for the sun; and the banded red agate that followed was bonny as a sunset; amethyst was next, which was said to be a charm against getting caught in drink; and then yellow serpentine, for the yellow berries of the ivy, like as not; and then clear green jasper; and finally I closed the loop with dark green malachite, with both greens for the ivy leaves, no doubt. And I set each of these bought stones in amongst the brightest bits of galena and spar that I'd come across. And somewhere along the ways I'd acquired a lump of amber, and I stuck that in right beside the green malachite, where it made a nice contrast, so I reckoned.

The quiet was broken again. Says Mop, 'Jenny was boasting today that William Lamb has gone to Spain.'

Says Mam, 'Spain! That lad's so daft he couldn't make his way to Emble and back.'

Says Mop, 'Oh, but he has! They reckon he's been and got the boat from Oldshield last week. They don't expect to hear from him now for two month, but, once he's settled and that, his brother Michael's going to join him . . .'

Says Mam, with finality, 'If you go to Spain, you'll have to can speak Spanish.'

Of course, we'd all heard about Spain, where the ore contained more silver than lead, and just rolled off the mountains into your hand, and the lasses were all bonny, and bottles of beer grew on every tree. Many were the miners who nurtured a secret plan to up and sail for the Sierra Almagrera, but the few who actually took such a trip tended to do so out of debt, shame or desperation, rather than out of hope. Except, it seemed, for William Lamb; and the idea of him packing his knapsack and setting out on the road from Whindale Town with a true determination to cross the sea made me feel – well, I couldn't put a name to what I felt. It wasn't as simple as envy, nor as mean as jealousy.

I tried to block out the chatter, and focus on arranging my spar box. In the centre, I'd had an idea to construct a free-standing bull, which I'd model out of wire first, and then fix stones on top. But over time this plan changed, and I set about making just a bull's head, consisting of firestone in the main, but with eyes of jasper, and horns encrusted with quartz, and ears of schorl, and a nose of jet, and cheeks of black jack, and a face and forehead of red sard, and all crowned with a poll of fool's gold.

Had you asked me, then, where I got the idea for all of this, I'd have said I didn't know. Or I'd have said that it simply occurred to me to make a bull's head, the fancy of a moment that I'd caught at on a whim, like any other affectation that a young man might grow into. But the truth was the idea for the bull came to me by way of a seizure-vision, just as the stone calendar scheme had. Considered in the light of what came after, I'm not so sure there wasn't more than chance at work.

Mop had given up trying to speak of William Lamb, and was trying a different tack. 'They reckon there's a lady preacher going to be visiting Whindale next week.'

Says Mam with a snort, 'The Lord help us!'

Says Mop, 'There's lots of lady preachers these days. Reverend Wrather said—'

At this point, Mam heaved a sigh that communicated a great deal concerning her church's allowance of itinerant female preachers, and the limits of Mam's patience with such newfangledness.

Says Mop, very quietly, 'Well, I was thinking of attending, to see what's what.'

Says Mam, 'You're needed here. Why do you want to be gallivanting off to hear some . . .' Here Mam paused, and regarded Mop, very like a poacher taking aim at a plover, and then, as Mam was sometimes able to do, she read Mop's mind. 'You're not thinking of trying your hand at it, are you, Mary?'

Mop said nowt, and she said it very guiltily.

Mam at once intuited that absolute interdiction might not be the most effective method in banishing this trace of ambition in her daughter, and said, 'Oh, Mary, don't be so silly. You could never preach to a room with your quiet little mousy voice – you'd be scared stiff! You cannot put God in their hearts if folk cannot hear a word you're saying. "Eh? What? Speak up, lass!"'

This poisonous counsel continued to drip for a while longer, but I fixed my attention more resolutely on my spar box, and tried to hold off the disturbing possibility that Mop might conceivably escape Mam's clutches afore I did.

It was some time the following week when word went round the village green that something was up, and that blacklegs were being brought in, which is to say miners from Wales who cared not a feather for our disputes and our strikes, and who would work for the mine owner and render our action ineffectual. The next morning, we all turned out at the picket line at the daisy – the daisy is what we called the entrance to the grove, it being the day's eye to a fellow underground – only to find that a gang of seven or eight candymen were already there waiting for us.

Now, the candymen were loathed as bad as scabs. They were bum-bailiffs, you see, and if a fellow on strike wound up owing over much back-rent, the mine owner, who was also your landlord, would send in a candyman or three to carry out the notice of ejectment. They were so called because, when they weren't running honest fellows out of house and home, they could be found ganging door-to-door selling sweeties to bairns, or cadging on Oldshield's high street, crying 'Dandy-candy, three sticks a penny!' – such being the only work they could find, apart from as cracksmen and fences. It was said that some of them had once been soldiers and had fought in Kabul, either surviving the massacre of forty-two or as part of the army of retribution that was sent in consequence, and it made sense to think of them having heard the cannon rattle too long while they saw their fellows being butchered in the desert, or while they themselves fell to butchering ... yes, it made sense to imagine them having escaped that, with their brains turned brutish and their hearts fed on horrors. They wore their candyman outfit of an apron and a top hat – to hide their jailcrop, like as not – as if it were a uniform.

I will not attempt to replicate the many oaths and insults with which they larded their every utterance, but they enquired as to our purpose in being there, seeing as we were a parcel of workshy fellows.

I will likewise not reproduce the means by which we coloured our riposte, but we asked them what *their* purpose was, for we had no need of sweeties.

They assured us that they had no sweeties for us today, only brass knuckles and billy clubs, but if we came again the morn-morn, we'd get to see their rifles.

We said we'd go where we pleased, and they could bring a cannon if they liked, we didn't give a tinker's wank.

The ensuing silence was first heightened and then broken by the distant sound of labouring wheels and the steady rhythm of horses, and presently a cart appeared over the rim of Tod Law.

'Here come the blacklegs!' bellowed George Henry, superfluously.

Some of the candymen were sneering now – the nearest their faces could manage to a smile, I thought.

And then, like that, the fight was on. Excepting Heavens-Evans, who had by then left us in disgust at our big swears, we acquitted ourselves with valour; but we were no match for the candymen, who had all of their military training and ten lifetimes' worth of brutality stored up inside of them. They tore into us like berserkers. Soon Mr Crow was lying curled up, covering his face, and I heard later that they had broken his cheekbone, and he never regained the sight in his left eye. Within minutes, the skirmish had been lost and won, and the candymen – albeit newly possessed of some black eyes and bloodied noses – had retaken possession of the daisy.

The cart pulled up at last. The blacklegs had seen enough of the fighting to know that they would have safe passage into the grove, but also that they'd do well not to hang about too long or speak to any of us. They piled out, careful to remain herded together as far as possible. We watched them warily. I poked a finger in my mouth and spat out a tooth that had been loosened. I felt strange and light-headed, as after one of my turns. I had of course received some blows to the head.

Now, what I did next requires some sort of introduction, or explanation, but I'm at a loss as to what I could offer you in that way. It was a thing that changed everything for me thereafter, as I would have anticipated had I given the matter a moment's forethought; but I did not. The idea simply came to me – or, rather, I found it waiting for me in my mind, like a forgotten key, long polished in my pocket. I could not then, and I cannot today, give a clear account of my motives. When I thought about it afterwards, I'd offer myself reasons, but – and I knew this, even as I was telling myself them! – in doing so I was merely speculating and imputing, as I might do had I seen a stranger do what I did. And I might even say that I became a stranger unto myself in that moment; in my mind's eye, when I recollect it, I always see myself from a distance of about ten feet or so, and always from a vantage point high in the air above me: I can see the look of shock and disgust and rage on the faces of my workmates, whereas in reality I didn't see this, for I didn't look back once I'd commenced walking. Today I can hear the things my workmates are calling me, whereas I did not, at the time.

I crossed the picket line.

The blacklegs were gathered at the daisy, jabbering in their backwards language. They were more than a little surprised to see me join them, and must have been half expecting a trick of some sort, and the candymen formed a wall in front of me, letting their arms hang heavy at their sides, as fellows do when they sniff there's a fight in the offing. What was my idea, they wished to know. I told them that it was no trick or foolery, and that I had merely differentiated myself from my fellows. This was a fearful moment for me, caught as I was betwixt my old life, in which I was as one defunct and exanimate, and a new life into which I was yet to be born. I was balanced on the still fulcrum of the machinery in spin about me. I hardly breathed as I looked into the head candyman's grey eyes, waiting to see if he would let me pass.

With regard to my workmates-as-was, they had – as if awakening from a troubled dream and remembering the reason they went to bed in such a twisty fettle – become suddenly animated, waving their arms and making gestures, and bequeathing me a variety of scatological epithets. Things was heating up again, and my position was looking a dubious one, but then there was movement, and the blacklegs and the candymen closed around me, protective-wise, and then, rather than test the stand-off too long, the blacklegs and I all scarpered through the daisy, and were soon blinking in the dark again.

3
The Scab and the Iron Devil

Having me with them convenienced the blacklegs a good deal, and they let me lead the way. Soon enough, we reached the face, where I was partnered with a hulking great fellow who stood about a foot taller than I. He always addressed me in good English, and soon established himself the spokesman for his group. I never knew precisely how much English the others had, for they spoke it as little as possible and with the thickest accent imaginable. With them, I soon discovered, there would be little in the way of a sharing of terms, which was a shame, as it's one of the few pleasures afforded a miner. For many years, the trade had drawn folk from all over these islands – and from beyond, too – and we'd been thrown together underground, hardly able to make sense of each other until, needs must, we enlightened one another as to whether the ore required ragging or cobbing or spalling, or whatever. We had to agree on such terms. You had to be sure that a fellow knew gubbin from grundy. But these blacklegs were sullen bastards in the main, excepting my partner, who seemed a good sort.

We asked each other's name, and I told him mine, and he said he was Aneurin Derfel.

'An Iron Devil! That's a good one. A very good one. At least you're not called William Williams or William Jones like the rest of your lot. And can none of them speak English?'

'I have a turn for the Saxon; they have not. Why did you join us, Caleb? If you don't mind me asking, that is. What made you cross the line?'

I felt the anger blow through me like a sudden wind. It's exasperating for a young man to be asked about his behaviour when he doesn't know the answer. I told him that I had my reasons, and said it in such a tone as to close the matter, but he affected not to understand this, and ceased his work to rest on his pick, giving me a more respectful hearing. In as peremptory a way as I could manage, I told him – oh, I don't know now what I told him. Anything, something. I said that I did it in spirit of contradiction. That I did it because all the arguments tended one way, and that it had to fall to a body to oppose the general drift. That we should not all behave like sheep; that Playfair was not a bellwether. The account I gave of myself disgraced the universe. And all this time the Iron Devil listened to my dreary ramblings with that same polite, lending-an-ear expression, until I was all but furious at my own inarticulacy.

Now, I will tell you something about Aneurin that, if events hadn't gone the way they did, I suppose I might keep to myself: he had the most pleasant and soothing voice you can imagine. Very low it was, very calming and reassuring, and these are qualities greatly to be valued in our line of work, which can be so maddeningly frustrating and precarious. I don't think I ever heard him utter a word without I felt the benefit of that voice, which seemed steadier at times than the rock we were quarrying.

And so the work continued, albeit with surly workmates who said little in my hearing and less in my understanding. But I knew that this would change, on account of me being so capable of attracting words and having them stick to me, and I was right: within a day or two, I was learning phrases such as *llais craic yn syrthiaw*, which meant 'the voice of a falling rock', which is to say the sound of blasting in a mine. And the Iron Devil said his home was in *pentref y dwr*, which meant 'the village of the water', for it had a river running through it, and he accounted it very pretty. It was to be found in an area called *bôn-y-maen*, which meant 'base of the stone'.

I said that every village within fifty miles of Windy Top had a right to be called *pentref y dwr*, due to the myriad waterways and forces, as we called them, that wend through the uplands and that all but constituted the region, rendering our human dwellings so many Neptunian follies . . . though, I said, I might better call them Coventinian follies, after the water goddess folk hereabouts used to believe in, in the long-ago. Windy Top, for example, was a wet mine – which was good, as you'll die the sooner in a dry one, on account of the dust and that.

At this time I noticed a few of the other fellows scowling over at us, and when I asked the Iron Devil why, he said,

'They do not like that a Saxon has Welsh words in his mouth.'

'Then I consider them to be *cenfigenus* fellows, to a man.'

'Ah, you mustn't hold it against them too far, Caleb. They were told, as I was, that a Saxon can never speak Welsh, his tongue being too short.'

'Aye, but I reckon you were too wise to believe all you were told.'

'Various are the people who believe the old tales,' he replied, and then he turned the conversation round to the rumoured wolf, for he and the other blacklegs had heard tell of it, and of Mr Playfair's body having been found all chewed up.

I sketched for him the positions on the matter.

'And the folk here believe there's a wolf on the loose, do they?' he asked, with that air of regretful kindliness he so often had.

'Folk round here, like folk elsewhere, believe and disbelieve all manner of things, as you have said. Like the Laidly Wyrm of Seven Springs, or the Hinkley Brag, which is a goblin shape-shifter that likes to appear as a horse . . .'

'And what about yourself? Do you think there's a Whindale Wolf?'

'For myself . . . well, as I see it, it's like this. There's been talk of a wolf going as far back as anyone can remember. My nana told me that *her* nana had told her that she'd seen it. And so forth. Now, that sort of thing makes some folk the more inclined to believe, but it makes me the less inclined, because it would mean that there's been a wolf pack big enough to breed and sustain itself living out here for a number of generations, but it's somehow evaded capture all this long while. And that defies belief. If it was a case of a single wolf, or big dog of some sort, living out there for a year or two, well, that would be one thing. But I cannot believe in a wolf pack. Not out here anyway, when there's Eshwood Forest to the north-east, which would afford it more in the way of food and shelter. And it seems that our wolf has only recently developed a taste for human flesh – now why should this be?'

'You've thought this through,' says the Iron Devil.

I said that belief in things like that would no doubt depend on the time of day and the locality of a fellow. To scoff at the idea of a Whindale Wolf when you're in a noisy tavern getting your drinking done is one thing, but it's another matter entirely to make light of it should you find yourself alone out on the moors at dusk. It was like the story we'd tell the washer-boys about the miner with no face, who would come sneaking up on any fellow caught alone and without a light down in the depths of the grove. Oh, they'd laugh all right when we told them of that! But the image – the thought of a fellow with no eyes, no nose, no mouth, no nowt – found secret purchase in their memory, and sooner or later, once they were a few years older and had become miners, they would find themselves in just such a position: last man to be leaving a level, who, lagging behind his fellows, finds that his candle of a sudden sputters and gutters out on him, plunging him into absolute darkness. And it's then that, in his mind's eye, he'll suddenly see the miner with no face a-creeping round the nearest corner, stealing up on him where he stands sweating and scrambling for a lucifer . . .

Well, we argued either side of the matter, finding ground upon which to agree, for the Iron Devil's people had superstitions to match those of my lot, which came as no surprise, seeing as the religious beliefs of our two tribes held much in common. In those days, you see, though there were some Anglicans scattered among us, dissent obtained to a great extent, and Primitive Methodism above all. I think we were affected by having lived so many generations in the uplands, far from cities, much like the situation of the Iron Devil's watery valleys. Even Oldshield was a place that many of us would never see in all our lifetime. Not that we minded the distance: preachers of every denomination never tired of telling us that cities aspired not toward Heaven but toward Babylon, and that all kings had been drunk with the wine of her fornication, and it followed that city folk were, so to speak, the *foci* of her fornication. And so forth.

We were born – and we lived, and we died and were buried – far away from the world, and you should not be astonished that we cultivated a preference for separatism in matters of the spirit, and saw the world as a hacky-dirty passageway in which we were dungeoned for a wink of time in the midst of God's eternal glory. *Wherefore come out from among them, and be ye separate, saith the Lord, and touch not the unclean thing; and I will receive you!* So the righteous believed, anyway. To them, the world was but a perishing tabernacle, and they longed to escape it for the haven of Heaven. And even the unrighteous, such as myself, had a superstition to much the same effect.

Once, drunkenness had been a great besetting problem among us – and, even though there were many in the Whin Valley still given that way, now there was also sprung up many temperance societies throughout the uplands, in which fellows such as Heavens-Evans would keep each other on the steep and thorny path to self-righteousness. Their point was that to drink and be merry was to love the world, and if any man love the world, the love of the Father is not in him, like it says in the Bible. I think it must have been because we were so short-lived that we were so given to excess or abstinence. It's not natural, is it, to be working underground all day like a mole, out of the sun and breathing bad air? A miner who saw his fortieth year was considered to have reached a venerable age. And with so little time in this world, and so much of that little being accounted for down the pit, we wound up veering to one extreme or the other, either thinking that our brief lives had to be enjoyed at all costs, or that such a temptation was part of the trial; so we wound up either all-out for revelry or all-in for soberness – dandies or puritans, and rarely owt in between.

I was cogitating on such matters next day in church where I had, in spite of their protests, decided to accompany Mam and Mop.

Mam had enquired, 'What possible reason have you to come to church? You believe in nowt.'

To which I had returned, 'Mother, to whom did the good Lord preach, if not to the heathen? And did he ask them their reasons for attending, like a county magistrate?'

'You wish to shame me. You live to shame me. You are my burden. I must not begrudge you.'

'Mother, you are truly the most begrudiest burden-bearer I can conceive of. Self-pity is the only pity you can produce. Now, let us skip along to the disembellished preaching box, and hear the good news, that we may be aggrieved.'

We walked the half a mile in pleasant silence, and then, alongside fifty other likeminded souls, we crammed ourselves into the church. I say church, but really it was the plainest, barest structure, adorned only with a cross that hung behind the pulpit. The idea was that nowt should distract you from the Word, but I always found words to be highly distracting in and of themselves. The programme got under way with a hymn. I hummed along.

To work and toil and strive and sweat –
Such is our lot until we die:
We pay our share of Adam's debt
And earn our rest in Heav'n on high.

But if we drink to quench the drouth
We soon start singing drunkards' songs:
The Devil speaking with our mouth
Puts bitter words upon our tongues.

> *So let us sing our hymns of praise –*
> *In strange hosannas raise our voice;*
> *From now until the end of days*
> *With temperate speech let us rejoice.*

Truth be told, I'd always despised the singing of a hymn. All them pluriform voices thrown together in a right pious and discordant gallimaufry, and all supposedly weighing equal on the Lord's vasty eardrum, when really it's plain enough that some of us are better voiced than others. I suspect the Lord would prefer it if the singing of His praises was left to those whom He'd favoured with a set of pipes, and who could therefore carry a note. Meg Lewney, for instance, had a voice like a cat in a mangle, and her husband, Philip, seemed to think that so long as he sang the lowest note possible he'd never be out of tune. I'm sure many of the congregation sang up so heartily just to drown out the pair of them. And, in particular, I didn't like those verses being so critical of 'drunkard's songs', for a Saturday-night sing-song in drink always rang truer to my ear than all this four-square piety that got itself pushed out betwixt the teeth on Sunday mornings. Anyways, we got the hymn fairly shouldered out of the way, and then Reverend Wrather stood tall in the pulpit, taking the measure of us, it seemed, and waiting for us to settle.

Reverend Wrather's complexion was of a burnt-red hue – as a child, when I first heard him speak of hellfire, I assumed it came from personal experience – and he possessed a magnificent pair of eyebrows that arose like smoke from the glowing embers below them. He kept a short length of purple velvet by his left hand, just so – I don't know if it was a bookmark or what, but he always had it with him when he preached – and when he got especially excited in his sermonising he'd strangulate it in his fist and thump it on the pulpit so as to emphasise a particular word. As a boy, I'd been fascinated by this display of righteous rage, and many's the time I lost the gist of his sermon on account of being so rapt in my focus on his left hand, and the purple velvet that would catch the light with the prettiest textures as he throttled it. It was the only bonny thing in the entire church. We had all settled in our pews, and the Reverend stood there until he had our attention, and then he began.

'Now. My sermon this morning is simple. It concerns *work*. Work is a good thing – only a loafer would deny it. But that is not my sermon. Work is our lot: it's what we got for Adam's sin, and it's the principal means by which we pay off his debt. Yes, indeed, you say. But that is not my sermon, either. My sermon is only this: every man among you has liberty to begin work, but it is my hope and earnest prayer that if any man do begin work *in connection with them that has already begun*, and here I mean them that has chosen to be *scabs* or *blacklegs*, that you will all have the goodness to pass by them without speaking to them, and have no further connection or communication with them whatsoever. For as it says in Ecclesiasticus, chapter thirteen: *What fellowship hath the wolf with the lamb? So the sinner with the godly.*'

I stole a glance at Mam and Mop, both of whom were

staring very fixedly at the preacher, and silently asserting a sort of barrier betwixt me and them. Wrather continued.

'If they be *sick* do not visit them; if they are in need of a *doctor* do not seek them one; if they *die* do not bury them but leave them for the *corbies*; if they are trapped and fastened underground in a mine, do not assist in seeking them out but *let them die*. Yes, let them die and go, as it were, from darkness into darkness, even into the fangs of the *Devil*, to be kept by him and his emissaries without remorse in the *fires of Hell* forever. It is your solemn duty to tor*ment* them every wise you can while they be here on earth, and when they die may the Devil tor*ment* them to all eternity.'

I had the shifty, prickly sense of every eye in the church being on me; but when I flicked my eyes about – not wishing to further draw attention to myself by turning about – not a soul met my gaze.

'I ask you, my brethren, what are these scabs and blacklegs, if not the very worst sort of hireling? And even as it says in John's Gospel, chapter ten: *the good shepherd giveth his life for the sheep. But he that is an hireling, and not the shepherd, whose own the sheep are not, seeth the wolf coming, and leaveth the sheep, and fleeth: and the wolf catcheth them, and scattereth the sheep. The hireling fleeth, because he is an hireling, and careth not for the sheep.*

'Brethren, there are wolves amongst us, even now. Wolves and hirelings. Be sober-minded; be watchful. Is it needful that I should say such things? May we not gather the evidence of our senses, and take heed of the signs and wonders that have been presented to us? Do we not know that there is a *real* wolf stalking high on the law, forever on the lookout for an easy meal? And even so, the adversary – and here I refer to Satan himself – the *adversary* prowls amongst us with a hunger that cannot be sated, seeking souls upon which to feast.

'To conclude, brethren, it is my earnest hope that you will, every one of you, do these wicked wolves and hirelings all the harm you can, and speak every manner of evil against them that is in your power. If one of them owes you anything, be sure to put him to all the trouble you possibly can. Let them be like *Cain*, for indeed they are like Cain; nay, they are Cain himself, deserted by the Lord and forsaken of their fellow man, doomed and determined to walk the earth, to toil for their bread, never knowing a home or a welcome or a kind word or a smile, all the days of their miserable lives. Aye, they are Cain, and also they are *Judas Iscariot*, fit for nowt but the taking of their own lives if none of you can do it for them: in this alone may you assist them in good conscience.'

Reverend Wrather had always interpreted scripture in his own manner. Just as when you find a lump in your cushion you solve it with a thump – why, he employed a like method in reconciling Biblical difficulties. But he wasn't done, having thought of some further godly counsel.

'Yes, I charitably hope that all you millers and shopkeepers, you cloggers and blacksmiths and tailors, deny them of *ev*erything; and even if they emigrate to Spain or to Australia or to America, there to dig for gold or for diamonds or such, with the sweat melting off their sinful faces, why, if any of you should pass that way or know a soul thereabouts, be sure to treat them in the same way, and so allow their name, which is like some evil matter, as of *pitch* or *dung*, to stick to them and defile them; for I tell you, my brothers, if I had a house full of bread and every other necessary of life to take and to spare, I would not give *one* of them a mouthful to save their lives if I saw them dying of want in *scores*. And I hope you will follow my example. Amen.

'There. Now let us sing "The Race that Long in Darkness Pined".'

At long last, we were done, and Reverend Wrather's piece of velvet could be let alone, having been punished enough, and the Lord could be let alone as well, to pick and choose His interventions according to His ever-mysterious scheme, and the bairns could be let loose to chase each other amidst the gravestones.

Mam and Mop and me maintained a politic silence as we made our ways home, for they had thoroughly approved of the Wrather's sermonising, though it had been squarely aimed at me, and none of us saw any gain in debating the matter. And then, as we neared our little shieling, we found the front door standing propped open. Something about it told me that mischief was afoot, though Mam and Mop seemed to think it nothing strange. I told them to bide outside, and entered the house very gingerly, and soon saw what had been done in our absence: some fellows had been in while we were out at church, and they had smashed my lovely spar box to pieces. Gemstones and lumps of purplish spar were scattered all over the floor, where all appeared as dull as any other muck and grit. Nothing identifiable was left of the bull's head that I'd so delicately constructed.

I let fly a volley of curses, and then howled, '*Beware of them that come in sheep's clothing, but inwardly are ravening wolves! Ye shall know them by their fruits!*' I was casting about for sayings to match the great anger I felt at my false friends.

Mam looked aghast when I said this, and spat a warning at me never to be so insolent as to apply those words to my own situation.

I bit back, and expressed my suspicions that the wreckage of my beautified spar box had not come altogether as a surprise to her and Mop, who blushed and looked away when I said this. She was still a child, after all, and her face was not yet brazen to deceit in the way that marks out the adult of our ignoble species. By the light of her blush, so to speak, I saw that, had I not on a whim accompanied her and Mam to church, I'd have been the one attacked, but, as I wasn't there, they'd took out their hatefulness on my spar box. And Mop and Mam had known or suspected all of this. I looked back at Mam and felt the venom singing in my veins – but she had an instinct for when a body was angered at her, and afore I could give vent she retaliated in advance.

'I should've dumped you in Siskin's orphanage and buggered off like your feckless excuse for a father! I should've drowned you at birth, like a kitten in Ridley's Tarn! Before God I swear it: I'd rather have died in the shame and agonies of childbirth than live to raise a bastard scab!'

So Mam was upset. But then, I thought, Mam was ever upset about something – and Mop was just doing what she always did on such occasions, that is repeating, under her breath, some of the more important of Mam's words a moment after they had first been uttered. In the speech reported above, for instance, she'd repeated the words 'dumped', 'orphanage', 'feckless', 'drowned', 'kitten', 'shame' and 'scab'. I suddenly thought how similar this was to Reverend Wrather throttling his bit of cloth for emphasis, and a great laughing fit came over me, and, though I tried to explain to Mop that she was nowt but a purple velvet bookmark in the paw of a zealot, I could not speak for the hilarity, and so, as the tears ran down my face, Mam and Mop left me, both very disgusted.

Even while these threats and reprisals were coming at me thick and fast, the news came that the strike had been called off. Mr Jobsworth had met with the chief blackleg at a neighbouring vein at lowse the night afore, and told him that, somewhat unexpectedly, the strikers had agreed to fixed working hours. This is how it often went, with strikes: the organising of them was like a great marching band with banners, but they ended with the feeble parp of a tin trumpet. Word was passed round among the Welshmen. Next day, back at the vein on Windy Top, the Iron Devil let me know that it would be our last day working together, and I let him know that I was sorry to hear it.

We talked no end that day, as men do once they know they'll never meet again. I asked him about Mrs Devil, for he had already given me to understand that he was married, though he had seemed reluctant to say more. But he must have been feeling the last-day licence and all, because he was more forthcoming now, and yes, he was married, he said, and she was a good woman. Her name was Gwen, and she had borne him three children. Once they'd got married, he and Gwen had moved, like many others in that part of the country, to Merthyr Tydfl in search of employment at the ironworks, but it had not been as they had hoped.

'When we got to Merthyr, we had to take lodging in the Cellars. You'll have heard of the Cellars? The stories are true. You cannot imagine the squalor, Caleb. I'd never seen such drunkenness and debauchery. I hadn't known there was so much misery in that behaviour. Every other woman was a nymph, every other man a bully. Nymph and bully: those were our words for whore and pimp. And the stench – human waste thrown into the street . . . we lived in it. In filth. Died in it. I still dream of the place and, first thing when I wake, there's often a horrible long moment when I believe I'm back in China.'

'China?'

'That's what we called the Cellars. So everyone called it: China. The worst part of the slum.'

I looked up, then, and not because I felt the eyes of the Almighty upon me, but more so that He might feel mine on Him. I told the Iron Devil that I'd recently heard a fellow talking about Mexico in a similar way, and telling us that we shouldn't strike, but rather be grateful, because there was fellows in Mexico who had it worse than us. And how it seems that, when things pass beyond the tolerable, our masters ask us to imagine an elsewhere – some place we'll never live to see with our own eyes – that is somehow even more hellish. And then, if things get worse still, they'll tell us that we're already in such an elsewhere, and not in our own land at all. It must be an old trick, I said.

'The trick wouldn't have got to be old unless it worked,' said my comrade quietly, and then recommenced his tale. 'China is what we who lived there called it, but outsiders called it Little Hell. That was a better name for it. Our first two children – two boys, Rees and Meyrick – both died of the measles before they turned three. And then we had a girl, Nest,' and here the Iron Devil paused a moment. 'If a child lived to be seven, then they were like to survive and get to be grown. You had to try not to hope too much before then. Nest lived to be six. When she died of the smallpox, it broke Gwen's spirit. She died, too.'

I laid my hand on the big man's shoulder and gave it a bit squeeze, but it felt strange so I stopped. Just letting the silence engulf us for a spell seemed the kindest thing. Something in the way he'd said that 'she died, too' made me think. He'd said it hurriedly, as you might say something shameful, to get it over with. There'd have been plenty of diseases for her to die from, of course, but I suspected that the fatal affliction in Gwen's case was despair. But, just as a fellow can't come out and tell you that his wife died by her own hand, a fellow can't ask if that's what happened.

This made me notice that neither myself nor the Iron Devil were the sort to talk around a thing, nor mutter to ourselves, nor address ourselves to nobody in particular – nor were we the sort to respond to such an address. Most people, it seems to me, speak in that manner twenty times a day, saying nothings-in-particular laced with approach and reproach, silly sallies that want to be made allowance for yet still expect to hit their mark. Such talk is piss and wind. No, it is better to be like the Iron Devil and me: talk directly to a body, or say nowt. So we said nowt.

And now I began to think. The strike had lasted barely three weeks, and failed. The blacklegs would be 'let go', as Jobsworth had put it, to return to China, presumably, or else to scrounge about for work where they could find it, and I'd be back with my workmates of old. All that day, I thought I could see the blacklegs reckoning up whether it had been worthwhile to travel all that way for so short a spell of work, and it was only at this point that I, too, started to consider the practicalities of my position. Only now did it occur to me that I'd cast off the bonds of friendship and kinship with every soul I knew, and that I'd done so for the sum of ten shillings, payable at year's-end.

Truth to tell, I had not, prior to that moment, understood very much about the world. I had not understood the nature of men, anyway. Of how much dependence I could place on my allies and of how much resistance I should anticipate from my enemies, I was equally ignorant; and even in distinguishing the one from the other, I was as a child, beyond the guess of folly. Nor was this the only deficiency in my education, as you shall see. My life was beginning to shake loose, the great clew of yarn beginning to unravel, laying a trail that would make my desultory wanderings the clearer for any who cared to judge the matter. But at that time it was beyond me to grasp my predicament. For all my vaunting, I avoided self-knowledge as though it were the Devil.

Next morning, with the blacklegs all packed up and dispersed, when I met with my marras of old at the daisy, I was braced for threats and insults and maybes fisticuffs; but, strange to say, there was nowt of the kind forthcoming, only a surly silence and a refusal to look me in the eye. Green as I was, I thought at first that this seemed the better for me, and that they might be going to let bygones be bygones, and that we'd be able to rub along as we did afore. Such was my relief at this, I found myself smiling foolishly while I worked, though it was too dark for anyone to discern it. But as the day wore on very ponderously, and the miserable silence did not dispel, I felt the weight of my sentence gradually descend upon me. Never afore had I been so aware of the sound of the great wheel as it turned interminably down in the depths; never afore had I realised what a maddening sound it was, should a fellow find himself with nowt else to attend to: no stories, no songs, no craic – nowt but cluck-clunk, cluck-clunk!

At last, having had enough of it, I threw down my pick with a clatter and indicated my preference to have it out with them there and then, rather than act like a bunch of twisty bairns who'd took the ghee.

Cluck-clunk went the wheel; cluck-clunk went the heart of the mine.

As one, my workmates threw down *their* picks and hammers, and the sound fairly made me jump. I watched them as close as I could in the gloom, and thought I could make out that they were looking to Mr Muffin to speak for them. Aye, I thought, as gravity fills in a goaf, so Muffin has stepped into the space left by Playfair. He was their leader now, and would speak for them, as presently he did.

'You think you're better than us, Caleb, you ever did. With your queer fits and your visions, and your fancy talk . . .'

'You're nowt but a bastard scab,' explained George Henry.

I ignored this, for George Henry was ever full of piss and vinegar, and turned to my old partner instead, Mr Crow, but he shook his head afore I could speak a word. He was wearing a patch over his left eye, because of our recent run-in with the candymen.

'You say you want to have it out with us here and now,' resumed Muffin. His voice was quiet, but in a way that sounded like he was choosing to keep it that way. 'We can have it out here and now. Here and now's as good as owt.'

They seemed to draw nearer to me at these words, and I began to regret having thrown my pick away so hastily. I implored, 'Crow! For pity's sake, don't tell me you're listening to these low-lived fellows. You know as well as I that Mr Muffin's a hateful manipulator, and George Henry hasn't the brains of a pony.'

But Mr Crow had gone over to their side and told me so in plain English. We addressed one another with a good deal of freedom after that, and it was intimated that I was shortly to sup on what I'd been brewing all my life. I gave as good as I got, I think, but I felt shaken to discover Crow felt this way, and had done so for quite a spell, it seemed.

Cluck-clunk went the wheel.

'What about you, Heavens-Evans? You haven't been persuaded by these filthy dreamers, have you? *Vengeance is mine, so saith the Lord,* and you know it's prideful for men to go seeking it out for themselves on earth!'

'Alas, Caleb, nothing I could say would change their minds. You have gnawed too much on the bridle, I think.'

'Have you forgotten the story of the Good Samaritan? The Good Book says it is divine to intercede on behalf of your brother!'

'Aye, and it also says that vanity is a quicksand, and a fellow will gang his own gait on his way to it!' says Heavens-Evans, with rather more pluck than he could usually muster. That boded ill for me.

'Heavens-Evans, you married the first lass you kissed, but you've been slow on the uptake ever since. I despise you, and heartily, you goat-faced Methodist shit-pot.'

Even at that he kept his countenance, and merely shook his head and said 'So the fool returneth to his folly,' or some such mewling platitude.

Cluck-clunk.

I couldn't think what else to do then but try to put a bit more wind up George Henry, and see if it might split him off from the other fellows, so I said that his mind was plainly addled from his excessive self-abuse. But my words found no purchase, and I think I knew then that they had already agreed on what they were about to do.

'Accidents are happening left and right down here,' says George Henry. 'It's the reason we need to band together.'

'Oh, aye, you band together, all right – in thuggish idiocy! Four against one: aye, I see why you band together!'

'Aye, four to one. So it'll be your word against all of ours, I reckon,' said George Henry.

'You band together like sheep! Like wolves!' I spat out. I

was a little delirious, I will admit.

'Why, even so you used to say to Mr Plover,' said George Henry, 'all those many times you disagreed with him. We heard you heaping scorn and derision on his head so often, and now he's dead, murdered most likely, and will they ever catch the guilty party?'

I think I staggered back at this. 'You cannot mean what you are insinuating. It is impossible that you mean it . . .' My heart was racing. I was so shocked by George Henry's remark that I felt dizzy and yet horribly clear-headed at the same time. What did they take me for, these fellows I'd worked with close as brothers for so many years? What sort of a web was I caught in?

'We're at the ends of the earth out here, and we must make our own rough justice,' said George Henry. 'We don't *know* that it was you who killed Mr Plover. Not for certain. Mind, if evidence should come before us, we'll give you more than a rap on the knuckles . . .'

I was innocent enough to take some comfort from that last remark, as a rap on the knuckles didn't sound so bad; but George Henry's tone was the clue. Like a child that is given to cruel ways, he addressed the prospect of another's suffering with unabashed relish. And then I saw with the tail of my eye how it was going to be, for he was still holding a poll-pick, keeping it half-hidden behind his leg, and the moment I spotted it, the other fellows rushed at me and wrestled me to the ground very roughly. I must have at least caught Mr Muffin with a good one, for I remember his nose was bloodied by the time he was kneeling over me, holding my right arm out at an angle. And now it was George Henry's turn. He swung the poll-pick and brought the hammer end down on my hand. I screamed blue murder, but he repeated this action thrice more all the same, every blow triggering a sort of blast in my brain; I felt them in white flashes – the worst and brightest light I ever saw down a mine: a thrill of pure agony shooting along every nerve in my body; I was a pain-tree lit up by a lightning flash. The last blow was the hardest, as though he were warming to the task. I thought every bone in my hand must be broken.

'There, now, Caleb,' says George Henry very nastily. 'You won't be drawing a wage for a while, now, will you? And you'll get no smart money, you know. We'd have to strike for that right, and what good would striking do when the valley's crawling with blacklegs? It seems to me you'll sharp lose all the pay you made scabbing. After that, well, it'll be off to the Sill for you, old marra, won't it! They'll take anyone there, you know. Idlers, loafers, magsmen. Low types. The thriftless, the worthless, the very refuse of community. The *residuum*. Men of no account. Best place for a rat scab like you.'

George Henry was a surly, tight-lipped bastard, but once he'd got himself excited, he never said a word when fifty would do. I'd have told him so, but I was so winded by the pain I couldn't breathe, and my eyes were already closing as merciful insensibility overwhelmed me.

4
an extract: *op. cit.*

[. . .] In one sense, ladies and gentlemen, Mithraic worship was regulated and restricted: it was the business of a carefully controlled mystery cult that existed within the Roman army; membership was only open to men. In another sense, it was a religion of principled excess: the Mithraists believed that all things, if taken to extremity, were good. It was an ecstatic religion: willed derangement, they believed, enabled direct access to the godhead, and we know their ceremonies to have been conducted under the power of wine suffused with hallucinogenic herbs, with many rituals culminating in outbreaks of violence, or sexual incontinence, or both.

The central motif of Mithraic iconography was undoubtedly the tauroctony: the slaying of the sacred bull. In every depiction, with remarkable uniformity, we see Mithras sitting astride a bull, plunging a dagger into its shoulder, while a dog and a snake lap at the blood, and a lion and a raven look on. A scorpion has attached itself to the bull's testicles. Our bull, we must allow, is not having a pleasant day. It will be observed that each of these animals represents a zodiacal sign: Taurus the bull, Leo the lion, Scorpio the scorpion; and the less obvious constellations: Corvus the raven, Hydra the Serpent, Canis Minor the dog. But who is Mithras in this symbology? I believe him to be Perseus – whose constellation sits astride Taurus in the heavens – which would explain his curious posture, that is, looking away from the bull he is slaying. For a hero to look at anything other than his goal would be unexampled in the classical world; only Perseus is famous for conquering a foe, Medusa the Gorgon, without looking directly at it. All of this to say: the Mithraists possessed a uniquely accurate star map, and one that fixed a point in time as well as space, for the zodiacal signs correspond to the constellations through which the celestial equator passed on the ecliptic when the spring equinox was in Taurus and the autumn equinox in Scorpio. This is where the constellations would have been situated in 4000 BC, and this, we must suppose, marks the point in time when the entity that came to be called Mithras introduced itself to the human race.

The Mithraic cult, then, understood the precession of the equinoxes, and celebrated Mithras as the one who steered the earth on its axis. Thus, the sun was compelled to kneel before him, for Mithras was the true sun, the unconquered sun: Mithras Sol Invictus. These were weighty mysteries, and the cult went to extraordinary lengths to protect them.

Initiation into the cult was difficult and dangerous. To join the order and advance through its seven ranks, the adept had to face a series of trials in a chamber of the Mithraic temple known as the Ordeal Pit. Trial by water, trial by fire, trial by combat and so on. Survival was not a given. One trial, for example, required the initiate to fight a bull, cut off a piece of its flesh, and eat it *during the combat*. Mithras was, in their mythos, simultaneously the one who slaughtered the bull and the bull itself, so this trial saw the initiate eating their god. The seven ranks were, in order, Raven (in Latin: *corax*), Bridegroom (*nymphus*), Soldier (*miles*), Lion (*leo*), Perses (the son of Perseus), Sun-runner (*heliodromus*) and Father (*pater*). Successful initiation into the community was marked by a handshake with the Pater, just as Mithras and the sun had once shaken hands, and so initiates of Mithras were called *syndexioi*, those 'united by the handshake'.

There was a further, final trial, one only taken up by the most devout of Paters, which required the initiate to have his right hand cut off. This was intended to be a gift to Mithras, and a sign of the Pater's courage, allegiance and faith in his god. As this was a god of contracts and agreements, the supplicant could expect his gift to be repaid – with special knowledge and with visions encrypted with wisdom. [. . .]

5
The Wolf of Whindale

I was lying on my back, unable to move, incapable even of turning my head. In the gloom, I could see – or I was somehow aware of the presence of – a figure standing by, carrying a lamp turned low and dim. This figure did not speak and remained in murky darkness so I could not tell its identity: guardian or captor, ministering angel or devil sent to torment me – I knew not. I wished to call out, but could not, so I lay still. Time was moving, so it seemed, very queerly – too fast or too slow, or somehow both at once, as when, in a panic, all around you seems to move thicklier, though this is but an effect of the celerity of your cogitations. I couldn't fix the figure in any wise: one moment I thought it a malevolent being, and the next I decided it was on my side.

Presently, I became sensible that the figure was approaching me, and I strained once more to make them out. For a moment, I thought it was Mr Crow, come back to see if I was all right, and for another moment I thought it was my sister, Mop – a very ridiculous idea, to think of her down in the grove. And then I grasped the reason I couldn't make out who it was. This was none other than the miner with no face. Long, long had he wanted to make my acquaintance, watching me make light of his existence and treat him as a jest to tell the young ones. Well, now I was to understand that he was as real as I. He crouched over me, and lifted his lamp to his awful no-face, that I might gaze upon its blank horror the more searchingly. I did so, feeling too terrified to breathe, and as I stared up into that vacancy, it, too, stared down into me – or so I fancied, for there was nowt to animate that face smooth as an egg, except the dancing of the lamplight – until presently he drew out a Barlow, which is a stubby little pocket-knife, and the way it caught the light bespoke how sharp the blade was, and he held it in one hand and with the other took hold of my chin. Of a sudden, I understood that he was going to cut off my face and wear it as his own.

I felt the blade – which seemed very cold, on account of how hot my blood was then, for though I couldn't move, my panic-stricken heart was pounding – press down on the side of my face, close to my ear. He paused, and I felt the tip of the blade dig into my skin. I think he was weighing up whether he should take off my ears into the bargain. The blade pierced my skin, and a quick trickle of blood shot down into my lughole, and while he held my mouth closed I tried my best to scream through my nose.

But presently I was released, and my oppressor turned away: a second figure was drawing near. The miner with no face stood back in deference to his approaching comrade, and slowly, slowly, he lifted up his lamp. Out of the gloom the second figure came, and I perceived that it was not stepping like a man, but rather swaying and loping in so stealthy and creeping a fashion that I did not realise how nearly it had come until I felt its very breath on my cheek – at which time I realised that it was a great dog, or, rather, a great wolf, very massive in proportion, and sniffing at me now as a prelude to taking a bite.

A fresh panic swept me up, and I strained once more to shift my ponderous body or at least cry out for help. And now the great wolf was turning in a circle just above my head; and now it stood over me; and now it settled down so that its great hairy belly smothered me. All was fear and darkness, and my lungs were ready to burst; and now the wolf clamped its teeth on my right hand and began to tug and tear at the flesh.

Who knows how long I suffered thus – a few minutes, a few hours – but at last the seizure passed (for it had been one of my turns, of course) and I came to alone, emerging from the gloom of my dream into the pitch dark of reality, where there wasn't a sound but the interminable drip-drip-drop of water moving unceasingly to find its proper level. My right hand felt like it was on fire – pain such as I'd never known, growing ever greater the closer I came to consciousness, bursting out like some sort of terrible blossom. When I touched it, right gingerly and that, it felt like some of the fingers were stuck pointing in the wrong direction, but, not being able to see, I wasn't confident of which way to twist them to get them true again. The very idea made me feel coggly, so I didn't touch it again.

Now, when I say pitch dark, that's exactly what I mean. Absolute, full dark. Your eyes don't ever adjust to it, because there's not so much as a glimmer to adjust *to*. How long I was on plouting about, feeling around with my good hand and trying not to dunch into owt with my wounded paw, I don't know. It seemed an age, and it occurred to me that maybes my workmates-as-was had murdered me after all, and that this was Hell, and that I'd henceforth be trapped here in darkness and eternal pain alone. I told myself to buck up for that. I would have given owt to have some light to see by though but.

After a deal of crashing about and bruising my shins, and discovering one blind end after another, I finally got a sense of my whereabouts, and very comfortless the knowledge was too: the way the walls were scooped and groined told me that these were ancient workings, made by the generations of miners afore us who used more primitive tools. The tunnel was so tight as to barely have elbow room, the miners not having used ponies to haul the spar in the olden days. Evidently, my workmates had dragged me and dumped me in one of the old coffin levels.

Whether they did so for their own amusement, by way of intimating that I was as good as dead to them henceforth, or if there was a yet meaner motive, I never knew, but either way a coffin-level was just about the worst place in the grove to have been left. Despite the name, every level in a lead-mine is in fact built ever so slightly *off* the level, not quite true, so that the water, which is continually shimmying down the walls and dripping from the roof, runs naturally away and out of the grove, down a central channel that eventually joins, tributary-like, another, larger channel. All of these channels converge until finally they form a steady stream of water that gushes, day and night, out of the daisy, which will be at the foot of a hill. And so, to figure my way out, had I been left in one of our modern tunnels, why, all I'd have had to do was reach down (with my good hand, of course) and feel for the direction of the water, and follow that, you see? But the exception to this was the coffin levels, so called because they gave you little more room than your long home, and which had been excavated by hand so many centuries ago, long afore anyone had properly thought through all the problems of drainage. All was catch-as-catch-can with our forefathers, and their tunnels spiralled madly underground through uncharted miles of the Whin Valley – I don't suppose there's mines anywhere in the world so extensively wrought. Whenever we broke through and discovered some of these old workings from past generations, we'd say 'The auld man got here afore us.' Some of their coffin levels was flooded entirely, some was blind, some had water standing long stagnant in them, and others still drained off into even older workings – and so to follow the waters that ran through them, that is, supposing a body was even able to do so, might lead you in precisely the wrong direction, and only deeper into the most hopeless darkness.

Well, I was feeling right sorry for myself by this time and, because I couldn't see it and assess the damage done to it, my hand was occupying most of my thoughts, and this is the reason, I suppose, that it took me so long to discover, tucked into the breast pocket of my shirt, the lucifer. Now, how it came to be there is a mystery, but I think my first guess – that Mr Crow had slipped it in there as a mercy after I lost consciousness – is likeliest true. I never had an opportunity afterwards to ask him; all I know is, I didn't ordinarily carry a lucifer but was very glad to have one at that moment.

Shielding my eyes so as not to utterly blind myself, I struck the lucifer on the wall, and found a candle and lit it, and things already seemed more cheerful – though my right hand was fearful to behold, with my fingers so twisted and knotted and barely hanging on. In the sobbing candlelight the hand seemed to perpetually twitch and jump and pulse and spasm, which made its deformity seem even worse. I tried to resist studying it.

Having divined my whereabouts, I made for the main level. As it turned out, I wasn't very deep in the grove, and had I not been so panicked and so pained, I'd have realised this sooner. Maybe ten minutes later I was making my way down the familiar first-and-last level, with the wet walls flicker-lit either side of me. The candlelight sent shadows leaping hither and thither, making me feel like I was in some enormous beast's gullet, and it was trying its best to swallow me down. I didn't care for that thought, but soon enough I could make out a piece of shimmery-blue night sky beckoning me on from the far end of the tunnel.

As soon as I stepped out into the fresh air, I doubled over and bowked. That often happens if you stay too long down the grove, breathing the foul stithe: at first, your lungs cannot tolerate the fresh air that they've been craving so long. But I didn't feel any better afterwards, as I usually did, only weak and light-headed, starved with cold, and my right arm a dead weight, with my destroyed hand twisting and complaining at the end of it.

The moon was full – a pearl of pure insolence high above me and my agonies and tribulations – and the uplands lay under it like a heap of blue blankets. There would be wind and rain tomorrow, I thought, maybes even snow, for the moon was haloed with mist. I looked east and west. The world seemed still as a stopped clock. I sniffed the air, which was beginning to seem fresh to me now, and looked up at the stars in their manifold formations. They fairly blazed. Yes, there was a great frost coming, late in the winter. I tried to feel lucky to not be down in the dark any more, but it was a pinching sort of night and that set my hand mounging afresh. I got a look at it in the moonlight, and it was properly mangled, so I set off walking and tried to keep my mind clear, for the pain was very bad and I had ten miles to walk and there was barely a farmhouse atween me and home. My great concern was that I might pass out again, for then the cold would surely do for me. I told myself to be glad that the night was so still, for a strong wind blowing against you high on the law will add two hours to a ten-mile walk and freeze you all the faster. At thirteen hundred feet above sea level, the cold bites you deeper than a starving rat, believe me. It was hard to feel glad of owt though but, with my hand looking like a smashed crab and throbbing as it was.

I hadn't gone too far afore the howl reached me, and, soon as it did, the fear took hold of me afresh, and with a grip that sunk into my marrow. The howl was like some terrible, long-imprisoned thing suddenly untethered; like a famished banshee let slip into the world. The sound hung on the cold air as though it had forgotten how to fall. Where could I run? Where would I hide? I looked east, where the land fell away by degrees to form Dardale Moss. It looked, that night, like a basin of mist, though I knew it to be the bleakest quagmire – a twelve-mile stretch with no shelter bigger than a birch or a dwarf oak. I looked north to the looming, irregular ascent of Cushy Law – but I didn't want to go that way, either, as there was something so very permanent about the great expanse that it made my little existence that night seem all the more fleet and vulnerable. At my feet, the pale grass trembled in a breeze I couldn't feel. I looked back at Dardale Moss, and thought how the mist looked like watery milk. And then it came again – the howl of the wolf, the hellish, melancholy clarion of the wolf, a ribbon of fury – and a wild fear thrilled through me again, and I thought I'd become frozen to the spot.

I shook myself free of this feeling and whirled about, and there, back the way I'd come, I saw it loping along, not five hundred yards off, head down like a guilty thing, its awful, yellow eyes blazing out at me. Strange how something in me knew it – straight off, categorically – to be a wolf rather than a dog. It was taller than any dog I'd seen – its legs seemed impossibly long. Its head and jaws were enormous, and its entire muscularity was different: front-loaded, it seemed to me then, as though it was permanently primed to leap.

It stopped dead when it saw me looking at it. I pretended that I was in the grip of a fit, and this vision was merely my imagination playing a trick – but no, that wouldn't do. The wolf was as real as I, out in the open, plain as you like in the light of the moon. There and then, I knew this was the beast that had killed Mr Playfair, and that I'd been in the wrong to scoff at the idea.

It looked at me, in the way such an animal will, with a sort of superiority, a sort of trivial interest; and then it seemed to incline its head, as if attending to a summons, or as if it was trying to get me in a right perspective. I took a slow step backwards away from the horrible thing – and then, as though it had only belatedly realised that it had every advantage, it bolted for me all of a sudden, flying straight as a dart, bounding along under its spine.

Judge if I showed a clean pair of heels! I ran like never afore, with my hand all but screaming at me to stop, as it was jarred every time my feet pounded the cold earth. Now and then, I'd step on a tussocky clump of rushes, which were damp and slippery, and so it was a flailing, plunging sort of run that I ran, and had there been anyone there to see me, I'd have looked a proper soft Johnny, escaped from bedlam in his pyjamas. What a terrible way to die, I thought, to be eaten alive by a thing like that, and then to be found next morning or the week after, pulled to ribbons, with your head bit clean off and planted on Windy Top like Playfair's was, and your eyes piked out by corbies, and through your white bones, once they've been picked clean, the north wind blowing forever more . . . My mind made time for such thoughts as I pelted along.

At first, I ran without direction, with the blood pounding in my ears and my teeth rattling about in their sockets. The only shelter nearby was our lodging shop, but that was back a-ways, near the entrance to the grove, and the wolf was atween me and it, and in any case I don't think I could have sheltered there, for shame of begging for help from the fellows who had lately mutilated me. But the wolf, I thought, must be closing on me by now, though I daren't look back for fear of slowing down. And then I saw the flue from the smelting mill, and so I made for that.

The flue was a chimbley about twenty feet high, and I thought if I could climb it I'd be safe up on the lip. How I was going to climb it one-handed, I had not a clue; but I'd no choice and must try. I ran flat out, every moment expecting to feel the wolf's great jaws closing around my thigh or tearing a lump out of my arse. The ground leading up to the flue was slightly inclined, and I cursed it for slowing me, though ever so little, but still I bounded up with my heart fit to burst in my chest and flung myself at the tower, my good hand thrust up and ready to grip at owt. My body slammed into the tower and the pain was like an explosion in my head. The breath was knocked clean out of me, but my good hand had caught on a helpful bit of stone, and with my last scrap of momentum I hoisted myself up, digging the toes of my boots in anywhere I could to steady myself. Somehow or other, I scrabbled to the top of the flue, defying the laws of nature to get there. And so I found myself lying on my belly, balanced on the lip of the flue with the blood singing in my veins, gasping for air, staring down at the great wolf that was snarling and snapping and panting and gulping and pacing about on the ground below.

In my mad climb up the flue, I'd torn up two of my fingernails on my good left hand, and they were now hanging on by little bloody hinges. They looked sore, but I couldn't feel them in my panic and with my brain already filled past the brim with pain. I tugged the two fingernails off altogether with my teeth, which was a miserable business. I spat them out, and the wolf immediately ran over to them where they fell and began sniffing and licking them, which made me cry out and curse it the more, the damnable monstrosity.

And thus I spent the night: prone, exhausted, the very target of the winter wind, feeling the starlight as so many needles of ice poking down into my bones, and always afeared to shut my eyes in case I lost consciousness and fell – either down the inside of the flue, where I'd be smothered in chokedamp, or down the outside of it, where the wolf was waiting, circling the base, all but examining it for any means of climbing up for some dinner. Its fur was brindled, freaked with greys and silvers – or so it appeared in the glamour of the moonlight – and, when it growled up at me, its teeth were white as birch and its eyes the colour of a miner's phlegm.

I've often thought how strange it is that sleep will insinuate itself atween a man and his thoughts, whatsoever thoughts they be, if only it is given time enough; that the most vexing worries and the worst cares must slide away sooner or later, and let King Sleep rule once more. And so it was that night: a stupor grew upon me, a great weariness about my heart, and, despite all my efforts to keep awake, I think I must have drowsed a little, because presently it was first light, and the stars were hiding, and the wolf was gone.

My whole body was stiff as a bone – oh, I was absolutely nithered! – but I told myself I'd sharp warm up once I got moving. Being elevated as I was, I could see a canny distance in all directions, and there was no sign of the beast. The morning sun glistened in a million brilliants on the dew. It gladdened the heart. Pockets of ground-mist nestled here and there. Nothing seems so very terrible once morning has got underway. I might even have tried telling myself that I'd imagined it all, if it weren't for the tracks I could see in the churned-up mud at the base of the flue. The wolf already seemed incredible to me, but it had been real enough.

My hand was a terrible colour now, mainly black, and it had swollen up fiercely. It was a continual ache and it weighed on me so. I'd have to get a doctor to look at it that very day or I was apt to lose it altogether. I'd seen what gangrene can do. I had to get moving. On top of that, my comrades would soon be waking, and I didn't want them to spy me perched up on the flue for their further amusement. So I eased myself over the lip and slithered down the side of the chimbley like a broken-backed rat.

Once on the ground, I got a look at the paw prints, which

were a terrific size, and I thought again of poor old Playfair, and what his final moments must have been like, and I was all but lamenting for him until I reasoned that I was only feeling sorry for myself in disguise, so I put a stop to that. Each paw print was a little larger than a man's hand, and I noticed the claws had left clean lines: they were sharp, unlike a dog's, which are typically blunted.

I'd a ten-mile walk in front of me, and for a time I wondered how I'd manage it – it was going to be hard lines; but then I hit upon a trick of an idea. I took myself by a circuitous route back to our lodging shop. There was a burn ran alongside it, where we'd go to wash at lowse, and I secreted myself underneath the little stone bridge, which, it being fornenst the lodging shop, meant that I'd be well hidden from their sight. I crouched there and stayed hid until my comrades emerged from the shop for their shift, keeping myself lively by inventing curses for them.

First came Heavens-Evans, marching ahead of the others, as was his wont, carrying himself as a great prize. Next came George Henry, deep in conversation with Mr Muffin, whatever they could have found to talk about. And last came Mr Crow, the great traitor. Mine own Judas Iscariot. My Lucifer – aye, my light-bringer indeed! They came blinking from the lodging shop, stretched, yawned, scratched and what-have-you, and then came wandering over towards the bridge where I was huddled. I thought I'd hear them talk of me, either to repent for the cruel turn they'd done me the day afore or to gloat over it, but not a one of them so much as mentioned me, which was a great insult to my vanity. I thought that this must be how it felt to be a ghost, supposing such exist, surrounded by life but reduced to the condition of onlooker and forced to understand how rarely the living pause to recollect them.

My workmates finished mortifying me with their indifference and all safely disappeared off over the moor towards the darkness of the grove. I bade them a tedious returning, and stretched my aching limbs out once more. Then I came out from under the bridge, and let myself in to the empty lodging shop. The door was always left on the sneck.

Inside, the pickings were thin, but there was a bowl of eggs and a great bar of black bread, and the skillet was still warm, so I helped myself to some breakfast. There was a little bacon, but it was oily, soft, wretched stuff. I ate as much of the eggs and bread as I thought I could manage, and then kept eating a bit longer just to be sure. At length, there was nowt left but a heel of bread, which I kept for my travels, and seven or eight eggs, which I threw against the walls of the shop. The hell with them all. Even after that, I still felt righteously aggrieved to have lost my right hand to them and got nowt back but pottage – like unto Esau who despised his birthright, Mam would surely have said – so I dragged the pillows from their beds, threw them all in a heap on the floor and pissed on them. May all their sons be tapsters. Soon I'd be gone, and I'd be long gone and all. If that meant I had to work at the Sill, then so be it. *Sill means trouble, Sill means trap* . . . Yes, yes, I thought, but if reports were true, and they would take on anyone there, then they'd not refuse me, and as long as there was a wage I'd keep body and soul together, and soon enough I'd be beyond the reach of any reprisals.

I threw open the door. It was a cold day, but the sun was in my eyes with a sort of vehemence. I chivvied myself up by minding on how I'd already outwitted a wolf, breakfasted, micturated on my enemies' pillows, and here I was still with plenty of day left. I left the lodging shop and went stepping forth like a calf fatted for slaughter.

6

The Pariah

'Mam, I'm home! Oh, me: I'm harmed! Me arm – maimed, Mam!' I wailed. How I could have joked about it is beyond me, really, but to do so has ever been habitual with me. 'Look, it's not my arm, really, just my hand. Look what they've done, the beasts.'

Mam and Mop barely gledged up, though I'd crashed through the door of the shieling and was waving my poorly hand right in front of them. So much for the famous Christian charity. They had already resumed their stitching.

Says Mop, 'I see poor Annie Granger's working as a washer now. Aye, she's dressing the ore. Isn't that a shame?'

Says Mam, 'It's improper's what it is. Kneeling and scrubbing in the dirt with all the young lads. But it's only to be expected, when her husband has a drink on him at nine in the morning.'

I tried a different tack. 'I will require monies to pay Dr Braistick to look at this,' I declared. 'Do you understand? I am in need of medical assistance, afore the black erysipelas takes hold!'

Says Mop, 'And then I saw Mr Croft, who said he'd have to think about raising his prices again soon.'

Says Mam, 'He's always mounging about his lot, but he does just as well as any and twice better than most. Last year his mutton was fivepence, I can tell you that. It's shameless! Old Croft must be turning in his grave . . .'

'Once again, you do not seem surprised at this misfortunate turn of events,' I said. 'It is enough to put suspicion in a fellow's heart.' With that, I gave up on conversational tactics and went hunting for Mam's money box; but when I found it, it had already been raided. I came storming back at them. 'What has happened to the pay I entrusted to you?' This got Mam started.

'It was unclean, so I cast it away.'

'You cast it away! That was all that remained of my last year's pay – what do you propose to live on, now that I'm incapacitated? The pennies you get from picking stones?'

'We will be compelled to show humility and live on the charity of the Church, which is the only family we recognise.'

I covered my eyes with my good hand. I couldn't bear to see the bitter fool a moment longer. 'You are telling me that you've given it to the Church. Jesus Christ!'

Mam shrieked at me never to use that name, and added, 'As for what's happened to your hand, why would I be surprised that the Devil has come for his due? *Whoever sows to please their flesh, from the flesh will reap destruction!'*

'*Destruction*,' added Mop, with a nod.

'Well,' says I, 'as it seems you have no regard for me, I will not tell you my news concerning the Whindale Wolf. It was very tasty news, and all. Very toothsome and nutritious. But maybe you'll learn of it another way.'

In the corner of the room lay the swept-up remains of my smashed spar box. My workmates had disdained the theft of the stones, as though my pariahdom might be catching and these items infected with my leprous scabbiness. I fished out the more valuable gems from amongst the mess of spar and whatnot, and pocketed them.

'I take my leave of you now, maternal parent. Fear not for the health and welfare of your only son, for even if I collapse on the road in pain and hunger, and sleep with my head in a puddle of cold horse piss, I'm sure that the rats and the kites and the ravens will come to nurse me; their hearts are not made of stone, and when they see a friendless man, so unhanded by his fellows, they will, I'm certain, cast off their savage nature and do me offices of pity. I leave you, too, Mop.'

I took my pocketful of tumblestone-gleanings to Harry Callan in Whindale Town, the same scoundrel from whom I had originally bought some of them, and sold them back at a very pitiful loss. Harry had a practised eye, knew a desperate fellow when he saw one, and acted no honester than his nature inclined – which is to say, crooked as a hound's back leg. He counted out the pennies while sucking his teeth, and the upshot was that I barely scrounged together enough monies to cover the fee for Dr Braistick. This was my next order of business.

'Now, Doctor,' says I, having taken myself over to his fine and fancy house, and having been admitted by his man, and having then waited – in a room that contained not a single book! and this was a learned man, supposedly! – an unnecessarily long while to see him, 'I'll put it to you straight: I don't like men of your profession, with their fatuous authority and do-as-I-tell-ye, when all the time they are changing their minds and swearing against the very thing they were professing last Tuesday. I don't trust a man who buries his mistakes and takes credit for hazards and chance. I don't take kindly to one who inflicts as many harms as he cures, and yet still expects a fee and a thanks-and-God-bless-ye afterwards. There: now I've been as square with you as I'm able, and I trust you'll be likewise with me. I hope that's plain!'

He took this canny well, all things being considered, merely saying that it was more plain than creditable, and then invited me to take a seat in case I hurt myself when I fell over.

I sat down, then he looks at my poor claw and pulls a face and says, 'Ghastly.' Now, there's a word I don't like: 'ghastly'. I don't reckon I've ever chosen to use it.

I was in a bad way, he reckoned.

I told him he'd have to earn his fee with something better than that.

He asked, could I move any of my fingers?

I could not.

He asked, could I move my wrist at all?

I could not.

My hand was very black now, and swollen like a pudding. After poking it and twisting it to his satisfaction, he sat back and exhaled through his nose for some time.

'So, Doctor, are you going to avail me of the prognosis?'

I did enjoy his look of surprise when he heard such words from the mouth of a miner with a tree root for a hand. But we miners were much beyond the average scale in education, as he should have known, and I was as far beyond again on account of my great bookishness and my contrarian reading programme.

The doctor proposed to bleed me, which would help with the swelling, and said he'd have to amputate my middle two fingers, which were hanging on by threads, but he'd do what he could to save the thumb. He offered to take off the hand entire, as it would make a cleaner job, but I says no, not if there's a chance that it might heal. So long as I've a thumb and one other finger, I can grip things after a fashion, and that means I'll can work. Reduced to one hand, I'd be lucky to get taken on as a farm labourer and eke out my days hoeing turnips and topping beets. He agreed to this.

Then I thought on, and asked him, afore he bled me and while I was still lucid, to tell me, as exactly and as precisely as he was able, how I might go about amputating my hand, lest I had to do it myself at a later date. He hummed and he hawed, and said how doubtful he was that I'd be capable of doing this myself, all of which got my temper up, so I assured him that not twelve hours since I'd already taken a bigger gliff than he could possibly appreciate, and that if it came to needing an amputation I'd try my luck with an axe and a hot poker, unless he gave me better advice.

So he told me.

After that, it was time to remove the two fingers that could not be saved. Since I couldn't afford his laudanum, he poured me a none-too-generous measure of brandy, which I knocked back at a gulp. He said he thought I'd pass out soon enough, being now somewhat short of blood, and that this was no doubt for the best; but in this he was wrong – he had said it as a sort of boast, and it's possible I stayed conscious out of sheer contrariness. He gave me a lump of leather to bite on, and then set about straightening the fingers that I wished to keep. I sank my teeth into my leathern bit very savagely, and at length he fixed some wooden splints and wrapped my fingers up in bandages.

After that, he had me place my hand upon a wooden block and produced his surgical instrument. I spat out the leather bit.

'A chisel! You cannot be in earnest!'

'It is the most apt instrument for the task.'

'A fucking *chisel*!'

'What would you have me use, Mr Malarkey?'

'I don't know! I don't swan around pretending to be a medical man, and charging folk a fee merely to swipe off their fingers with a tool that could be found in any fellow's house!'

'Let me be clear: you paid for the advice and the brandy

and the logs I added to the fire. The surgery I perform *pro bono*.'

'Ah, I see where you're going. You're thinking I might refuse to pay you. You are a chiseller indeed. Get to work, damn your eyes!'

He jabbed the blade close to my middle-finger knuckle, and then produced a mallet. With it, he whacked the end of the chisel so hard that, having severed my finger, the blade got jammed into the wooden block. Once he'd pazed the blade loose, we did it all again for the other finger. I was breathing very heavily by this point. My fingers had been causing me grievous agony, but I was sorry to see them go, all the same.

Then he sauntered over to the fireplace and drew the poker out from where he'd positioned it in the heart of the fire, then he brought it over and instructed me to hold my hand still. I pressed down on the bloody block, and got my bodily weight behind my hand in an effort to hold it steady. Then he dabbed the poker on each of the stumps. The pain was like a gimlet driven into my brains, and I nearly bit the leather through. There was now a faint aroma of frying on the air, or I thought there was, and I felt quite sick. At last, he dressed the wounds.

Having done me this service and received his fee, he warned me against drinking too much tea, as, according to a recent medical article he'd read, it had an injurious tendency. This was as gratuitous and insolent a piece of advice as ever I received, and I reciprocated by advising him never to let the same bee sting him twice, and then roundly accused him of quacksalvery – and then he sent me on my way.

I stepped outside, and the daylight swarmed upon me like a million white ants. Being so tired and sore, and having lost such a deal of blood, I felt about as weak as a kitten, but I had another eleven miles to walk afore I reached the Sill. Eleven miles over Driver's Law, which was a high, inconvenient road that afforded no shelter from the elements. Elements that included, I now knew, a wolf – one that had stepped, as it were, from the unwritten page of poor men's superstition and into the world of the actual. And would the wolf be able to smell the blood on my bandaged hand? Was that why it had chased me the night afore?

Such morbid musings led me to alter my plans. I wouldn't walk directly to the Sill, I decided, but rather, I would take the straight road north to Rutherchester. This would still be a ten-mile walk, but the road was straight and flat and easier-going and busier; I might even cadge a lift if I were lucky. I had a few pennies left in my pocket, so could stay a night or two at an inn, and then, once my hand had healed a little and stopped weeping, I could walk from Rutherchester along the Empingham road as far as it would take me in the direction of the Sill. This seemed a better plan altogether.

I breathed deeply and commenced my journey, humming an air to myself – I believe it was 'Foxes on the Mountain' – but as I was making my way through town, not in the least bit minded for trouble, I saw Malcolm Tyler. Malcolm was a milliner, so I used to call him Malliner. He was stood outside his shop, knocking the dust off one of his felt hats. Waiting their turn were several other hats, all stacked one on top of the tother on his head. He'd been passing the time talking to Meg Lewney, but when she spied me she turned her back and scurried on her way. Malliner's look soured and all when he saw me approaching. Very risible he looked, glowering at me from beneath his seven-hat chimbley, so I hallooed him, all friendly like.

'Well, good *day* to you, Malliner!'

'Is it? I can't say I noticed.' He looked like he was keeping his eyes trained on either end of his moustache.

'Oh, it's a good day for me, at any rate,' says I. 'It's the day I blow out of the whole Whin Valley for good. It's a seat of roguery, you know, full of treacherous backstabbers and chiselling doctors.'

'It'll be the Sill you're heading to, is it?'

'What's it to you?'

He said it was nowt to him, one way or tother.

'So why ask?' I replied, and called him a fopdoodle. And a cunt.

He said there'd be plenty of folk glad to know I was moving on, and I said there'd be plenty of dry eyes at his funeral, what of that? He didn't answer, which is lucky for him: there was nowt wrong with my left hand, and, even feeling coggly as I was, I reckon I'd have yarked him just to see those hats fly up in the air. But he said nowt, so I passed him by, and Malliner was the last I saw of Whindale Town for several years. He was a proper fool. The whole town was a prying, tattling nest of ninnies and calumniators when all is said and done.

If all the young men was bulls in the heather
How many young girls would skin them for leather?
Sing fol-de-rol de-rolly-oh!

If all the young men was mice in the kitchen
How many young girls would put traps out to catch them?
Sing fol-de-rol de-rolly-oh!

If a young man turns into a stock or narcissus
Would a young girl come running to snip him with scissors?
Sing fol-de-rol de-rolly-oh!

If all the young men was birds on the wing
Would the young girls encage them to hear them sing?
Sing fol-de-rol de-rolly-oh!

If the young men was foxes with high bushy tails
How many young girls would set dogs on their trails?
Sing fol-de-rol de-rolly-oh!

The inn I stayed at in Rutherchester was called the Three Shoes, and if you should happen to pass that way, please take this recommendation that you find lodgings elsewhere. A ditch of slurry would be preferable to the Three Shoes – if indeed it is yet standing, which seems unlikely, as its architecture when last I saw it seemed about as robustious as that of a house of cards. The filthiness of the place is not to be told: the reek was worse than my old lodging shop, and that had smelt worse than the grove. I'd wanted to order a boiled chicken for dinner, but they said they'd nowt left but trollybobs and mutton chops. I said I wasn't going to pay good money to eat a cow's arse, and ordered the chops; but when they finally came, they were vile. I tried to strike up a bit of friendly chatter with the innkeeper, a burly fellow with a great clump of wiry grey hair on his head, but I was met with silence and suspicion.

'I believe Mr Walter Corlett came from hereabouts,' says I. 'Now, did you happen to know the fellow?'

'Aye,' says he, leaning his weight on the counter afore us, as much to say *what of it?*

'Well, then, you'll maybes know what became of him. Is it true, as I heard, that he upped and left for Spain?'

I'd no reason at all to think Corlett really was in Spain, but I intuited that the innkeeper might be the sort who liked to correct a fellow when he could. But he was too wily.

'That's right: Spain,' he says.

'To do what, when he gets there, though but?'

'Play cards. Had enough?' He gestures at the remains of the chops.

'Enough? Aye, I'll say enough's enough – like there's enough water in your whisky; enough sand in your sugar!'

'And I've had enough of you. Sup up and fuck off.'

'Sup your blashy beer? I'd as soon you kissed my arse, you puff-guts bastard!'

Like as not, we'd have resorted to fisticuffs, and I cannot imagine I'd have given much of a showing on that score, but then this blowsabella pops up and starts making light of it all, and saying she'll open a fresh barrel of beer and bring me another, and not to mind her husband, for he was only so shaken up on account of them finding Walter Corlett's head on Driver's Law the morning afore, and hadn't I heard about it, and Mr Corlett had been a friend of her husband's, and really everyone was shaken up, so when a stranger comes in asking about the poor fellow, well, it—

She rattled on like this for a bit, and when she took a breath I managed to ask, hadn't Mr Corlett been missing for a number of months?

'Aye,' she says, 'He was, true enough, and that's why the head was right grisly and raw and that, so's we'd not've known him if it hadn't've been for his teeth – for, you know, Walter had those terrible buck teeth, poor thing, and folk would make game of him, though he always took it in good fun, to be fair, aye, he'd boast that he could eat an apple through a letterbox, and one time—'

'So Mr Corlett's head had lain exposed to the elements for some months . . . ?'

'Aye,' she says, 'And there's not a trace of the body, which is very strange, and no way to make sure of the manner of his death, you see—'

'So you mustn't be sure if it was the work of man or wolf, as was the case with Mr Playfair.'

'Who?'

'Mr Plover.'

'Oh, aye. For myself though but, I think it was the wolf. My husband thinks it the work of a man who hides behind the stories of the wolf, but . . .'

I looked on Mr Puff-guts with a more sympathetic eye,

then. Once, I had thought the same as he did. But I'd been disabused of such rational views, and now knew the world to be a wild and terrible place that condescended to logic only occasionally, so as to dupe us more deeply elsetimes.

Mrs Puff-guts was so complete a church bell, it took me some time and several pints of beer afore I could escape to my room. No sooner was I ensconced there than I understood that sleep was not to be found at the Three Shoes, for it was a parcel of shofulmen and fiddle-duffers – gambling, fighting and fucking all night – and so, having lain and sweated on hacky-dirty blankets waiting for the morning's light, I rose at last with a headful of discomposed cogitations, and made a long business of rising and dressing. The milk they gave me for breakfast was loppered, so I braced myself with a cup of the worst coffee I ever tasted and went on my way.

Having no Montaigne to chivvy myself up, I set forth thinking very gloomily on how that was two of my fingers in the grave, and I imagined them buried six feet under, a V-sign lying in wait for the rest of me to catch up. I didn't like this thought, but couldn't get it out of my mind's eye for a time, so I sang a few verses of 'The Rose of Whindale' until I'd raised my spirits somewhat.

Still I see my true love's eyes
Laughing ever silently;
And in whispers deep and wise
Still I hear her telling me:

Never tell of all you've seen,
Do a job until it's done:
Make your bed with all things green,
Love is easy lost and won . . .

The land climbed higher, and the elders gave way to stunted, bushy shrubs and heather. Whatever grew there grew in despite of the conditions, and had known conflict afore it knew owt else, and, I tell you, there's a part of my heart yet that loves that country. Amidst the desolation and the smattering of coarser flowers like the whin, you'd chancetimes spy a maiden-pink – or a flash of spring gentians, blue as lapis lazuli, or the more delicate hues of the mountain pansy and birds-eye primrose – and all the more precious it would be for its rarity.

It was at this time that I was, of a sudden, put in mind of my money bag, and, stood there in the wilderness as I was, I scrambled in my pockets till I'd found it – and discovered that the last of my pennies had been thieved. I thought again of the strange friendliness of the barmaid after I'd so nearly come to blows with her husband. I raged at the wilderness, and decried the inherent wickedness of the universe. I shouted at the butterflies, and told them, if they ever expected to live happily, they should not trust these three things: an adder when he's sleeping; a fart in a hurry; a woman when she smiles. I cursed my folly as though I'd been given no prior warnings of it.

And then I sat down on a rock. I felt no benefit for having theatricalised my rage. Did I ever? It was simply my character to behave thus. Maybe Mrs Puff-guts had lightened my pocket, and maybe she hadn't: I might as easily have lost my pennies by negligence. Realising my impoverishment, whatsoever the reason for it, had quite put me out of sorts. Where was the advantage in climbing so far, if the heart does not obtain a broader horizon of feeling to match the view? I was, as they say, at the end of my tether, if I hadn't slipped it entirely. And though I had but little love for the people and the circumstances to which I'd once been bound, there was a kind of grief about my heart now that I was out of the known world. Within a matter of weeks, I'd exhausted my every last point of human contact, as if my life were a heap of dry leaves or other such tinder, and suddenly I'd dropped a lit match and up it went: *whap!* When I crossed the line, I set a course of action in motion, all right, but how long would the consequences play out? Can a fellow's life be nowt but an endless swerve in the wake of a decision he can barely understand?

I pressed on for another hour or two, and the road became very slippery and inconvenient, but I kept faith in it, needs must, though I had to ramble over rocks and wade in water and march through sparty mud. A wastrel back at the Three Shoes had given me the vaguest of directions for how to find the mining offices, which were situated in an old bastle house, he said, which stood in front of a muckle-great outcrop of whinstone. You see, whinstone weathers slower than limestone or other surrounding rock, so it will tend to form jags and cliffs and outcrops where the rest of the land has sunk and worn away around it.

Well, at length I reached this bastle house. I'd seen no smoke or flues or other evidence of a smelting mill on my approach, which was a shame, for that was the line of work I reckoned I could best attempt, given my injury and that. Smelting or washing and dressing the ore. Something like that, I thought. The house was evidently being used as an office, and through the window on the first floor I spied a fellow sat working at a table, so I took myself up the stairs and knocked for entry.

There being no answer, I opened the door. The fellow I'd seen from outside was a secretary or some such, and he was scribbling in a great ledger spread in front of him on a desk that seemed too big by half for any purpose he might have found for it. This must be the place, all right. Forefinger raised in the air as though testing the breeze, he made me wait until he got to the bottom of his row of figures afore acknowledging my presence. Then he hopped down from his chair and hurried around the desk to meet me, searching my face as though he expected to find the latest news written there in brief.

I tell him I'm looking for work and he says yes, yes – very brusque like – and asks my name and I tell him: Caleb Benjamin Malarkey. (Did I tell you I had a middle name? It's of no consequence.) And then he asked if I knew my birthday, which I did, the twenty-third of December, though I wasn't sure of the year – eighteen twenty or twenty-one, something like that. And then he asked for my experience, so I told him how I'd mined lead, coal and tin; how I'd got my start washing and dressing the ore, and would be happy to do it again for a spell; how I'd smelted lead and knew the desilvering method of congelation and what-have-you, and I added that, to put my cards on the table, smelting was the line of work I'd been hoping for. I knew that the Sill was composed of trouble, which is to say whinstone, which is a bothersome tchew of a thing to quarry, and, given my injury, I'd prefer to have a go at smelting.

'There's no smelting mill here, Mr Malarkey. By the sounds of it, you've taken up a number of trades. Not found one to your liking, is it? Not that it makes any odds here at the Sill, I can assure you. We take all comers, even an itinerant labourer—'

'I'm not a navvy, you impittent get!'

He takes a step back and starts picking at a hole in his knitted spencer. It had been a while, it seemed, since he'd been called a get. Too long. Eventually he says, 'And why did you leave your last employment, Mr Malarkey?'

'A difference of opinion with my colleagues.'

And then he spies the bandage and asks, 'And what happened to your hand?'

'Difference of opinion.'

He sighed and shook his head and said that a pre-existing injury would complicate matters as far as he was concerned. I assured him that losing the use of my right hand had already complicated matters for me, as he'd appreciate if he'd ever tried to wipe his arse with his left.

He ignored this and asked if I knew what they were mining here at the Sill, and I answered truthfully and without animation that I'd never yet met with a soul who knew what was mined there.

'I always ask, because I find it amusing to hear people's ideas of what we're up to. I'll tell you what we're mining here: nothing!'

He evidently expected to be entertained by a reaction to this, but all I said was that I'd sharp get the hang of it.

'We're not mining, you see. We're searching.'

'Discovery? Fathom-tale it is, then. Dead work, that's all I need to know.'

'You may call it fathom-tale or dead work, or you may call it flat rate, but it's all there is: three shillings per day, to be paid every six months. You see, we aren't searching for a seam or a vein. The Sill is, strictly speaking, beyond the bounds of the mineral field; so, there! What we're searching for is an artefact – an object.'

I assured him that I knew what 'artefact' meant. I was finding him more wearying than the whinstone could possibly be. But I was also thinking of how quickly those three shillings a day would add up.

'Well, the artefact we're searching for is buried here, somewhere, and it's waiting to be found. It has come to be known as the Knack. Now, you'll be expecting me to tell you what the Knack is, or what it looks like – but I can't, you see, because I don't know! Nobody knows. The Knack is a mystery, utterly. But I'm given to understand that the finder will know it when he sees it. It might be that the Knack would appear in a different form to me, should I be the one to find it, than it will to you, if you're the one it chooses. A strange job and no mistake, eh? Not for everyone. But you'll be well remunerated . . .' And then he laughed a silly, unbecoming laugh, and added that I'd find that the men were 'fascinated' (his word) by the work. He was certain that, soon enough, I'd be fascinated too.

I ask how long they had been on this fool's errand, and he says 'Oh, five-and-twenty years is as far back as the records go,' and he gestures towards the shelf of ledgers behind his desk.

He put a lot of store by these records, I thought, as he made his way back to his chair. The earliest of them might have been the same age he was. I ask how he could be so certain that this 'Knack' really existed, if the only two things he knew about it was that it was well hidden and might look like owt.

'Oh,' he says, 'It exists, all right! Don't you worry about that. Master Siskin wouldn't have paid for so many years of labour for nothing.' And that's how I confirmed the rumour I'd heard that Siskin was the mine owner at the Sill, just as he had become the latest owner at Windy Top.

If it wasn't all for nowt, I declared, pointing at his ledgers, then it was for seven-eighths of nine-tenths of fuck-all. I disliked this fellow's whole manner, and I let this be known, and asked him what sort of an enterprise this was, men being paid to search for the Lord knows what.

He twitched and frowned, and, finding himself at a momentary disadvantage, shifted his meagre weight in his creaky chair afore he rallied. 'Well, so long as we're paying you, what are the odds to you? I'll tell you one thing: the men here don't complain, and they don't give up. None of your fore-shift and back-shift here. None of your Chartists ganging together in combinations and electing a steward. No place for loafers – everyone mucks in and doesn't let up!'

He'd found a combative note and was piping it for all it was worth, but seeing how far I was from qualifying as the target of his sneering, being the one fellow in my whole partnership who wasn't set on forming a combination, I paid him little heed, saying simply that I reckoned they'd let up at lowse, and maybes then I'd enjoy a more sensible conversation.

At this, he gives that silly laugh of his again, and says I might be waiting a good while for lowse, as I'd soon see.

I made no answer to that, but up and left the quill-driver in his bastle-office, surrounded by his ledgers and his accounts, all neatly shelved in sequence for the great audit that would never come.

7
At the Sill

A quarter-mile further down the road, I found the entrance to the Sill, though it was half-hidden and the path leading up to it was green and overgrown. Now, the daisy at Windy Top was a proper entranceway, and when you walked in under the inverted horseshoe of slates, which had a keystone at the top and everything, you'd feel a wee bit reassured that human hands had shaped it thus. But here at the Sill, there was nowt but a crack in the whinstone shelf, only big enough for one man to enter or leave at a time. It looked, for all the world, deserted; but this had to be the place, for it was surrounded by an efflorescence of queer polypetalous yellow flowers that I couldn't identify, as the quill-driver had told me to watch out for. Well, I thought, I can have a keek and see if owt's stirring inside, and if not I'll head back to the quill-driver for an explanation.

Sill means trouble, Sill means trap . . . I couldn't shake off the saying as I ducked and entered and began to make my way along the level. As I did so, I remember feeling a great sense of unease and foreboding, as though I might never again see daylight. Perhaps that sounds like an everyday sort of concern in my line of work, but it is not so: you cannot afford to be entertaining such timorousness willy-nilly; you must hold it off if you're to keep a clear head. But there was no resisting it on this occasion, and I'd the strangest conviction, as I crouch-waddled along, and the sound of the wind and the birds fell away, and the closed-in, pent-up pressure of the air increased, that I'd passed a point of no return.

It was a roughly excavated level – not a horse level, as they weren't mining here and therefore wouldn't have any spar to cart out – and it was more like a naturally formed cave than a grove. Nothing about the place was proper. The roof was so low that even I, who will never be tall, had to stay crouched much of the time. (I call it a roof, but it wasn't formed of sandstone slabs: it was crudely dug out the same as everything else.) There weren't enough supporting posts for my liking, and those that were there appeared coated in woolly, snow-like mushrooms, so I knew they must have been rotted through, and unworthy of the trust that had been reposed in them. Also, there were far too few candles and lamps. Ordinarily, a mine's first level will be well lit, comparatively speaking, and the candlelight upon the regular posts as they recede into the distance can easily trick the eye so that you momentarily think yourself in a great and tenebrous cathedral; but the Sill could never create this effect, being too irregular and too dark altogether. Water dripped and ran down the walls, and flowed and trickled about my feet, but there was no central drainage channel, and the lack of one had led to the creation of vast pools through which I found I had to wade, sometimes knee-deep.

It was not until I made my way further into the Sill that I saw any other miners, and, when I did, the feeling of foreboding at once rose up in me again. Men worked here and there, seemingly without arrangement, picking and chipping and scraping. They reminded me of a schoolroom full of scapegrace rattlescawps made to stand facing the wall – and then I realised why it had struck me so strange: each man worked alone, as though he had cavilled himself where he pleased, and not in a partnership or a team as was usually the case. It might sound queer if you haven't been engaged in that line of work yourself, but in a good, efficient operation there is a sort of thread that connects the men to one another, of which the chatter and the songs are merely the most obvious manifestations. The thread might be, as it were, slack much of the time, but as and when required it lets you know of its existence through a thousand little tugs and twitches, as the fellow you're working alongside might pause and feel about for a turn-bat, and you naturally fall in step with him and place one in his hand without him having to ask for it. And if a fellow should cry 'Put nowt down!', then all within earshot would stop work at once, as though spellbound, for this was our watchword. Such was the power of the thread. The only thing I can liken it to is dancing, though it's true I've little experience of that.

One Christmas, when I was fourteen or fifteen year old, there was a dance in Bob Little's barn, and they had a fiddle player and a fellow playing the small-pipes, and when they struck up 'The Fair Flower of Northalbion' I caught the eye of Kitty Charlton, and asked her to dance. She was, it was universally held, the bonniest lass in the valley, with the sweetest dimples when she smiled, as she often did, and as she did when I jumped up and asked her to dance. She was two years older than me, and more than two inches taller, so I reckon it was an indulgent sort of smile, but it was sweet for all that. Anyway, I knew the steps all right and though I passed through them at something like the correct interval, I learned there and then that I was no dancer. But Kitty assuredly was – graceful and easy, as though her movements were all natural and inspired and, as it were, only coincidentally those that the dance required. And that's like the difference between work when it's going well, as it should, and all are moving in tandem according to the directions of the invisible thread, and work when it's going poorly, stop-start like, and everybody getting in each other's way. And the Sill was as ungainly and uncomfortable as a floor full of dancers such as I had shown myself to be. Work was getting done here, but in about as unsatisfactory a way as you can imagine. All of this I grasped intuitively right off, though, had you asked me, I couldn't have put it into words.

I goes over to a fellow half-turned in my direction, and ask him cheerily, 'How, marra, who's the gaffer round here?'

He acted as if he hadn't heard: nor look nor answer gave he me, only he kept attacking the wall with his poll-pick, with no concern for the sharp chips of whinstone that flew hither and yon each time he swung. He was whispering and muttering something to himself, but not in response to my words. I'd soon learn that all of the men at the Sill were continually muttering, but at this time I thought it peculiar to him.

'I says *who's in charge*?'

Again, I got nowt back in reply but the *sotto voce* murmuring.

I say, 'Look, how's a bloke supposed to know what's needing doing?' and I ask him if he's deaf, and so on.

He continued to stare at the face of the shaft, pick-pick-picking away at an area that he seemed intent upon. I considered giving him a wee rabbit punch for his insolence, for that's the way of it sometimes: when you're the newcomer you have to step up the first time a fellow gives you any lip or else you'll be dogged with all sorts of cheek ever after. But this place didn't strike me that way. It seemed too strange for such conventional shenanigans. So I marched off – marched isn't the right word, crouched over as I was, but there you go – muttering various oaths in a somewhat theatrical manner, as you do when you've been met with silence and you're making up for the lack of response you received.

The walls consisted of a dark rock I couldn't quite identify. It was black in colour, fibred with blue, and wet as a tooth; it was like whinstone, but not quite it, and it wasn't felspathic: no tea-gold sparkling fissures, no glint of quartz to catch the tail of your eye. Instead, a strange yellow oxide like whin flowers festooned the walls in various places, or leaked through the sandstone bricks that constituted the roof, much as thill would leak through the sandstone back at Windy Top.

Down the way was another fellow, wrapped up in his work. I gave several great sighs and coughs as I approached him to ensure he heard, and tried my luck again. Well, to make a short story of it, I got precisely the same insolence from him, and from the next bloke I tried – and he was one of the blackleg Williams-Joneses that I'd worked with the month afore. But his features – insofar as I could judge of them in the candlelight, for his visage was thickly begrimed with all sorts of muck – showed not a hint of recognition when I spoke to him: he'd a wistful half-smile about his lips, but I was a rank stranger to his sight. I tried a phrase of his language that Aneurin had taught me – '*Bore da, ffrind, sut wyt ti?*' – without noticeable effect. Even when I grabbed him by the shoulder, he stared straight through me, and then gazed over my shoulder at the shaft behind me, more interested in that than in the fellow sufferer that stood in front of him.

A wondering kind of despair began to creep upon me. I began to conceive that this wasn't mere unfriendliness on their part; it was more akin to sleepwalking, being an involuntary and uncanny condition, only stranger yet for its afflicting such a great raff of folk all at once. The further in I crept, the more fellows I saw in like condition, and never a one would speak or acknowledge me in any way. Some of them laboured in nigh-on absolute darkness, the sound of their picks dull and regular and thoughtless as clockwork;

some of them were stark naked or nearly; and some of them carried fearful wounds, I knew not whether self-inflicted or from a fall of stones or if they sometimes attacked each other, and I thought of my own maimed hand and imagined us all in a vast underground hospital. When next I happened upon a poll-pick lying on the ground – for there were many such tools strewn about the place – I took it up, as much for self-protection as owt else.

I'm a reasonable fellow, and I won't say I don't relish a reasonable amount of resistance, but to have encountered this queer vacancy time and again was fairly nibbling at my resolve, which had held up canny well till then. I saw several more of the blacklegs I'd so recently worked alongside, but they did not or could not see me, and so I passed like a wraith. What sort of a place was this, where men worked without direction, without coordination, without speaking or even seeing each other? They seemed – it eventually occurred to me – to be in a state of seizure: this is how I must appear to those around me, when I took one of my turns, I thought. I felt my way, plouting forwards, for on top of all else it was just the gloomiest grove I'd ever visited. The water lay everywhere in vast pools and puddles, sometimes draining off every which crazy way down hidden faults, sometimes streaming down from the roof – I was never wholly confident that the whole place wasn't about to come crashing down upon me like impending doom.

And then, there he was. As soon as I saw him, by the light of the candle he held, I, too, brightened: the Iron Devil! True, he looked strangely haggard, I thought, as if he'd lost weight in the brief time since I last saw him. His belt seemed to be pulled tight at his waist: he looked like an old man grown too small for his clothes. But I knew by the hunted, apprehensive look in his eyes that he had still a human soul inside him. I imagine my face must have taken on much the same cast. I wasted no time in asking what was wrong with the other fellows, what was wrong with this blamed hole, what was wrong with everything.

'As you see them now, why, so they become, within a few days of getting here. There's not a man down here who could give you a sensible word, nor know you, even were he your brother. They work, and they work without ceasing. And you can hear them mumbling and murmuring the whole time, though it has no more sense than the sound of the wind in the trees.' His words were not comforting, but his voice was mellifluous and steadying, as of old. I found I'd rather missed hearing it.

'These are not men,' I declared. I thought of George Henry with his mean little mouth saying that the men who worked here were the *residuum*. But I spurned his word, as I did all of his sayings and doings. 'They are automata,' I announced.

The Iron Devil was right about the murmuring: the place was like a whispering gallery. Little by little, your ear attuned to it, against your will. When I asked him where the face was, he smiled and shook his head and said it was everywhere. I knew by that that there was no normal procedure here, and didn't trouble to ask any such questions again.

Most of the automata were incapable of owt so finicky

as lighting a candle, which were less and less numerous the further you ventured. It seemed that the creatures worked by touch alone, which was just about possible, for even at its greatest depth the Sill was never altogether dark, much of the rock giving off a very pale blue glow. This was imperceptible if you had a candle on the go, but blow that candle out and eventually your eyes would adjust to the queer blue gloom. For this reason, the Iron Devil and I were scrupulous in keeping a candle burning at all times: we didn't want our bodies to adjust to the place any more than was inevitable.

I asked the Iron Devil how long he'd been down here, and he looked at me sheepishly and made an evasive reply. Hitherto, I'd have pressed the matter, but something in me knew to let it drop. Strange, to have been promised three shillings a day, but to neither know nor care how long you'd been at work! A change was working its way through me. Everything about the place was dubious and contrary to any other workplace I'd known. The air down there seemed filled with the oppressive sense you get just afore a thunder storm, when you can scarcely catch your breath and everything crackles with suspense: that was how it was every moment, except it never broke.

As it seemed we could talk of little else, we talked about the Knack; but our conversation was unlike any I'd ever had or heard. Truly, we knew nowt about the Knack. We have been sent here to search for it, but the quill-driver's instructions were next to useless, and each of us was as ignorant as the tother. Regardless of that, we tried to talk our way through to knowledge, as though we were two men sunk in a mire, hoping we'd be saved if I pulled on his bootstraps while he pulled on mine. One of us would ask a question, and one of us would endeavour to answer it, using reason, deduction, imagination, guesswork, supposition, nous and whatever else God gave us. It seemed a natural way to pass the time, for we were deep underground, where everything begins. Where the water that slakes your thirst is first forced up betwixt galvanic pressures until it bursts out as a spring. Where the coal that makes the steam that powers the engine that brought you here comes from. Where the seed that grows the tree that makes the wood that makes the cradle that dandles the bairn that grows to be the man that kills you takes root. We were there, pick-pick-picking away at the shale and the schist, looking for we knew not what, surrounded by automata soulless as though, on the day of creation, they had remained tight-lipped to the heavenly insufflation, and never been owt but clay. And so in this almost total darkness, by which I mean an almost total darkness of every kind, our words went twirling and whizzing up like sparks.

At first, we spoke of practicalities and such things that men of our trade would want to know, and so one of us – I think it must have been me – asked, 'How heavy is it, do you think?'

And one of us – I think it must have been the Iron Devil – answered, 'Not so heavy. It must be light enough for one man to lift, for these fellows never work together, so they'd never twig to lift it jointly.'

'Will it be faceted like a crystallised carbonate of witherite?'

'No, it will be flat, as I suppose, or lenticular.'
'Is it not sharp and jagged?'
'No, I say it is round as a cat's chin.'
'I think it will be of an impossible design, as of a six-sided pyramid or such.'

But as time wore on, our questions became untethered, and in the end ranged freer, perhaps, than either of us would have liked. Too gloomy, down there, to tell if the other man was smiling as he spoke; our words took on, by turns, a simplicity like the talk of children, and a complexity that bewildered our own selves. Ignorance as regards the practicalities of the Knack had not prevented us from speculating; why should it now be a bar to our enquiries into its abstruser dimensions? Well, they say the heart of the foolish is like a cartwheel, and his thoughts like a rolling axletree, and even so it was with myself and the Iron Devil as we toiled in the pit.

'Is the Knack a natural thing, do you think, or a human product, as of a talisman?'
'It is an inhuman product. It is the *signatum* of the forces that made it.'
'How will it feel to find the Knack?'
'Like a conversion.'
'The gladness of it, I suppose?'
'Like a conversion. Or like the way something once believed, though long disowned, is apt to come echoing back to you, as though it were imploring you to hold it just once more in mind.'
'Like a conversion.'

'Like a conversion to the point of view that the world is a created thing; that God entered, once, only to withdraw, leaving behind nowt that didn't bear His signature.'

'His signature?'

'His *signatum*.'

'Leaving nowt behind, you say?'

'Nought that didn't bear His signature. As when a thaw unlocks the river that feeds a waterfall.'

'His signature. As when winter comes, and the waterfall grows fangs.'

'As when winter comes, and we wait for spring and think it will never come, but, at last, there's a morning when the south wind breathes upon us while we sleep, even before the window has been opened . . .'

'How I miss the sweet south wind . . .'

It was all as Timaeus said, according to Mr Plato anyways: we reasoned rashly, and our discourses, like our lives, had great participation with the temerity of hazard, and went shooting about scatter-brained all over the place. Truly, I think a sort of fever had come upon us, attacking us both at an equal rate, so that we were both patients, and also both each other's nurse. The best way I can describe it is to say that, for better or for worse, we ministered to each other.

'I think we are in the belly of the whale, are we not?'

'In the labyrinthine entrails of the leviathan.'

'And is the Knack very perfect?'

'It is perfect or it is nothing.'

'It is perfect. Such a labour as this was never set in motion merely to find a flaw. Master Siskin owns the Sill, and Master Siskin is a man, and to prize a flaw is a womanish thing to do.'

'I knew a woman who took such an attitude to her buttons and duffels and what-have-you: she wouldn't wear a plain one. She had to have the ones with flaws, and took more pride in them than a soldier does his scars. And even I, who call this a womanish thing, must admit that it is the flaws that linger longest in the remembrance. So it is with this woman: her other ways and habits, I suppose, will come back to me if I think on her awhile, but what I remember best about her is this strange habit of hers to seek out the flaws in seashells and in flowers.'

I looked at him when he said this, and saw in the candlelight that a tear had left a clear line down his cheek – and so he appears to this day when I recollect him.

'Why are we not like the others who work here?'

'A better question: why are we not altogether different?'

'A better question? Are we not altogether different?'

'Not altogether. You should have noticed that all this time we've been digging – and who knows how long that has been? – we have not stopped to eat or sleep. See how thin we've grown. You are a death's-head on a mop stick.'

'As are you.'

'As am I. And yet, I think it must be with you as it is with me: we don't feel the need of rest or nourishment. Now, how can that be, unless this place is exerting some force upon us, which is having something of the effect it has on these other creatures?'

'We have not even stopped to drink. We don't carry so much as a bottle to swig. How can that be?'

'We soss the water that runs down the walls. We browse on the mushrooms that grow upon the rotten wood. It's shameful to speak of, but that's what we have been doing.'

'I saw you do so. I didn't think you had seen me doing so.'

'I saw you do so. And I have seen the automata doing so. I think it is the only way to stay alive down here. It's shameful, to soss at dirty water like a dog, but that's what we've been doing.'

'But I think I must have slept a little. I must have rested and shut my eyes, even if it were standing here and leaning on the wall.'

'If it comes to that, I could say we both might be sleeping and dreaming at this very moment.'

'And maybe we are! But to have worked so long without proper food, without a bit of bait, that is very strange. I think we have not been at work for so very long, after all.'

'It might be that more time has passed than we realise. When you first came here, your hand was bandaged. See it now: the bandage has rotted away and perished. Your wounds have healed and scarred. It might be that we are exactly like these others. The voice you hear as I say these words might be no more than a phantasm of your brain. You might be flattering yourself that you're unaffected by this place, when in fact a visitor would discern no difference between you and any other of these sleepwalkers.'

'You must not say such things. Do you mean to send us both mad? We've nowt in common with these frightful hideosities. I cannot believe that they are human beings. I think they have no blood, no bones.'

'Nor mind, nor heart. Nor soul.'

'Nor soul. I think if you were to break one of them open with a pick, you'd find nowt inside, just as, when you break open a rock, you find inside nowt but more rock.'

'That is well said.'

'Some say the living body is the grave of the soul.'

'I say this place is a grave for the living body.'

'The living. We are here to make a living. How do you think we are to be rewarded for the finding of the Knack?'

'With our heart's desire, like as not.'

'With our heart's desire, like it or not.'

'With a great pay, beyond our dreams: take it or leave it.'

'Far beyond?'

'Over the hills and far away.'

'And will it be beautiful?'

'The fear that we're bound to feel upon finding it might blind us to its beauty. But this will pass. We will remember it as beautiful, no doubt. If we live to tell of finding it, we'll not can describe it without saying it was beautiful.'

'If we live, you say? If we live to tell?'

'Why, look at us: skin and bone, my friend. See my arm, now, it is withered away! It was twice as thick, once upon a time.'

'Once upon a time.'

'See how often we must stop and breathe.'

'We are not the men we were, once upon a time.'

'We've weakened for the want of sleep, I think.'

'Our bodies cry out for it.'

'Will finding the Knack be more like meeting a man or meeting a woman?'

'Like a child, surely, but like no child that ever lived.'

'One that was never naughty, nor ever good, nor ever kissed.'

'Nor ever scolded when it was bad.'

'It was bad.'

'Will it be bad for the one who finds it?'

'It must carry a deal of luck within it; whether good or bad, who can say?'

'There are times in our life when we can divine that our luck has changed, but whether for better or worse might not be clear until much later.'

'Might not be clear. Our thinking might not be clear. Montaigne says the mind, unless it's busied about some subject that can bridle it, is apt to scatter itself through a vast field of imaginations.'

'A vast field? Scattered? Like stones?'

Often I knew not whether I was speaking the words or hearing them spoken; I suppose that talking in the darkness under such conditions can play tricks on a fellow's brain. Some of our questions went unanswered, not from rude impatience but simply because we could not frame a reply.

'What does Brinsley Siskin want with the Knack?'

'What does the Knack want with Brinsley Siskin?'

'If we find it, will it save us?'

'And if we do not find it . . . ?'

'Does that which is past and gone still exist?'

'What song did the sirens sing?'
'Who cleft the Devil's foot?'
'Why did the Lord make trees and grass afore He made the sun, moon, and stars?'
'Where shall wisdom be found?'
'Wherefore is there a price in the hand of a fool to get wisdom, seeing he hath no heart to it?'
'What do cats fight about?'
'What's the smell of pear drops?'
And many's the song we sung, and sung it through and around again, until its end coincided with that of our patience, and we sang hymns and all, for all my mislike of them. We sang 'See How Great a Flame Aspires' which had been written, I'd heard, by a fellow after he'd been preaching to the colliers at Oldshield: *Still the small inward voice I hear!* And we sang 'Out of the Depths I Cry to Thee', while at our feet the dirty water hurtled and snorted, snickering and hockering.

Time passed in this fashion. We picked and dug as and when and where the fancy took us; and if we found some charge, we'd make use of it. Our fingers fluttered over the walls like those of a blind man over a plate of food. And never a lough loaded with jewels, as we'd find at Windy Top and elsewhere in the mineral field, nor even so much as a lump of spar to catch what light there was. But at length, hewing away as we did ceaselessly and without division into day and night, we found it. We found the Knack.

It was nested in rock, glowing bright blue like an airy chunk of sky, coruscating madly down there in the depths.

Indeed, the glare was such that I should have been feared it would be scalding hot, but somehow I knew that it would not be so. It was about the size of a man's fist, which they say is about the size of a man's heart, and it was shaped – that is, it had been cut and polished, though by whose hand I cannot conceive – into the semblance of a bull's head. An ugly shape for such a marvellous bright gem, I thought; and then I remembered my spar box and the design I had chosen for it, and the coincidence stranged my mind. The yellow oxide all around the site where I found it was very thick, and, being lit by flickers as it was, the yellows seemed to sway, and I thought again how like flowering whin it was, shivering in a brusque wind.

Thoughtlessly, I reached down and seized the Knack – and still I don't know why – with my maimed right hand. And as I gripped it, it gripped me: it felt quick, and warm, and I found I couldn't let go of the thing, and the more I struggled to unclasp my birdlike thumb-and-two-fingers, the more resolutely fixed my hand remained. The Knack seemed to be oozing a sort of gum that gave the palm of my hand all sorts of ticklish sensations, and which welded it even more firmly to me. I almost grabbed the Knack with my left hand to wrest it free, but I was afraid to, lest it should stick to that one just the same.

Holding the Knack felt like being bled: all the precious vitality seemed to be draining out of me, and in its absence a horrible sort of clarity seemed to be unravelling in my brain. I tried to work my pick between the Knack and the flesh of my hand, but I couldn't get any purchase on the damned thing, and any pressure I applied sent the pick stabbing directly into my fingers. It was as though the Knack was glued to me, tightly and absolutely, and had been so for some time.

Panic was rising in me, but Aneurin was pestering me about the automata, and saying that a change had come over them. Really, I was too concerned with the change that had come over my hand to attend to owt else, but I gledged up, and saw one or two of the creatures stepping back from their work, as though suddenly puzzled to find themselves here, underground, staring so intently at a wall. There was a slight sense of relaxation about them, a loosening of tension about their shoulders. I saw one of them touch his chin as though for the first time, and then I noticed that their interminable murmuring, which had accompanied our labour all this long while, had fallen into unison. Their words were no more intelligible for that, but it was unsettling to be down there with an army of waking sleepwalkers all murmuring the same thing of a sudden. It stopped me from thinking about my poor hand for a moment, in any case. It was as though the thunder that had seemed to be threatening all the time we were down there had just started to break, with at first the most distant rolling, far over the horizon, but headed our way all the same.

'*Fy duw* . . . I think they are waking!' cried Aneurin.

I said aye, whatever was left of them was waking.

Next, they became cognisant of me and the Iron Devil – maybes they sensed that we were not as they were – and they began to shuffle towards us. At first it seemed they moved without volition, or according to a mysterious group logic, as a school of fish might zig and zag in unison. But it was towards us that they tended, which was a sight to quicken the liver.

I cried out 'Put nowt down! Put nowt down!' at the top of my lungs, for these were the magic words of old that would bring all work and movement to a sudden stop, anywhere within earshot. But alas, such sorcery did not obtain down in the Sill, and the creatures kept stumbling towards us, jostling against one another now, with no more regard than the leaves blown on a breeze – at most, maybes one or two of them shook their heads, as if momentarily distracted by some ancient association still attached to the sound of the phrase, but that was all. In my despair, I repeated the cry a number of times – 'Put nowt down! Put nowt down!' – until my voice cracked and I thought I'd start bawling and bubbling on like a bairn.

Awake they might have been, but the automata were yet beyond language and reason, and still they closed in on us. But presently Aneurin had a better thought, and taking up a jumper-rod he began to whack it against the nearest supporting post. This is what you did when you needed to send the signal of 'Put nowt down' a greater distance than your voice alone could cover: you would beat on the rails or on a post five times, the first two slow and the next three quick. This would bring work to a cessation. *Slow . . . slow . . . quick-quick-quick.* We called this jowling.

This is what the Iron Devil now tried – *slow . . . slow . . . quick-quick-quick* – and I cannot tell you the relief it was to see this tattoo give pause to the creatures' motion. They stood afore us, the nearest but a few yards away, frozen utterly, even as though God had poked out one of His long and holy fingers and stopped the pendulum on the great clock of the world. Were they so much as breathing? I knew not. Aneurin looked at me and I looked at him. *All's still at the Sill*, I thought, and the silly phrase immediately lodged in my thoughts and there began to beat and repeat its own mad tattoo throughout much of what I'm about to tell you.

We both understood that we needed to make use of this strange lull and try to find our way out of the Sill altogether, though we had nowt but a hunch as to which was the proper direction. Nor did we know how long the automatas' bewilderment might last. And yet neither of us had made a move. So I said, 'Look sharp!' and started forward.

'What if they wake up once more?' the Iron Devil murmured from close beside me.

'If they do, you make sure and jowl the signal again, quick smart!' said I, though I think, in fact, I might have used some coarser turns of phrase.

And so we began to weave our way among the stilled creatures. They were statues, very like those of saints in a cathedral, for they had a queer, beatific blankness of expression, and some of them had hands raised as though in almsgiving – and they were all, as it were, arranged for our perusal: they faced us, even those who had initially been beyond our sight. It was an eerie thing, to walk among a herd of statues all turned in our direction. It meant that they had all, every man Jack of them, been making their way towards us at the moment when the Iron Devil stilled them.

We moved as nimbly and speedily as we could. Presently, a hissing sound arose, like a long-drawn wave breaking on a shaley beach, and suddenly they recommenced their awful, eager-sounding whispering. It was our time to freeze now, and we stood still and watched them, saucer-eyed, to see what would happen next. The creatures made it through one round of their whispered incantation (for that is what it was like, after all: an incantation) and then suddenly, as at a signal we had not perceived, all of them turned to face us again – just spun on their heels, pivoting in regimental unison as though the pair of us were magnets and they were nowt but iron filings. At that, my companion and I nearly leapt into one another's arms in fright.

'Jowl!' I cried, and the Iron Devil came to, as it were, and lurched for the nearest post, and even as he was beating out the signal – s*low . . . slow . . . quick-quick-quick* – the automata were shuffling forward, and reaching out their arms to apprehend us. But thanks be to fortune (I say fortune, for I cannot be persuaded that God was watching the events down at the Sill) the old trick worked again, and the creatures were spellbound and fixed in place once more. *All's still at the Sill.*

At about this time, I became aware of my right hand again, or, rather, I became aware that I was *not* aware of it, as it was now completely numb all the way up to my elbow. I found myself looking at it to make sure it hadn't dropped off altogether; but it was still there, and still grasping the Knack.

Before me on the ground, I noticed a discarded pick, which I took up with gratitude. I only had the use of my left hand now, and in order to control the pick I had to grasp it half way up the shank – in consequence, it would only be of use at close range, but I was glad to have it all the same.

'How long was that? How long does the spell last?'

The Iron Devil said he wasn't sure; he thought it had been a minute or maybes a bit longer, but he wasn't sure.

'I think it was two minutes,' I declared. 'Not long. Not long at all. Well, we must make the most of it!' And so we pressed on, dodging atween the creatures, moving more nimbly now that we had a sense of how little time a jowling would buy us.

Thus we made our progress, stop-start, through the army of stultified ex-men, the automata. Sometimes they were grouped close together like skittles, and we had to shunt and shoulder them out of our way. They would put up no more resistance than their bodyweight, but that slowed us all the same, and a feeling of panic would quickly arise if we found ourselves surrounded too thickly by the herd and with no post in sight.

When we started to suspect our time was running low, we'd linger by the nearest post and wait for the tide of whispering to rise once more about us. That was the worst time of all, I think, when we were standing and waiting, on the twitch for the least bit flicker of motion in the gloom. As soon as it began, the Iron Devil would rap out the signal – s*low* . . . *slow* . . . *quick-quick-quick* – and that would silence and still the creatures for another minute or two. *All's still* *at the Sill.* If he left it too long, they would complete a line of their evil whispering, and then all suddenly spin on their heels to face us: it was too disquieting; neither of us wished to ever see it again.

I cannot say how often we repeated this procedure. Time, as was indicated to me later, and as I suspected even then, behaved very differently at the Sill. But it seemed to me that we were making good progress, and, certainly, we had a system that worked well enough, and was allowing us to pass through the herd of creatures unmolested. All was going about as well as we might reasonably have hoped, given the straits we had been in when we first found the Knack in the deepest level of the Sill. Yes, all was going well, until it all went so very wrong.

Suddenly, the creatures were whispering again, and this time it seemed only a moment had passed since our last jowling. We stared madly at each other, the Iron Devil and I, and fairly charged ahead, clambering past the swaying bodies of the creatures in order to reach the next post on our way. But, as rotten luck would have it, there was not a post to be seen for the longest stretch, and the creatures were grouped afore us in an especially tight herd. With horrible clarity, we saw that we would not make it to safety, and bellowed questions at each other, such as whether we should turn back and head for the last post we rapped; but I think we both knew instinctually that heading back into the depths would have been the worse folly.

By now the automata had completed their catechism, and, as we had come to expect, all of those not already facing us executed their pivot – every one at the same instant, every one obedient to the same will – and now they resumed their shambling gait towards us, with wasted arms lifted to embrace us, blackened lips blowing kisses as they whispered horrors.

In desperation, the Iron Devil rapped the jumper-rod against the wall of the corridor – *slow* . . . *slow* . . . *quick-quick-quick* – but it hardly made a sound, and so made no odds to the automata who crept ever closer. We had both known that this wouldn't do; the noise must carry for it to have any effect. Why hadn't we found some object we might have used as a sounding block, something we could have brought with us to avoid just this eventuality? I don't know, but we hadn't thought of it, and now it was too late.

The foremost of the creatures had reached us now. Unthinkingly, I let the Iron Devil stand in front of me: he had the jumper-rod to fend it off, and all I had was an uncertain grip on the pick that wobbled unpromisingly in my left hand. My right arm was now a ghost to me – I could but slowly lift it; it would avail me nothing in combat. With the automaton in range, and clutching at us with its blackened fingers, the Iron Devil took a great swing at it, and whacked it across the head with the jumper-rod. It made a sound that put me in mind of windfall apples in September, when Mop and me, back when we were bairns like, would have at them with sticks and watch the rotten ones fly apart. Well, the creature's head made much the same sickening sound. It stopped dead in its tracks for a moment, and its head fell forward bonelessly, but its body stayed upright, whereas a man so stricken would surely have fallen down dead or unconscious anyway. And then it raised its head once more and grabbed the Iron Devil by the throat.

My companion gave a squawk, for the creature had moved with unexpected speed, and – it being too close now to allow him another swing at it – he raised up the jumper-rod and drove the pointy end directly into the creature's left eye. Nor did he stop at that, but pushed on bodily until the rod was sunk very deep in its skull and might even have pierced it through. And then, without a sound, the creature collapsed at last, sinking to its knees before the Iron Devil as if in supplication, with the jumper-rod still sunk into its face. My saviour planted a foot on its chest, and pulled and twisted and tugged the rod free. It was dripping with gore that looked, by the dim light we had, like blackcurrant jam.

We stepped back. We – but I should say 'he', for I had contributed nowt – had felled one of the automata, but there were maybes scores more to get through afore we got on bank. I said as much, and said that we could not hope to succeed by felling every one of our adversaries in like manner.

Three more creatures were nearly upon us.

'We cannot make our last stand here,' I yelled.

'Then let us try a little further on down the road!' our hero replied, and, plucking up heart at that, he charged forward, breaking through the creatures and jabbing either end of the rod at them as he did so. Most of them overbalanced and fell, but it seemed they took no hurt at this and at once resumed the chase, though they moved much more slowly than we. I fairly scurried after my protector, and thus we made it along a good stretch of tunnel, with the Iron Devil stotting the creatures aside like skittles or walloping them with the rod – I saw one creature take such a crashing swipe to the temple, the eyeball popped from its socket – and always with me at his heels, swiping at the herd with my pick, about as effectual as a little dog yapping at the heels of a marching band.

We were making some progress, but expending a deal of energy. When next we found a likely post, we jowled it, and since we could see no creatures near to us, we had to hope that it had taken effect. We leant upon the walls and gulped in breaths, our lungs churning and our skinny legs trembling. I felt sick at heart, and I think the Iron Devil was the same. We could scarce afford to breathe for long, however, as the automata behind us, back the way we had come, would be in pursuit of us, and, though they moved but slowly, they did not cease to move unless we had them spellbound. It was impossible to avoid imagining them, deep in the darkness, out of earshot of our jowling, crawling and staggering towards us, even now.

Soon after we had started to make our way once more, having rapped out the signal again for good measure, we happened upon a thing that seemed to us a great gift, and we thought for a moment that all our luck had turned: here was some charge. How it came to be there, and how we had missed it during our prior excavations, I know not; for whenever we'd found some charge, we'd made use of it at once, and certainly the creatures hadn't the know-how to so much as recognise the stuff. But here it was. I don't suppose many heavenly intercessions have been so wholeheartedly welcomed as were these packets of black powder.

Well, our joy was like so much kindling: it went up in a great blaze, but it couldn't last. I saw the gloomy thoughts resettle on the Iron Devil's brow, and he asked how should we make use of this, for it wouldn't be safe to carry it any distance, when we had to fight our way through the creatures; it was too unstable a compound to be jiggled so.

'We cannot leave it here, though but. It is a boon. I say we use it, here and now, and try to bring down the roof. That way, as we press on, we will at least know that there can be no more creatures approaching us from behind.' I was talking myself into the idea as I went along. It sounded like quite a good idea, really, to my ears.

So that's what we set about doing. We laid the charge all around the post, and in the vicinity of what seemed to us to be the supporting rocks. We worked breathlessly. Setting charge was a fearful business at the best of times, but doing so in such a hurry, and with little light, and surrounded by enemies as we were, it's a wonder we managed to avoid blowing ourselves to kingdom come.

We cut the wire into lengths, making a fuse for each packet of powder that we'd jammed into the rock and the post. The lengths looked right to us, though you never knew for sure how much clearance you'd have, because there was no telling how fast the fuse was going to burn: three seconds or fifteen — you never knew until you found out. At last, we touched the ends of each one with the flame of a candle, starting with the longest and working our way down to the shortest, and once they had all commenced to sparkle we made a run for it. We had but cautious hope that our plans would carry. And if they did not, we could not return and try again; it would be too dangerous altogether.

It was time to be gone from that place, and to cover the most distance, but my joints and my legs were stiff from having been crouched over, laying the charge for so long, and I was alarmed at how sluggish I seemed to be moving. The Iron Devil seemed to be faring little better, but we ran as fast as we were able, in any case. Perhaps, had we not been so stiff and sore and weary by that time, things would have ended differently.

We were scurrying along, squatting under a low roof, when we saw a group of them coming at us, flat-footed, unbalanced, but en masse. We stole a look at each other, me and the Iron Devil, and I think for a brief moment he smiled. And then, at our backs, as though the gates of Hell had been thrown open, the blast came.

The hurricane picked us up lightly as though we were may blossom, and flung us forwards. The creatures in front of us were likewise thrown back the way they had come – I saw them, for a second, mid-flight, like stick-figures in a bairn's drawing – and then all light was extinguished. A fraction of a second later, it seemed, the noise reached us, as though the earth were tearing itself asunder for Judgement Day, and then I passed from darkness into darkness.

The last thing I had felt was a sensation of flight; now I was waking, in patches and flashes of time, and all I knew was aches and sharp pains that thrilled into my mind from every direction. I was being ground in the teeth of a monster, or so it felt. All was bleakest darkness, and I was buried alive.

How much time passed, I know not. My thoughts were apt to race and churn, and then fly away like startled birds. At length, however, I found myself digging my way out of the shale in which I lay buried. My right hand – which felt numb, and yet also bigger than its natural size, and which still seemed to be holding on to the Knack – my right hand was digging and scooping and delving, as though it were now merely a shovel, and it seemed to be doing so without conscious motivation from me. Very strange to awaken thus, and to find oneself in the throes of exhuming a corpse, when the corpse is none other than yourself.

My shovel-hand finally shifted enough of the rock for me to sit up a little, and I set about unburying my legs, now using both hands. My shovel-hand still worked as though it had a mind of its own, but it was doing the work I'd have set it to, had I been capable of thought.

Once I was free, I crawled up out of my rocky bed, and began feeling about for owt useful. I was far from forming a plan. I wanted to call out for my companion, but my voice was gone; either that, or I was deaf – I seemed to be deaf, but was too thick-headed to test the matter. At least the blackness was not so absolute any more: as I have said, the rock in the Sill was faintly luciferous with a queer blue glow, which provided just enough light for me to discern the lay of the land in a general way.

For a spell, that was all I did: I crawled about like

Nebuchadnezzar in his madness – I'd maybes have browsed on grass like a ox, had there been any there for to nibble. My shovel-hand seemed to be leading me, tending me now this way and now that, and I followed it as docilely as would any beast of burden.

Suddenly, I was digging again, scooping at the earth like a mole. I seemed to watch myself doing so, like one stunned or in drink. I leaned my weight on my left hand, and dug furiously with my right. I did not seem to be properly awake, nor properly thinking.

Now I'd found something.

Now I held a candle stub in my left hand; my shovel-hand was back to digging.

Now I'd a box of matches in my left hand, alongside the candle.

I might as well tell you now that I cannot account for any of this. Just how I'd known where to dig for the candle and matches is a mystery, and if that upsets you, I have yet greater mysteries to unfold, as you shall hear.

I struck a match – very tricky to do this one-handed like – and lit the candle stub. My thoughts were steadying, and now my vision cleared.

The blast had brought down the roof, and turned the tunnel into an irregular cavern, as various nearby tunnels were now combined with it. I sat and marvelled at it all for some time, until I thought my candle stub would soon be burnt out, and I'd have nowt to show for it. So I got myself stood up, and, swaying and staggering like a galloway fit for the knacker's yard, I began to stagger about.

Here again, it seemed that I was led by a kind of providence, for there were a number of avenues I might have explored, and, as I've indicated, there was no system to the tunnelling at the Sill, so it would have been the easiest thing in the world to have lost my way there, but this did not come to pass. Rather, I chose one tunnel, which looked objectively no more promising than any of its siblings, and I pursued it.

That's where I found him, lying against the wall with his body all folded up: the Iron Devil. I knew, from a ways off, that he'd been killed by the blast. His neck was bent so far out of true, there wasn't a chance he'd survived it. Still, I knelt a moment and felt for a pulse, just to be sure. He was dead as earth. I thought what a vast and terrible grave this was, in which to abandon the body of my old companion. For the form's sake, I rolled him over on his back, and set his head where it should have been – and very horrible it was, to be moving his head and to feel as though there were no bones in his neck – and I folded his hands over his chest, as I've seen it done. Well, perhaps those miners in Mexico had had the right idea, after all, to have built a church down in their grove, but we'd no such thing here. My candle was guttering and down to barely an inch, and so, sheltering the flame with the great lumpen mitten that was my right hand, I had to leave him there, both buried and unburied, his grave sanctified only with a sinner's disbelieving prayer, and so I staggered on.

I saw no more of the creatures, but of course my nerves were all a-twangling, for I expected to see them at every moment. The horrors still felt close behind me, and a grievous sorrow for poor Aneurin was near to my heart, but it felt good nonetheless to perceive, as presently I did so, that a faint white light was blending with the yellower rays of my candle – and then to turn that final corner in the Sill, and see, at the distant end of the tunnel, a tiny key of daylight, surpassingly bright, and to know that in just a few minutes I would pass through that keyhole and back out into the wide world, like a camel through the eye of a needle, like a rich man entering the kingdom of God – oh, it felt good indeed. I think I crouch-waddled that much faster, now that my goal was in sight.

There were tears on my cheeks, and above me, to match, the roof was all sparkly and silvery with pendent drops of water. It was hard lines that the Iron Devil wasn't with me to see it; he'd have been as glad of the sight as I was. So many sensations were fighting for mastery of me as I made my way along that final stretch of the Sill.

And so, at length, the Sill begrudgingly released me, and now I was staggering back out into the air, where the horizons seemed stunned, far off, cold and permanent. The world smelt absolutely and indescribably vile to me, and I doubled over, retching and heaving, but with nowt in my stomach to bowk up this time. The sky was banked with white cloud, painfully bright to look at, and I thought I could feel my eyes turning like screws, trying in vain to adjust to being back in this almost-forgotten ocean of light. The wind was not so very high, but it chilled me all over.

In the daylight, I could get a proper look at myself. With

so little clothing that had not perished during my time at the Sill – barely enough left to preserve my dignity, a mere loin cloth – I could see how depleted my body now appeared. My ribs were clearly accountable, and my legs so skinny they looked corded with the most meagre portion of muscle imaginable. I was covered thickly in all kinds of muck and dust and blood from the thousand times the shale had cut me in the blast. How far would I get in such a weakened state? I didn't know, but I would have to try, and for much the same reason as the last time I'd set out on an uncertain expedition from a mine: my right hand had been destroyed, and the pain was growing, as though fed by the cold. I would have to get to a doctor and have him remove the hand, or do so myself, so soon as I happened upon a blade fit for the purpose. It looked like it had all but melted and fused with the Knack: nowt but an ugly ball of fleshy stuff frilled with blisters. I felt righteously aggrieved to be, alone of the human race, the man who had twice lost the same hand to torture.

I tried to recall the way back to the bastle house, and, though it didn't cheer me to think of asking the quill-driver for assistance, I began to totter in what I guessed was the right direction. It was no great distance for a healthy man, but for me as I was then, a living skeleton, it felt like many miles. With my right hand held afore me like a lantern, as though it were leading me and chivvying me on, as though I were a modern Diogenes searching – in the least propitious of places – for one honest man, I somehow made it to the bastle. I had not the energy to attempt the stairs that mounted the side of the building, and thought for an unlucky moment that maybes I'd die there, just a few feet from human help. But then, as luck would have it, or maybes (who knows?) as the Knack would have it, the door opened, and the quill-driver stepped out and saw me.

My hearing must have been returning, because I heard him give exactly the sort of girlish shriek that I'd have expected of him. I watched him shrink back into the doorway. It took him a moment to gather his wits, but presently he recognised me in my tatterdemalion guise, or seemed to, and began to creep down the steps towards me. I think I must have looked as monstrous to him as the automata had been to my sight. And, though I hadn't the pluck to think much of it at the time, his appearance was also greatly changed, for there was grey in his hair and he'd grown stocky. He was staring at the top of my head a good deal, and when I raised my hand to it I discovered that I was now completely bald – not so much as a wisp of old-man's fluff behind my ears! No wonder I felt the chill of the wind. But I was too stunned with pain and exhaustion to think very deeply on this, with all of my energy being expended on just standing there, balanced on my poor stick-legs.

Once we were face to face, I managed to tell him, in a sort of whisper, a sort of whistle, that I had found the Knack, and that I held it now in my hand, which I waved slowly in front of him, though it was merely a fried mess of skin by this stage, blackened with dirt from all of the furious digging it had done.

He staggered back again when he deciphered my words,

and asked, in a voice that sounded far away, why in Christ's name had I touched the thing with my bare hands? I felt my temper rise at this – a feeling I experienced in my enfeebled state as a great wound opening in my head – and I declared that I did *not* recall him warning me against this, or imparting any such useful information; but by then I could barely speak. He shook his head and disappeared for a moment, and reappeared pushing a wheelbarrow. Bringing it up behind me, he gestured to me, and I let myself collapse into it.

Quill-driver or no, he kept up a good pace, though I don't suppose I was any great weight. I felt looked-after, like a bairn again, because I thought, then, that he was hurrying along for my sake, trying to get me to safety afore I expired, I mean. Thinking about it now, I doubt that this was his primary motive; but you can judge.

I remember being trundled past a great field of buttercups, and the smell, which I knew should have been sweet, was so powerful it made my head wuzz. And that great mass of yellow minded me too much of the encrustations at the Sill. Off in the midst of the field there nodded a single white campion – a grave flower, as some call it – and I remember thinking that I was like the white campion, alone in an ocean of unlikeness, and I felt right sorry for myself as I jiggled along the track. I tried to tell the quill-driver that I wished I could be a buttercup, but he was wise enough to ignore my foolish ramblings.

After an hour, or maybes two, I saw that we were approaching a great house that had miles of whin flowers to defend it from the world, and which appeared to cling to the side of a great outcrop of whinstone like a barnacle on a ship's bow. Our pace slowed as we began the climb up towards it. *Brink House* was carved into the gatepost, and I knew this was the place for me, for verily I was on the brink of life and death, and it seemed that I had pitched my little tent there for many a day. And so, even on the threshold, overcome with relief at thinking myself in a safer place at last, I let myself slip from consciousness, and as the door swung open the world swam away, and I was lost to my dreams for the longest while.

8

At Brink House

As regards the events of the following weeks – if indeed my convalescence took weeks rather than months or years – my recollection is misty and partial. The world all but passed, as it were, beyond my ken; I had not slept, it seemed, for many weeks at a stretch and I was now exhausted past imagining. So I lay insensible for a deal of days and nights, and then, when I first began to come to consciousness, I was not truly awake nor yet fully asleep. All my thoughts hung suspended in a teasing sort of dream that continually uncoiled with no indication of whether it would end pleasantly or in outright nightmare.

At first, I woke only fitfully, for the briefest of intervals, and it always seemed that I had been woken by the sound of thunder rolling overhead – but an orderly thunder, arranged in short and distinct bursts, administered like a bailiff's knock upon the door. Half-awake, I raved on these occasions, and, shameful to say, I cried sometimes, and then I would drink as much water as I could, bawling that my throat was gizened, afore my nurse came and administered a tablespoon of brandy laced with laudanum, and then back I fell into delirium, whereupon I'd be visited by an assortment of beings, only some of which, I later understood, were actual.

Mam and Mop were often with me. Though they never spoke, there were times when, though I was all but insensible and could not so much as open my eyes, the silence in the room seemed suddenly so dismal that I thought, yes, surely Mam and Mop must be there, praying for my very soul, boring the angelic hierarchies into submission. At other times, I saw the wolf that had so nearly made a meal out of me on Windy Top: he'd be sat at the foot of bed, glowering at me with his awful eyes, and me all laid out afore him, no more able to move or cry out than a Sunday ham. But other visitors were more friendly: I saw Mr Crow, and all was well with us once again, which made me glad, and we played cards and sang songs and talked of the old days, though afterwards they said I'd done no more than pluck at my blankets and smile foolishly; and I saw the Iron Devil himself – my last workmate, Aneurin, poor sod! And very crestfallen were we both that he should be forced to visit me like this, as a ghost rather than a fellow of flesh and blood.

Strangest of these visitors was my father, who so rarely troubled my waking thoughts, but who stopped by to pass the time with me all the same when the fit was on me. As usual, we had a long conversation, the details of which slipped beyond my recall subsequently. At length, he asked if I would take a turn with him about the garden, and I said yes I would, and gladly, and next thing we were outside in a bright light – I don't recall seeing the sun, but I remember the glare of the light – and he was telling me of his many travels, and I was up and walking with ease at last. And next thing after that, we were down beneath Brink House, deep in shadow and cobweb, for this was a crypt, and the cogs of the dream were turning and bringing round the old, familiar climax, and now my father was pointing to the inscription on the side of the tomb, which I understood to read *ex homine commutatus nuper in lupus*. And then I looked to see whose grave this was, and when I read the name, I awoke with a great cry, sweating in my bed.

Once, in these strange days, when I lay dreaming of the moment the Iron Devil walloped one of the automata on the head – and how the creature's eyeball was knocked out of its skull, glib as a newborn's meconium – a punctual round of thunder woke me to the sight of a man, or something in the shape of a man anyway: very tall he was, with a face as sombre as a judge, but with long hair that hung shaggy to his shoulders. A great weight of loneliness seemed to hang about him, made the more acute to my perception by the way he himself appeared to be oblivious to it. He was a stranger to me, but he stood over me like a sentinel, as if my welfare was his concern, and I got it into my head that this was Death himself, dressed in the modest apparel he wore for Everyman. Of course, this unsettled me and I started trembling, but the next thing I knew he was gone, if he'd ever really been there at all.

In time I began to wake more properly, and I became more aware of the room in which I lay. First, there was my bed, which was about five times the size of any bed I'd seen up to that point, for I was used to the narrow bunks in the lodging shop and at home in our shieling. The bed-frame was made of oak, and it had a carved wooden owl standing guard on each of its four corner-posts: the tutelary spirits of my sleep! And there was a fireplace, and the fire was kept in, which I appreciated, as it seemed that I felt the cold these days, as I never had afore. And there was a great bay window, and very pleasant I found it to lie abed in the daylight – another new experience – and the ceiling was panelled with oak, which looked very fancy to my eyes.

I also became more aware of my condition. My right hand was wrapped muckle tight in a great bandage, which I somehow understood I was not to undo, despite the discomfort it gave me. I knew not whether the Knack remained in my grip, or if it had been prised from me in my sleep; the former seemed more likely, as I often had the sensation of grasping a foreign object, and in many of the dream-visions that I had in those days I was holding on to something very hot or very cold and wouldn't let go, or else I was wearing manacles and chained to a madman – always some such nightmare. My mind lurched from one fit to the next, throwing up one queer vision after another, until I thought I must go mad.

But at length, as I began to seem tolerably myself once

again, two somewhat more material presences came to my sickbed, the first of these being Master Brinsley Siskin himself. He was an old man, and walked with a cane, and he wore a black broadcloth suit and what would today be called a Gladstone collar; but his otherwise sober appearance was dominated by his oversized white moustaches, which stood out like an unexpected flourish at the end of a neatly printed signature. Maybes he'd once been a dandy, and the moustaches was the last vestige of his crazy days. I could just about imagine him as a young man – I fitted him up in my mind's eye with a canary-yellow waistcoat, green velvet trousers and buckled shoes. His eyes, hazel in colour, were kindly, and his brow was furrowed, and his eyebrows were never still, so that I could never be certain of his expression; his face was like a deck of cards that he never ceased shuffling. When he spoke, it was with an unpleasant shushing, lisping sound – the effects of an apoplexy he had lately suffered, he explained.

Master Siskin kept but few servants, and the only one I was permitted to speak to, then or at any later date, was a tall, stern-faced woman from Algeria by way of France, who went by the name of Madame Laguiole. This was my nurse, though she was also Siskin's housekeeper, butler, secretary and factotum. Master Siskin told me carefully enough how to pronounce her name – *lah-yol* – but, once I knew how the word was spelt, I called her La Ghoul when he wasn't around. She called me Monsieur le Con, and worse, and didn't make a secret of her mislike of me. I liked her voice, queerly accented to my ears with emphases I could never anticipate, but I thought her aloof; only much later did I come to understand that what I saw in her was merely the composure of misery and subdued fury. But in those early days I straightforwardly disliked her, being her patient and her prisoner – I was all but her baby, truth be told, and doubtless that made me more thoroughly resent her. She spooned me soup whenever I was awake long enough to take some, and I'd glare at her if she dribbled some down my chin, and even as I did so I would wonder at my own petulance. I'd seen invalids afore – bed-bound, drawing on the time and effort of others and giving nowt back in return, lying there alone, out of the swim of things, with their queer surliness, their secret determination ... I'd never guessed that I might one day be of their number; but here I was, and it was a miserable state of affairs.

Maybe we'd have been able to get along not so bad, La Ghoul and I, but something happened, soon after I'd begun my slow process of waking up to the world once more, which soured things, or provided purchase for the instinctual mistrust we each felt towards the other. One afternoon, as I lay there reading, La Ghoul entered the room to replenish my drinking water, and at her side – my guts ran cold when I gledged up and saw it – loped the huge beast that had so terrorised me on Windy Top: the Whindale Wolf itself.

To see the creature like this, indoors, in broad daylight, when I knew myself to be fully awake, threw me into an overmastering panic. I made a sound I cannot rightly describe and went hirpling out of bed backwards, away from the horrible thing, though I was so enervated I could but barely walk at that time. I groped my way across an armchair, and when I looked back the world seemed to slow, and my startled eyes drank in the details, as the beast lowered its head and stared me down, the fur about its neck shivering lightly, with La Ghoul standing by its side, as though oblivious to its presence, holding her jug of water and gazing evenly at me to see what fresh outrage to her sensibilities I'd concocted.

What was wrong with me, La Ghoul desired to know. I'd pressed myself into the corner of the room by this point, and was trying ineffectually to drag a large leather chair in front of me as a sort of shield. My throat had turned dry as snuff, but I gestured with my bandaged club and managed to tell her that it was the Devil himself that walked by her side, and that she was no more nor less than a witch.

'This is the delirium. Too much medicine, I think. Monsieur le Con raves.'

Without letting gentlemanly manners confuse clear speech, I bade her depart and take her familiar with her. The wolf, for its part, didn't like my tone and began to emit a long-drawn growl, its black lips twitching back to reveal flashes of white teeth.

'This is a dog. Has our guest never seen one before? Dog. *Le chien.*'

'Witch, that is no dog. It is the shepherds' bane, Satan's emissary, the Whindale Wolf!'

'Ha!' La Ghoul's laugh, which was rarely heard, erupted in a single rasp; I will say now that every time I heard it, it sent a thrill through me like I'd just glimpsed a sepulchre illuminated by a flash of lightning.

'I have seen it afore, and it has seen me, aye, and chased me halfway up the Whin Valley by the light of the moon. This is the very beast that tore the head off Mr Playfair. It is wild, violent and untamed!' I remember saying this and feeling that the words were being spoken through me, as though I were not their author but merely their mouthpiece, so fearful an impression had the wolf made upon me.

'This is not possible. Our guest knows not what he says. *Le chien ne quitte jamais le jardin.* Master Siskin is highly particular on this. The dog does not leave the grounds. We have a walled garden, and there the dog plays. Is it possible to see him on the moors, where he never goes? It is not. Our guest says he has seen the dog before: I think our guest was in drink that night, perhaps? I think our guest is often in drink, and he struggles now without it, no?'

I scarce had a moment to consider her insolence, for I was thinking how she had as yet made no effort to restrain the black beast, much less take it out of the room, and how long, I wondered, we were to hold to these positions – until my legs gave way beneath me? That would be the matter of a minute. I was leaning on the back of the chair and trying to conserve my energy when, coming to my rescue as it were, Master Siskin entered the room, took a survey of the situation, and fairly growled one word, 'Absalom!', at which the wolf ducked its head lower and, tail curled under it, slunk out of the room in shame. He told La Ghoul that that would be all for now, and she followed after the wolf, and in like manner, I thought.

Siskin politely turned his back, and busied himself

pouring the water from the jug that La Ghoul had left, while I crawled back into bed, an undignified progress with my stick-legs quivering and trembling. Once there, I composed myself, or tried to. He made some apologies for the fright I had received, and said that Madame Laguiole ought not to have allowed the dog (for it certainly was a dog and not a wolf, he asseverated) into my room. He was very strict about where the dog was permitted to roam, he said, and insisted that I could not possibly have seen it anywhere beyond the bounds of Brink House – which told me that he'd overheard that part of our conversation, at least.

For my part, I hadn't the pluck at that time to contest the matter further, and so let it go. But I found that the gliff had blown away the last of the cobwebs; I felt properly awake at last, and in need of gaining a truer sense of my state of affairs. First and foremost, I had to acknowledge that I was nowt but skin and bone. My legs were very thin, my forearms so wasted away that the skin hung loose. There was no mirror in the room, but I could feel that I had next to no hair on my head. In summary, I was become like an old man: this was the simple fact of the matter. My life seemed to have vaulted over its middling portion, and delivered me from my too-long-hoarded youthfulness into the quag of extreme old age.

And so I asked Master Siskin, as it were by the by, where the Knack was now.

He answered, as it were by the by, that it was quite safe.

Well, at once I saw how, in asking for its whereabouts even afore I'd asked after my hand, I'd made a poor show of hiding my interest in the Knack. The truth was, I still felt as though I had the thing in my grasp under the bandages, but I couldn't be certain, on account of my hand being somewhat benumbed. So my question was intended to test my interlocutor as much as anything; but he'd returned the test to me very easily. And of course, I *did* want to know other things about my condition, such as why I now seemed so changed, how long I'd been toiling at the Sill, how my hand was doing, and why it had reacted to holding the Knack as though it was burning and melting almost . . . And what, in any case, *was* the Knack? I couldn't think why one of these questions hadn't been the first thing on my lips. Siskin assured me that I'd been seen by a doctor while I was unconscious, and that this doctor had dressed my wound and given his opinion that I would, in time, make a full recovery. But in the meantime I was not on any account to remove the dressing, as some sort of powerful unguent had been painted on my hand, and must be left to do its work. The best thing I could do was rest and eat – 'put some meat back on my bones' as he put it – and let myself recover. I told him that it was very liberal of him to allow me to stay in his house while I did so, and he very graciously said how responsible he felt, seeing as I'd suffered such an injury while in his service, and I marvelled at this, hardly able to credit it, but not wanting to encourage him to reflect on it any further.

Still, he hung around the room, walking to and fro, examining a vase of lilies, taking in the view from the window, and working himself up to say something. But when he did speak, it was mere blether at first.

'Malarkey ... Curious name...' Siskin's lisp fairly mangled the word 'curious'. I suppose I could remind you of his impediment at every turn by spelling 'curious' as 'kooreeyush' and so on, but I cannot abide how Mr Dickens does this whenever Mr Peggotty speaks, therefore I will refrain. 'Is it, if you don't mind me asking, from the Hebrew, *Malachi*? One of the minor prophets. *Malachi* meaning angel – angel or messenger. Or is it Irish, from *Maoileachlainn* or *Melaghlin*, one of St Patrick's first companions?'

That was how he went on, Master Siskin. People such as he think that they're different in kind to the common sort, when, really, they're only different in quality, not in kind. A fellow lead-miner would have simply asked me directly if I was a Jew or a Mick – and he would have done so without attempting to hide the idle curiosity and suspicion that I knew were behind Master Siskin's kind-old-uncle eyes. You have to dance about with this sort. I wasn't about to tell him about my dad being Irish, but I didn't want to tell a lie about it either, in case he already knew the truth. So I merely noted that Malachy *was* an Irish name, but it was a forename, and maybes that is what he was thinking of; to which he says 'ah' and 'of course, of course', as though I had stamped my foot and made him jump.

'Our dear Madame Laguiole takes her name from a village in France. And my own name must be German, I suppose,' he says, as if he'd never considered it hitherto. 'From *Zeischen* ... or perhaps from *Süskind*, meaning sweetheart! Yes, Germanic and, before that, Slavic. And, to be sure, the bird with whom I share my name has curious migratory behaviour . . . Not quite a wandering Jew! But curious migratory behaviour, all the same. Or Siskin may be related to Erskine, I suppose, which is a common enough name. At this rate, I shall reason away my ancestors' good work before bedtime!'

So he might have rattled on indefinitely, but just then, La Ghoul reentered with my dinner on a tray. To signal her displeasure at me, she would not condescend to English, and merely said '*La tarte aux pigeonneaux*,' and then promptly left us.

Well, I've had pigeon pies in my time, but none as formidable as the one I faced that day. I could smell the mace and the cloves and the Madeira in the gravy very distinctly. It had been so long since I'd eaten solid food that even the sight of three pairs of pigeon feet poking out of the steam hole on the top of the pie (a silly affectation, I think, and a poor tribute to the birds who have given their all to the dish) could not put me off. Evidently, this was a house of plenty. Confirming the matter, Master Siskin rather disingenuously said that it was 'Very nearly a humble pie indeed!'

'It is fit for Caranus' wedding feast,' said I, earning a baffled smile from my host as I took up my knife and commenced attack. I will admit that, throughout the ensuing conversation, which touched on matters of no small importance to me, my attention frequently tended in the direction of the pie. I make no apology for this. It's a fool who holds forth on his hobbyhorse to a hungry man. Anyway, while I ate, Master Siskin talked of the Sill, and of his people's interest in it.

'The Sill is a field of force. The name of the Sill is misleading, for "whin sill" would indicate a regular stratification of the rock, which is not to be found here, as you will have observed. The Sill is not, in fact, composed of dolerite, which you would call whinstone, at all. It resembles dolerite, but is a more rare variation. But we shall call it the Sill for convenience. And the Sill has a number of unique properties, Caleb. We are still in the process of discovering them, or, perhaps I should say, *re*discovering them, for I believe its properties were known and appreciated, once, long ago, hereabouts. Trajan's Wall, it is generally believed, was built to annex the coal field and the mineral field – and so it does, and we know the Romans mined coal, lead and silver here; but the Wall also encloses the Sill. Now, why do you suppose the Romans would care to lay claim to a vast slab of apparently worthless whinstone, some seventy miles wide?'

'You buy meat, you buy bones; you buy land, you buy stones,' said I. I was, at that moment, crunching tiny bones atween my front teeth: the cook – La Ghoul herself, I later learned – had made resourceful use of every part of the birds, not excluding hearts and gizzards and necks. What with the quail eggs and the spicy forcemeat, it was an exceedingly rich dish.

Siskin indulged me with a chuckle and said, 'Very good,' and then said no, there was more to it than that: 'I believe the Romans knew about the Knack. Certainly, they knew more than they are credited with knowing. They had the capacity to learn. Not all cultures have this. They understood that conquest is union, and that it changes the conqueror as much as it does the conquered. You have heard of syncretism?'

Of course I had: it was something of a dirty word in my part of the world, where it was used to refer to those who wanted to immix the various dissenting sects of Christianity into a single brotherhood of crackbrains. Mam held, or she repeated anyway, strong views on the matter. But as my mouth was crammed with an especially large and dry bolus of piecrust at that moment, I merely nodded sagaciously. It transpired that Siskin was referring to an older sense of the word.

'When the Romans conquered a people, they adopted their gods. They absorbed them, folding them into their own beliefs, which were capacious and forever proliferating. That is syncretism. Clearly, they reasoned that if people could continue to worship the old, familiar gods by the old, familiar names, then they would scarcely notice that they had been colonised at all. And, generally speaking, it worked. So a cynical sort of religious toleration was enforced, and disrespect for anyone's gods was severely punished. This strategy wasn't seriously opposed until the Jews and the Christians came along with their jealous God, hence the tireless persecution of these peoples by the Romans.

'It has been said that the best things in life are to be found at its edges. A versatile phrase! – the meaning of which depends entirely on what is meant by "best" and "edges". But, at that time, Trajan's Wall was certainly an edge: the northernmost reach of the Roman Empire. And if not the best, then the strangest things in life were certainly to be found here. All along the Wall you can find the remains of temples, the remnants of a hundred heathen cults, each with their believers, each with their sacred rites, howsoever blasphemous. Temples to demons such as Armadiel and Demoriel, to the water goddess Coventina ... to Mithras ... For all I know, there may have been a synagogue or two among them! And there were Christians, too, but of a kind that you and I would hardly recognise: gnostics, mystics. More pagan than anything else. They worshipped strange gods, Caleb.'

As he described it to me, back in the second and third century, here on the margins of a decrepit empire, the process of syncretism was churning away, with all of the devouring and the digesting and the synthesising and the excreting that this entailed. Those were the words he used, with the upshot that I instantly equated the concept with the pie I was then eating. At what point does the pigeon become part of the pie? At what point does the pie become part of its devourer? Musing upon such questions, I became a little distracted, but the gist of what he said was this: in our day, men of science would conduct experiments and write up their findings in great books for other likeminded fellows to read; and three hundred years ago, or thenabouts, the alchemists would be busy at their version of this same endeavour, mucking about with their wax tablets and black mirrors and their bottles of piss, and maybe, once or thrice in a lifetime of ignorant gloom, they would glimpse the merest chink of truth; but further back, in the days of the Romans, there was nothing of science whatsoever, and this was the only way owt got worked out: through faith. Northalbion, back then, was a vast crucible of beliefs and superstitions, in which the truth would be ground up and powdered and solved. Siskin outlined various theories as to the origins of the Knack: some said that these faith-experiments had led the Romans to discover the existence of the Knack buried deep under the vast lid of stone we called the Sill; some said that the Romans happened upon it some other way and then buried it there themselves for safekeeping; and some said that their experimental rituals had somehow or other seeded and incubated the Knack.

Something in his manner told me that Siskin's own view on the Knack's origins was very much made up, and did not exactly coincide with any of the views he had so far described; but he didn't show his hand, so to speak. All he said was that the Knack was an artefact of pure force (having the power to effect change), of pure fortitude (having the power to endure change) and of pure fortune (having the power of celestial ordinance, which could not be changed). In sum, it was a pure *fors*. This was a word he delivered rather sumptuously, so that I was to understand he had achieved it at some cost.

'The Romans, or one of them anyways – Marcus Cato – recommended pigeon meat for the convalescent,' I said cheerily, my mouth full of the stuff. Well, I'd felt that I should add something to the conversation – and at that time I still assumed that everyone liked to learn a new thing as much as I did. What a long road it is that leads us to the realisation that others are otherwise! Master Siskin ignored me, and resumed speaking.

'Having once discovered or created the Knack, the Romans quickly learned to be fearful of it, and so it was banished and buried under the vastest, hardest rock they had encountered: the Sill. Truth to tell, history was never my strongest suit, but *geology* . . . My people were geologists before the term had currency. We learned that the Sill has a certain property, a certain *masking* property. It occludes – it *occults* – it renders absolutely untraceable the very thing for which we searched . . .'

'The Knack,' I said, and more respectfully, that he might know I was following along indifferent well.

'The Knack. Our philosopher's stone! It has the power to join and the power to separate: *solve et coagula*, as the alchemists used to say. But it isn't esoteric purposes that I have in mind. Imagine a doctor able to separate a man from the chronic disease that afflicts him. Or imagine if we could bring about new unions that would extend the category of the human: if we could make the miner stronger and the mine owner wiser – or the soldier braver, or the maiden more comely! The problems of the ages might be answered. Consider the criminal: presently, we may hang him, which seems wasteful; transport him, which merely shifts the problem it cannot cure; or imprison him, which is now the fashion, albeit an expensive one of doubtful benefit. Why, they say a released prisoner reoffends in four cases out of five! But once we have unlocked the secrets of the Knack, we could straightforwardly draw out the man's criminality, as easily as drawing his blood. Well, well. Forgive me my enthusiasm, Mr Malarkey! I am an old philanthropist, and if not a scientist then at least a *dilettante*. My family has been searching for the Knack these many generations, knowing all the while that it would not be found until the time ripened, until fate forced our hand, but searching hopefully all the same. To be so close to our goal makes me a child again!'

'At the Sill, there were creatures,' I said, but my throat dried of a sudden, and I had to take a gulp of water afore I continued. I really had eaten a prodigious quantity of pie. 'There were other miners. But they were more like creatures – automata, I called them – than real men. After I dug up the Knack, they almost seemed to waken, and they pursued us . . .'

'Once it was free of the rock, the Knack would have been able to call to them. They would have been pursuing it by instinct. You did well to evade them.'

I sat on the bed and stared into the fire. I didn't feel that I had done well. I was thinking of the Iron Devil, buried forever at the Sill. A guilty feeling began to dispute with my full belly, as of something uncoiling and tightening at the same time.

'The Knack, you see, has a peculiar power. Or rather, it *is* a peculiar power. I speak of harnessing this power for the progress of science and the common good, yes, but let us state the matter plainly: it is a metaphysical artefact, for all that. It turns what is merely the case into that which was inevitable. It chose to be hidden, and it chose where and when to be found. It chose its discoverer. It chose you, Caleb, and then it brought us together, here at Brink House. How can I put this so that you will understand? With regard to the Knack, whatever happens, happens on its say-so.'

My mind turned at once to consider my decision, a lifetime ago it now seemed, to cross the picket line, and the suffering that had followed, and that had led me to this room. My thoughts bottomed out into the vast mysteries of which all human natures, not excepting my own, are composed. I wondered how many of my contrarian doings and sayings had been the Knack working all along. When I looked up, Siskin smiled as though he had read my mind.

'Then: now. Action: consequence . . .' he said. 'Such co-ordinates will not help you to navigate this terrain. Terrain from the Latin, *terra*. Earth. When *one* person touches the Knack, the result is simply fusion – absorption – as you know all too well. But if *two people were to touch it simultaneously*, the result would be quite different. Transference, Caleb. Fluency! Escape. The stronger essence synthesising the weaker, breaking it down. Stealing its gods.'

Maybes it was the laudanum, and maybes it was because I'd already seen some queer things, and maybes it was because my stomach was indicating to me that I should consider bringing this interview to a close, but I was readier to accept all of this than I might otherwise have been. I looked at my great swaddled hand, wondering again what state it was in under the bandages. What good was all of this talk about the Knack's strange power if it was yet glued, stuck fast to my hand? Again, Siskin followed the drift of my thoughts, and assured me that there at Brink House he had the means to remove the Knack, very safely and without pain. There would be no pain at all, he said softly.

'And what is your intended method of removal?' I asked, but just then La Ghoul entered the room and interrupted us, and the next time I looked at him his face had all of its old amiability. Why didn't I trust him? Was he a sincere fellow speaking gibberish, or a deceiver telling the truth with bad intent? I could feel my mind searching and searching, busy as a hundred weasels' noses, trying to determine the matter. But then, I didn't altogether trust my mind, either.

La Ghoul collected my empty plate and put it back on its tray. She spoke not a word, only watched me, I thought, with quick, wide, expressive eyes, and then she left us.

'Well,' said Master Siskin briskly, 'I hope you enjoyed your dinner: alas, we've nothing sweet to offer you afterwards today . . .'

'No bother,' quoth I, 'As the poet said,

> *It is the fair acceptance, sir, that makes*
> *The entertainment perfect, not the cakes.*

Siskin laughed politely but perplexedly; or was he peeved not to see the joke?

I told him that it was Ben Jonson.

Ah, of course, of course, says he – but I don't know whether he recognised the name, much less the lines or the misquotation.

Having a great deal to consider, I felt a sudden need for space and time to mull it all over. I had to decide how I felt to be thus declared the pivot in such a cog in such an engine. That's what all of this talk of the Knack and the

Sill and all the changes that could now be wrought put me in mind of: a vast, geological engine, slowly turning over, though it took nineteen centuries to do so. What bad luck to have been born at just the right time to be caught up in it all, and to have the Knack fall into my grasp . . . I sighed and looked about me, and Siskin again caught my drift, and apologised for so deluging me with discomforting thoughts, and promised to give me time to think and recuperate. He said he hoped that I was being properly looked after, and so on and so forth, and at length he left me.

Once alone, I considered what little I knew of my new abode. It's true, I was being fed and watered and nursed back to health very carefully. La Ghoul (for all my mislike of her, I had to admit it) knew her work well enough, and as for Master Siskin, well, I thought, he was doing his best to play the role of the genial old cove, but did this reflect his true nature? He'd even made play of laughing at my foolery, and I didn't suppose that *that* was how he'd made his fortune, howsoever he derived the word . . . But then, I reminded myself, I knew little of the ways of rich folk. Maybes this was just how they went on. Or maybes all anyone truly is is the person they pretend to be . . . My thoughts were very easily diverted into paradoxes at this time, though I've ever been a conundrumising fellow.

Looking back now, I would say that I was turned upside down in the fulcrum of my crisis. I'd gotten so quick to seek out and laugh at the shabbiness in people, that I couldn't tell what my actual feelings were any more. Could I tell friend from foe? Back at Windy Top I'd made foes of my friends

– and ever since, perhaps, I'd been wandering the paths of confusion. But here was an old fellow, I told myself, who had done me more than one good turn, who took an interest in the deeper mysteries of the world, and who could therefore sustain a bit of conversation: why not simply enjoy what I could of him? Why scrutinise? In lieu of data, why suppose?

I wanted to give in to such a line of reasoning, or sleep on the matter anyway, but my guts's long-drawn gurglings disconcerted me and, for the first time at Brink House, I didn't care to close my eyes and sleep just yet. Instead, I heaved myself out of bed, swung my bony legs over the side, and, with the help of the cane that was propped at my bedside, made it to my feet. Waddling like a lame duck, I crossed the room (the carpet – so deep and luxuriant! – was my first) to the great bay window, and stepped between the thick curtains. I looked up at the cloudless sky full of stars winking down upon me in a friendly fashion. Below me, the walled gardens opened like a grand amphitheatre. It was a fine night, I thought.

And then I saw, loping along at a terrible speed, the great black dog that had been at La Ghoul's side. Its paws pummelled the earth, and sods of dirt were flung up when it took a corner. Its spine looked ready to crack as it flexed madly, and its tongue was hanging from its jaws. It whistled down one long row, between the high hedges, and disappeared from my sight. Some instinct in me thrilled to see it moving with such power and urgency, and I had to tell myself sternly that it was not hunting, and certainly not hunting me, and that I was quite safe being indoors and so high above it, and that it was only . . . exercising. Playing, for want of a better word. My heart had picked up a pace, nonetheless. I could feel it in my throat.

At this time, there was a noise from a floor below as bolts were drawn, and then I saw a spill of yellow light as the front door was opened. Out steps Master Siskin, in need of a breath of air, it seems, as he raises his face heavenward, the way you might if you wished to feel the rain on your face, though there was no rain that night, nor a cloud in the sky.

The dog returned from its circuit of Brink House, galloping back towards Master Siskin, slowing its pace when it saw him, until it was trotting, and presently all but skulking past him. It crept back indoors, as it were sullenly, and Master Siskin followed it in a similar manner. I pitied the beast, and thought what a poor heart it had, that despite all its fierce looks it should quail so afore an old man, and I wondered at how it had managed to scare me, as truly it had, that night on Windy Top. By then the door was shut, and the gloom was over the garden once again, and to be indoors was so preferable to my experience that terrible night, I almost felt glad to be at Brink House, and able to step back through those fine, heavy curtains and retreat to my bed, which was so comfortable, and sleep once more . . .

But the devil of perversity that dwells within me had another idea: it made me head for the door to my room. Even though I knew that I lacked the strength to get far or explore much of the house, I felt the need to at least poke my head out of my room, which I was already growing too familiar with, and have a look up and down the hallway, which I'd not yet seen. To acknowledge my room's boundary in this way would help me, I reasoned, to lay claim to my little domain, and get to sleep in it. So, with the help of my cane, I waddled across the carpeted expanse to the door, and turned the handle—

But the door wouldn't budge. I was locked in. My keepers were my gaolers.

9
The Tour

Can a body be said to be in prison if the body doesn't realise the fact? And if a body learns that they are locked up somewhere against their will – be it howsoever comfortably and with howsoever much room to wander – can they ever henceforth be anywhere but in prison?

    I passed the time idly musing on such matters, as a prisoner will. Chancetimes, when I remembered how content I had been until the moment I tried the door, I cursed my devil of perversity afresh. And yet, I must confess it, there were other times when I sojourned there in no terrible distress, and the days continued to slip by in a languid, laudanum-assisted monotony, and all was as it had been afore. I drowsed and dozed, until I'd be smartly woken by the thunder-bailiff.

    At length, I was made aware that I was to be granted day release: it being decided that I was well enough, I would be given a tour of Brink House. Still too weak to walk further than the compass of my room on foot, I was therefore portered down Brink House's endless corridors – not one of which had been suffered to go without at least one vaulted archway – in what Master Siskin called a bath chair, this being a wicker seat fixed to a set of iron wheels. La Ghoul was the captain of this little vessel, with me as her cargo, and she steered us from room to room with Master Siskin leading the way, talking all the while about the improvements he had made to the house, or planned to make very soon.

Wrapped in a rug and installed in my perambulator, I must have looked every inch the invalid; but I wasn't entirely helpless, and I was endeavouring to form an imaginative map of the house. This was instinct to me, as it would have been to any miner, and I was already thinking of how I could maybes escape. Had you asked me, I think I would have used the word 'escape' even afore I learned that I was locked in my room each night. But I found it hard going to grasp the geography of the place: there was a room for every day of the year, and so many blind corridors, and windows where I'd have thought a window couldn't be, and rooms of such proportion that it put all sense of geometry to the strain. At the time, I told myself that this must be on account of my being more confused than I realised; but the fear-thought was that every room was merely a front for the real room hidden behind it.

Master Siskin explained all of this away, or tried to. 'Something of a warren, isn't it? It's certainly a challenge to new staff: indeed, I think some of them may have wandered off and never been seen since! They may yet be stalking the corridors, trying to find their way back to Madame Laguiole! Now, to be serious for a moment, my ancestors kept extending the original house, generation upon generation, following the whims of the day – Bavarian-style towers, Gothic facades, Venetian bridges to nowhere – until eventually they were left with the higgledy-piggledy concoction of nooks and spires in which we stand today . . .'

One of the first of the grander chambers we saw was the dining room, which was on the same floor as my bedroom. Inside, one wall was taken up with a great cabinet all filled with porcelain, much of which was Chinese, Master Siskin informed me, glazed in the bonniest colours, so that the effect of the whole was like the most lavish sweetie shop in the world. The dining table was of a mahogany so deeply polished it resembled a still pool, and the Ormolu candelabrum was reflected in it very exactly. But most impressive was a very massive marble mantelpiece, which took up the easternmost portion of the room, from wall to wall and floor to ceiling – and the ceiling was very high. The inglenook alone seemed the dimension of my old shieling, with two settles on either side of the blazing fire, and above that rose the bulk of a marble slab, which must actually have been multiple slabs cunningly pressed and fitted together, ornately carved with forest scenes and classical figures – the centrepiece showed a fellow wrestling with a bull, holding it by the nostrils; elsewhere was depicted a fellow being born out of a rock, and whatnot – and the whole thing framed with a row of fluted marble columns. It was like a house within the house, and this was not even on the ground floor. I was quite taken aback at all of this marble, and stood a moment trying to calculate how much it all must weigh, and how the building could possibly support it, and how the devil it had been transported to so remote a location ... it baffled me. I felt sorry for the poor bastards who'd been tasked with constructing so ponderous a folly.

After this, I was shown the billiards room and the smoking room, but all my thoughts were taken up with that enormous marble fireplace and the labour of constructing it, so I paid little heed to what I saw. And then, well, I will not describe the indignities I endured in being transported down the wide, palatial staircase, but they were of an order that would have made a good man weep, a bad man laugh and a Christian offer to help for a shilling. Anyways, we got down it, and into the Great Hall, which was a vast, squarish, high-ceilinged room, with stone pillars supporting balconies around the outside. Behind the pillars, the walls were decorated with frescos that celebrated Northalbion's history. At least, I thought initially that they depicted scenes from Northalbion's history: as I was wheeled along them, I saw that some of them did, certainly, but others were decidedly more esoteric, and even the more conventional frescos seemed to be inflected with other meanings, as though their historical anchors had been loosened, so to speak, resulting in a polysemous cauldron of imagery. Here, for example, were the Romans directing the building of Trajan's Wall – but wasn't the focus more on the temple to Mithras that was being constructed at this particular point on the wall?

Here was painted a hunting scene of terrific violence, showing black-caped riders atop monumental steeds, and with a tumult of hounds swirling about the plunging hooves – but no sign of their quarry. It bore the legend *Trahor Fatis*, and must have been a depiction of old Sir Guy de Ville riding on Lenterencleugh Moor, but I reckoned it might as easily have been the Wild Hunt, led not by de Ville but by the Devil himself, and those hounds the hounds of hell . . .

And here were the Vikings in their longships descending on the Northalbion coast, being met in battle by my forefathers with their war dogs at their sides, and this fresco bore the legend *They shall take who have the power: they shall keep who can*. Another painting showed a partnership of six miners, and one in particular looked quite astonishingly similar to me, I thought . . . and then, the longer I looked, the more I seemed to espy similarities between the other fellows in the painting and my old workmates, Heavens-Evans, and Mr Crow with his black beard and even his eye-patch, and Mr Muffin and George Henry – all of them labouring in a lead-mine, except the tools they were using were not exactly accurate, with the handles on the picks being too long and so forth, and evidently the artist had never worked in a grove himself. This fresco bore the legend *The Men of Northalbion Show the World what can be done with Iron and Coal*.

Other frescos were more mysterious in their subjects. Here was an eagle of unearthly size; and here was a behemothian bull with, scattered upon its hide, hawthorn blossom like constellations of stars. Here was the wyrm of Seven Springs – Mop and me'd been frighted by tales of it when we were bairns. And here was a painting of a sundial made of polished granite inlaid with coloured minerals and decorated with all sorts of queer sigils. I'd been looking at this picture for some time afore I realised how closely the ordering of the coloured stones on the sundial matched those of my old spar box, and I felt a pang at the memory of it having been smashed into smithereens. Upon the sundial lay a pair of riding spurs, and the fresco bore an especially strange legend: *The Sundial warns the Border Chief that the Larder needs replenishing.* Another painting showed a giant whose body was all made of leaves and branches – a Green Man, with a huge axe in one hand. The final painting in the series depicted a creature that looked like a cross between a young man, a lion and a bat, all encircled with flames.

I asked La Ghoul to stop a while here, though she seemed unwilling to do so. I was struck with the particular care the artist had evidently taken; the astonishing beauty of the youth compelled the eye, and yet there was the merest – though undeniable – trace of cruelty to his smile, which seemed, the longer I studied it, a deliberate touch. The youth's hair turned into a mane, and his body was that of a lion. He held his right paw aloft and his left paw low. Behind him were stretched his two huge bat-wings. Beaming out of him were rays of light and fire. The painting bore the legend *Mithras Sol Invictus*. I thought that, had I been the artist and had a free hand in the matter, I'd have titled it *Daybreak in Hell*, and I set my brains to retrieving owt I knew about this Mithras, who was, I began to conceive, the *genius loci* of Brink House.

Between these forbidding scenes and portraits, like a healing balm for the eyes, were more tranquil paintings of wildflowers native to Northalbion: here was wheat, wild oats, cornflower and yarrow, with bachelor's buttons, the melancholy thistle, and winter aconite that we'd call New Year's Gifts. The ceiling was all painted a deep blue, decorated with stars in so exact a design, I found, that I could recognise the constellation: here was Perseus and, below it, Taurus; at the centre of the ceiling sat the star Algol, as it were organising the rest. A damned unlucky star for any sailor to set a course by.

Although Brink House was now a collocation of architectural styles and fancies, its first intended style, I was informed, was Italian Renaissance, the primary models being Palazzo Schifanoia in Ferrara and Tempio Malatestiano in Rimini. According to Master Siskin's story, his ancestral seat had originally been built to be a centre for artistic, scientific and intellectual pursuits. I thought then that Brink House seemed, for all its quips and finery, altogether too lonely and godforsaken a place to be the centre of owt; but what I said was, 'Ah, yes: intellectual pursuits. Hence Mithras. He was a god of the intellect, wasn't he?'

Master Siskin appraised me, and I felt that I had blabbed. When he spoke, he said, 'You are knowledgeable about Mithras . . . ?' Which is the sort of open-ended question a fellow asks when he's withholding something.

I said I couldn't claim to be knowledgeable, but that Mithras seemed to be an important figure in the frescos.

'What first made you think so – if you don't mind my asking?'

I mulled it over, but answered honestly. 'In the painting of Trajan's Wall, where they're building the Temple. It's not that the subject itself is such a giveaway. But there are two fellows holding torches: one torch pointing up, the tother pointing down. I've seen them afore, in a book somewhere. And they're called . . . let me think on . . . they're called Cortez and . . .'

'Cautes and Cautopates.'

'Ah, I was nearly there!' I laughed, though Master Siskin didn't join me in my laughter. 'Cautes and Cautopates. The torch-bearers. I won't forget again. They're symbols of . . . of something as regards Mithras . . . but he was a sun god, wasn't he? So I suppose torch-bearers would be important to him: light-bringers. Lucifers, of a kind . . .'

All I had achieved here was to inform Master Siskin of the extent and the limits of my knowledge. So it is with fellows such as I: we get so sick of fancy folk taking us for nincompoops that we give away much free information about ourselves, which only benefits our adversaries, who come at us forewarned. Having sounded my depths, and considered the matter for more than a moment, Master Siskin let me know that Cautes and Cautopates symbolised the two points in the moon's orbit when it cuts the ecliptic. Then he recommenced the tour.

We passed through the drawing room, where there was a piano made of very beautiful walnut, its pattern all beswirled like a tabular cross-bed of sandstone, and a vast tapestry that covered the entirety of one wall, and a high ceiling filled with rococo plaster. My eye was caught by a portrait of Master Siskin, showing him standing proudly beside a boy of sixteen years or so. In truth, there was no family resemblance, and yet the boy looked familiar to me somehow, so I asked if this was his son: perhaps the boy was presently away at school . . . ?

'Ah, I would be proud to call the boy my son,' said Master Siskin, smiling, as he so often did, as though he were magnanimously talking to a child or simpleton, 'but no; that is Thomas, and he is only my ward. And yet, I have almost come to consider him my flesh and blood. You will be meeting him very soon.'

And finally, the room I'd been especially looking forward to: the library. Here, again, the house's geography had misdirected me, for the library stood, Siskin informed me, immediately below the dining room. We passed through an antechamber into an unexpectedly large room, rectangular in shape, furnished in light oak, and with a series of cumbrous wooden pillars supporting the ceiling: twelve in all, running the length of the chamber. Like everything else in Brink House, they had been carved and ornamented as thoroughly as possible, each one showing a man with the head of a lion. It occurred to me that the entire house was really a rich man's spar box, but I kept the thought to myself. The library was lit by a pair of tall windows, and I was wheeled over to them so as to admire the view. This side of the house was built on the very side of the crag – the brink for which the house was named – and I felt a little vertiginous to look down so steep a precipice. At last, I was permitted to spend a moment perusing the books themselves, which filled shelves from floor to ceiling along two of the walls – a magical sight for a bookish fellow such as I – but the awe I felt was soon tempered with disappointment when I discovered that only a fraction of them were in English. My disappointment was not in the library, but in the limitations of my learning. The library's magnificence was the work of many generations, and could not be accredited to its present-day custodian: I jealoused as much when I asked Master Siskin a question or two, and heard him hem and haw. Technical manuals stuffed with tables and charts were the reading matter he preferred. He all but ignored the books, and talked instead about how the fireplace was made of fancy Egyptian onyx and red marble and blue majolica tiles.

But though Brink House looked fine and fancy, I had the strangest sense that it was somehow like – or, no, not 'like' as such; more that it had an air of, or had once, long ago, *been* – a tuppenny brothel presided over by a hard-faced procuress. Yes, it was as though all that I could see was merely a mirage, and if a man were to take out his Barlow and scratch the florid oak panelling that covered the walls, he'd find that it was mere veneer – and rotten underneath. It had no life to it. It was like a house after all the children have left and grown up and never returned – it was like that, only more so. It couldn't breathe, as if it had paused mid-sentence and then forgotten what it had to say, and suddenly two centuries had stolen by. It was trapped in an endless afternoon that stretched on forever and never reached teatime. Maybes it needed more windows or mirrors; it had too many places for gloom to congeal. I didn't know why I should have had such misgivings, especially as Brink House was by some way the finest lodgings I'd ever seen. Nor have I since seen finer. But there it is: I didn't like the place.

At length, it was time to go outside. Master Siskin was very proud of his gardens, but, once in them, I could hardly refrain from twisting about to take another look at Brink House itself. It had been built directly into the side of a great mass of whinstone, so that certain portions stood quite proud of the hill, while others seemed half-sunk, or more than half-sunk, into the rock itself, with the effect that the structure seemed to be straining to free itself, and the earth seemed to be trying to gulp the place back down. Some of the house's facades must have been shallow indeed, for behind them surely lay a solid mass of whinstone, unless the builders had blasted it all out – but what a deal of extra work that must have been! Well, I mused as I was trundled about the gardens, they do say that fools build houses and that wise men live in them. It was about the size of three shooting lodges bashed together, with various additional towers and bridges sprinkled about it; but even this was strange to me, for the house had seemed far bigger on the inside.

At this time, a maid – I might say *the* maid, for I'm not certain I ever saw a second in the house — came scurrying out to us, and whispered something to La Ghoul. Then the maid scuttled off again, and La Ghoul informed Master Siskin that a messenger had arrived from Rutherchester with the telegram he'd been waiting for.

Siskin fairly jumped at this news, and I watched his

features to see what he looked like when he was getting something he wanted, as this can tell you a thing or two about a fellow. In this case, there was, I thought, a dark edge to his glee that I didn't like. He said the telegram would require an immediate answer, and in a gabble of words he told me how he himself had established the telegraph office in Rutherchester the year afore, and how fortunate this was, for it would not do to keep his Highness waiting ... All of this was said absently, so I felt no obligation to feign an interest in his connections, whether social or telegraphic. Now he was all for hurrying us back indoors, and offering mock apologies for it, the way some folk do. But I'd an idea.

'Might I be permitted to remain out here a little longer, Master Siskin?' I asked, and flattered him that his fine gardens had so captivated me that I wished to further admire them. I must have looked sincerely enthused, for truly it felt wonderful to be outside in the fresh air, under the vast bowl of clouds once more. Something about my request seemed to make him uneasy, but he agreed, and, shooting a meaningful look at La Ghoul, disappeared once more into his house. La Ghoul and I watched him go. The look he had given her emboldened me: it bespoke no trust, only mastery. He might be aged and encumbered with physical infirmity, the look said, but he expected nonetheless to be obeyed absolutely.

'And which of the gardens does Monsieur wish to further admire?' enquired La Ghoul once we were alone, but in a tone that told me she didn't believe a word of my reasons for remaining outside.

'The cellar,' I said frankly. 'Brink House has a cellar, I take it?'

La Ghoul acknowledged that it did.

'I have heard a strange story about the cellar here. I have heard that it is, in fact, a sort of crypt.' This was true, in a manner of speaking; I saw no reason to specify that the story had been communicated to me in a dream by my long-lost and probably dead dad.

La Ghoul did not blink, but assured me that, as far as she was aware, it was not used for so unusual a purpose.

'Perhaps you will indulge me, nonetheless? Something about this place is awry, and I would like to find out what it is.'

La Ghoul looked at me differently, then, I thought. I will not say that her expression softened, for I cannot conceive of such an occurrence, but something inside her relented. She knew the house's secrets and I did not, but I had twigged something was off, and this impressed her. She was unhappy here, but apparently could not leave. Perhaps she saw in me an opportunity to make an ally. Brink House would have afforded her few such opportunities: it had the still, stale quality of a place but rarely visited. Whatever her reasons, she gave a shrug and wheeled me back towards the house.

Again, I will spare you the details of how we managed to get the chair down the cellar steps, but, briefly, La Ghoul managed it while I sat on my arse and watched, and then I scuttled down after her. Anyway, we got ourselves into the cellar, and there was a lamp hanging by the door and we got that lit and, after all that faff, wouldn't you know, it was an utterly normal and conventional sort of cellar, with the usual dusty bottles and other cobwebbed detritus, but no graves or tombstones or what-have-you. The apparition of my dad was nowhere to be seen.

La Ghoul looked at me and I looked at her.

'There has to be something more . . .' I said. Nor did I doubt that there *was* something more. I think I had La Ghoul half-persuaded and all. She wheeled me further through the gloomy rooms.

I sniffed and observed that the bacon was reesty, and peered up at the ceiling to see where it was hanging.

La Ghoul was asking what 'reesty' meant. She spoke English indifferent well, but her grasp of our most excellent dialect was deplorable.

'It means *on the turn* – as when bacon goes oily and starts to smell.'

'We do not keep meat down here. The kitchen is on the eastern side of the house.'

La Ghoul and I stood there sniffing like a pair of imbeciles for a minute or so. At length I said, Well, surely she could smell there was something rotten down here. She didn't deign to give me a nod, but the search was on. As quickly and as quietly as possible, we turned the place upside down, trying to nose out the source of the queer rotten stink that seemed to get worse the more you sniffed around for it. I wasn't much use, but I waddled here and there, and poked about with my stick, and did what I could. Every now and then, we'd stop and test the air again, to make sure we weren't losing our minds. But we weren't, and at last we located the source: behind a wine-rack filled with nowt but cobwebs there stood a barrel, and behind the barrel, which was empty and easily shifted, we found a small door, maybes four foot in height. The smell was more noticeable here, or so it seemed.

I asked La Ghoul if she'd a key, and she said yes, she had a skeleton key to the entire house, and then we realised that there wasn't even a lock on the door, so my question had been idle.

'We have little time,' I reminded her. 'Let's get it open.'

As soon as the door began to move, we were engulfed with the stench. We retched and covered our mouths and noses – she with a handkerchief, I with my sleeve – for all the good that did, and when I raised the lamp, I found I could not keep my hand from trembling. But we had not come so far only to turn back. La Ghoul wheeled me in.

I thought that I was back at the Sill, or down some sort of mine, and that the scene was the aftermath of an explosion; and then I thought that I was in a sculptor's studio, and the floor was strewn with anatomical studies and discarded attempts. My mind shuffled through a deck of images, trying to find one that could make sense of what I was seeing. The reality was this: the room was scattered with the remains of human bodies. All were torn asunder, and in many cases the head was missing entirely. Some of the bodies had been there many years, and for cerements had nowt but the crumbling wool that once had been their clothes. Elsewhere were the remains of more recent kills, as I surmised by the putrescent smell. It was altogether a loathly midden of carnage and decay. Behind me, I heard La Ghoul gasp and exclaim and make big swears in French.

'The wolf did this. You cannot deny it, now. Absalom, as you call it, is nowt but a wild animal,' I said, stating the case very simply in a voice that I struggled to hold steady.

Shock and anger were vying for dominance on La Ghoul's face. 'Absalom is innocent of this!' she spat out, and then covered her mouth again.

I could not pursue the matter then and there, lest she, in her indignation, abandon me down there and leave me to crawl my way out. I saw a gleam upon the ground, and pointed to it. 'There: what is that?'

La Ghoul reluctantly retrieved it for me. It was a gold coin.

'Give it here,' I said. 'It will not be missed, and I wish to see the date on it, and I cannot read by this light.'

La Ghoul had evidently spotted something else of interest when she picked up the coin, for she knelt again and lifted up what I later learned was a small doll made of rags.

In addition to these items, I saw some more coins lying scattered here and there, and a tattered pamphlet entitled *First Principles of Political Economy*. I pocketed these items. Strangest of all, we saw, grinning up at us, the skull of a wolf. It had been there many years, by the looks of it, as the rats and maggots had long since polished off the gore. La Ghoul stared at it so long, I thought she might be waiting for it to speak.

We had been in that cell scant minutes, but suddenly it felt like an age; I asked La Ghoul to take us away from the horrible place. So she spun me around as quickly as she was able – which was not so easy in my impractical chariot, and the sound made by the wheels of my bath chair as they crunched and squeaked over the carpet of brittle bones will never leave me – and then, once we were turned about to go, I saw, by the swaying light of the lamp, sitting on the floor, half-hidden by the door, the quill-driver who had brought me to this blighted house. We'd passed him by, unregarded, when we'd entered. His face wore a look of surprise – an expression that would last until, by slow degrees, it gave way to the grin that mocked us from every corner of that room, for he was dead as earth. The heart had been ripped from his chest, which seemed to have burst open like a ransacked jewellery cabinet, all of its precious jellies and syrups congealed where they had spattered and spilt. Not knowing the dead man's name, nor remembering if he had in fact introduced himself when first we met, I uttered only the name of his creator, and covered my eyes until I'd been wheeled out of the cursed cell.

La Ghoul and I were back in the complacent daylight of the gardens afore either of us could speak. All now seemed unreal to my eyes. I watched Master Siskin's honeybees go about their business from bloom to bloom on the purple heath-bells, sweetly oblivious to the horrors we had just witnessed. I tried to focus on them and their doings. I'd missed the year's may blossom, and the roses were not yet out. But at least I had the heath-bells. And the honeybees. My thoughts slid about; my brain was a creel of eels. From my new perspective, I looked back at Brink House where it stood, evil and brazen. We had only closed two doors between ourselves and the horrors that it held.

'So Brink House has a crypt, after all,' said I at length.

La Ghoul nodded. She seemed momentarily dumbfounded.

'Now,' I resumed, 'I must be frank. I don't mind folk thinking me a fratchy and disgracious fellow, but what I'm saying now, I'm not saying to make sport. The dog that you dote on, Absalom, is not a dog at all. We must now surely call it a wolf, and admit that it has to be responsible for the carnage we have seen.'

La Ghoul kept her composure this time. 'The story that you heard – about the cellar being a crypt – the story was true. And yet, I was not aware. You are wrong about Absalom, but you were right about the cellar. And you were right when you said that something is very wrong here. And there I can enlighten you. I know many of this house's secrets. Before today, I believed I knew them all, but now . . .' Her voice trailed into silence. After a spell she remarked that the door had not even been locked, but she spoke as if to herself.

She had the sorry look of a woman who had long since accommodated herself to things being bad, only to now be forced to realise that things were, in fact, very much worse. I was satisfied that she'd been as appalled as I at the sights we had just seen, but why she should be so stubborn as to deny that a wolf was a wolf? Indeed, the only other suspect I could conceive of was the tall, long-haired, sad-faced fellow that I'd seen in my delirium; but he might have been all shadow and no substance.

La Ghoul said, 'The man we saw – when we turned around, the dead man who was sitting by the door – you started as if you knew him?'

'I knew him . . .' I said, but couldn't find further words for the quill-driver or his sad end.

I reached into my pocket, and drew out the pamphlet and the coins, and regarded them in the daylight.

'What can we learn by these tokens?' asked La Ghoul.

'Well, here are pennies – mites and groats – but here is a gold sovereign. This tells us that the murderer did not discriminate between the poor and the moneyed. And a sovereign left lying where it fell suggests the murderer was not driven by earthly motivations.

'And then there's the pamphlet, *First Principles of Political Economy*. It is of a kind I recognise. My old gaffer, Mr Playfair, was forever reading this sort of thing, and I reckon his marra, Walter Corlett, must've been the same. I'd bet that this was in the possession of one or other of them when they were killed.'

La Ghoul made an announcement. 'We must keep what we have seen today between ourselves. We cannot tell Master Siskin of this, do you understand what I say?' She was all urgency, now. 'It would mean our lives, monsieur, do you understand? I will tell you how I came to work for Master Siskin. I will tell you what I know of the house's secrets. I will tell you—' and here she paused and looked back at Brink House, afore changing tack for her concluding word: '. . . tomorrow.'

I looked back up the hill and saw, framed in the doorway

to Brink House, Master Siskin. Evidently, our presence was requested and we could not dally. I couldn't make out his features, but I thought, or imagined, to judge from his posture, that he was smiling down at us. He raised his cane in a slow salute, and, since I too had a walking stick lying in my lap, I raised it in reply.

10

La Ghoul

Whether by chance or by Master Siskin's policy, La Ghoul and I did not get the opportunity to speak for the rest of that day, nor on the morrow. Always, La Ghoul was wanted, was needed, was accompanied. And so I spent the time alone, sitting in my bed or in my chair by the window, looking down into the amphitheatre of the garden but seeing nowt but the images from yesterday that I could not stop recollecting: the heaps of broken corpses; the scattered bones; the quill-driver's perplexed last look at the world; the way Master Siskin had saluted me with his stick, as if to signal the commencement of the joust.

On the second morning, I sat there and watched the clouds sweep in, trying to guess how long Brink House had afore it was wrapped in rain. I thought of how the Sill had been hellish, but at the heart of its madness and misery was a kernel of friendship with the Iron Devil; and how Brink House had seemed paradisiacal by comparison, but all its luxuries were founded on horror. I balanced the costs of the two worlds against each other, so far as I was able.

At last, my musing was interrupted. La Ghoul slipped into my room to tell me that the house was ours, for Master Siskin had gone to Empingham and would not return afore dark. That I might have a change of scenery from my room, she suggested that we establish ourselves in front of the fire in the library. And so we went down, and La Ghoul dragged an armchair for herself close to the fender, and wheeled me to face her there.

The rain now lashed the windows, and it seemed to draw all of Brink House's inmates the closer together. Absalom, as ever, lay on the floor beside La Ghoul. When I'd seen him come padding into the room, I'd started and squirmed, and for a moment I'd thought I was about to give a repeat performance of the histrionics I'd shown the very first time I saw him; but La Ghoul had snapped at me to calm myself, and said that what she had to tell me would exonerate Absalom absolutely. I'd looked at the muckle-great hound, and reminded myself of how timid it seemed, for all its bulk. It had seemed much bigger and more fierce out in the Whin Valley at yon time of night; but this was no doubt because of the tremendous fear I had felt upon seeing it. It moved more freely when Master Siskin was gone from the house, more nobly, I thought, with none of its habitual skulking.

In a short time, La Ghoul had got the fire in and poured herself a glass of water. I sat opposite her, bundled in my ridiculous wicker contraption, while she perched on the edge of a high-backed leather chair, eyeing me and tapping her fingernails on her glass, building up her nerve.

'My story begins before I began,' she said at length. 'Before I was born. But I must begin somewhere. So I begin in Algiers, and the fall of the city.'

'Ah, yes, the empire-building of those damned French bastards!' said I, with sympathy.

'No, monsieur. This is fifteen years before the French bastards came. I speak of English bastards and Dutch bastards.'

I will admit that this chastened me enough to consider the merits of shutting up, when I was able. Perhaps my predicament was teaching me, at long last, subtlety.

'This is eighteen sixteen. It is the story I have from my mother, who was there. Back then, Omar Agha was the Dey of Algiers. Dey is *uncle*. Omar Agha had once been a corsair – what you'd call a pirate – and now he was uncle to a city full of pirates. That is how the Europeans saw it. They found a thousand reasons why our ships could not dock in their ports, and why we could not trade with them. In the end, my people did what people do when driven to extremity. We took instead of trading. We boarded European ships. We sailed to European towns and took all we found there – and then we took the people who had tried to stop us taking it. And where there was plenty, we took plenty, and where there was little, we took all.

'At this time, you Europeans were very hot against slavery. Your people had only just passed a law that banned the trade; but, of course, the trade continued all the same, and your great empire could not survive without its slaves . . .'

I bristled at being lumped in with such a hodgepodge, for it smacked of nowt but another forced combination to me, and one that I wanted no part of. I broke my short-lived vow of silence on the matter, but the woman merely shrugged, and said that we were all much of a muchness in her eyes.

'*I* never forced anyone to be a pirate!' I cried. '*I* never passed a law blocking Algerian trade! I was too busy digging for lead, if I wasn't digging for coal!'

'Lead and coal, monsieur. As you say. And to what end did you dig?'

'To what end? Why, as it happens, I did it so as to keep two ignorant women in the misery to which they'd grown accustomed.'

'I mean, where did this lead and coal go? Do you know?'

'How the devil am I to know that?'

'Well, *I* know. I know at least some of the uses your people found for your lead and your coal. And that is part of what I have to say. So. You had passed a law against slavery. And now you were very hot against Omar Agha, and against the Beys of Tunis and Tripoli – a Bey is like a Dey – and you told them they all had to stop being pirates and enslaving your people. And the Beys of Tunis and Tripoli said all right they would stop. But Omar Agha said, why should he stop? You had outlawed every means by which Algiers could buy and sell in Europe – how else were we to get any money?

'So the Dey of Algiers continued in his lawlessness, and then, in eighteen sixteen, the British and Dutch ships set sail for Algiers. Algiers is a coastal city. A fortified port. But now there were many ships sailing for it – and among them were the four great bomb ships: the *Infernal*, the *Fury*, the *Hecla*, and *Belzebub*. *Belzebub* led the convoy. On that ship was Master Siskin.'

The fire gave a crack and I started, causing Absalom to sit up on high alert for a moment, afore he whuffled his displeasure and settled again. I pictured Siskin, his mortars arranged all about him, standing on the prow of *Belzebub* as it cut through the ocean, its sails bellied forth with a fair wind sent from the opened doors of Hell.

'Master Siskin would then have been six-and-twenty years of age, and in those days the family went by another name: Tarin. His father was still alive then, and his branch of the family were living in France, and it was Tarin *père* who ran the family business, which was making guns and bombs, then as now. Tarin *père* had sent his son along on this mission to oversee the operation of the new exploding shells. That's the sort of devil he was: he sent his son to war for no better reason than to see the carnage his weapons would cause.

'So the ships were sailing for Algiers when, as they were rounding the Iberian Peninsula, they encountered one of our corsair ships, the *Ajenwi*, carrying ninety souls – mostly men, but some women, and one of these was my mother, who had me in her belly. The *Ajenwi* tried to flee. We could not hold out against a single European war ship, and certainly not a fleet of them. So the *Ajenwi* tried to flee – but: *Belzebub* opens fire, and the ship goes down. Some of the women on board were lifted from the water, to be used for the amusement of the English sailors; my mother was claimed by Master Siskin. All other souls were lost. Any who didn't go down with the *Ajenwi* were picked off with rifles. That is how my family died.'

The fire cracked again, and the coals shivered and resettled. It seemed a more eloquent response than any I could have managed. After a moment, La Ghoul resumed her tale.

'When I was very small, my mother would tell me a version of the events of that day, and she would say that Master Siskin had saved her out of mercy. By then, she knew that this was not so; but she let me continue to believe the story that she had once told herself. I will say this: he did not use her the way men usually use women they have captured. Not then, and not later. Perhaps, at first, it was because her belly was big with me. Perhaps, later, it was because he had not done it at first. I do not know. But, whatever the reason, her trials were to be of a different kind.

'My mother was now Master Siskin's captive, stowed aboard *Belzebub*, which sailed on, along with the other British and Dutch ships, heading for Algiers. The convoy arrived on August twenty-six, eighteen sixteen. They began shelling at three in the afternoon. It took them seven hours to destroy our fleet, our arsenal and our port. Master Siskin told me, many years later, that the European ships had fired fifty thousand rounds of shot, and used more than one hundred ton of gunpowder. The four bomb ships had, between them, fired one thousand explosive shells. He enjoyed reciting the numbers. He likes to have everything – how do you say?'

'Accounted for,' I said heavily, thinking of the quill-driver's shelf of ledgers.

'Counted for. Yes. My mother said that by ten o'clock the air was filled with smoke, and the sea was filled with the wreckage of our ships and with the bodies of our fallen. Wherever she looked, she said, she saw the ghastly smiles of sharks and Englishmen.'

'Your mother had a canny turn of phrase,' I noted.

'Algiers was broken, so Lord Exmouth – he was the leader of the navy – he offered peace terms. And now, along with the design of the bomb ships and the guns and the shells, this was Master Siskin's other contribution to the work of that day. For it was Master Siskin who told Lord Exmouth to threaten the Dey that, if the peace terms were not accepted immediately, they would proceed at once to bombard the city itself, and utterly destroy it. This was a lie – a bluff, I think you say? They had already exhausted their munitions. But the Dey didn't know that, so he signed the peace treaty.'

It was almost enough to make a fellow sorry for the poor old Dey, I thought, even despite him being a pirate and a wicked enslaver of Christians. I said as much to La Ghoul, who shrugged. And then I asked what became of him, the Dey of Algiers?

'After the ships sailed away, Algiers survived, but, ever after, the city was smaller, weaker. And then – my mother told me this, though she was far away by the time it happened – within a year, the plague returned. That was the summer of eighteen seventeen. They say one person in three died of the outbreak. My people can tolerate a tyrant, but they cannot abide one with bad luck. By September, Omar Agha was no longer the Dey of Algiers; he'd been strangled by his own janissary troops. The men buried him within an hour of killing him. He had ruled for two and a half years.'

'Two and a half years,' I mused. 'A poor showing, I think?'

'His predecessor had been assassinated after two and a half weeks. So, no.'

'Fair enough,' said I. 'So that is how Algiers fell . . .'

'That is how Algiers fell. Master Siskin's guns. Master Siskin's lies. And that is how my mother – and how I – came into his service. I was born, a month before my time, the morning after the bombardment, on board the *Belzebub*. My mother told me that the first breath I took was yet bitter with the smoke.

'Master Siskin took us to France after that. I needed a name, but when my mother told him the name she had given me, he said it would not do, and so I was given the name of the village we were passing through at the time: Laguiole.'

When I heard this, I felt bad, for maybes the first time in my life, at having bequeathed someone a nickname. Laguiole was hardly a name to begin with, having been inflicted by a captor, so I swore to myself not to call her La Ghoul again, and asked her what her true name was, if she cared to tell me.

She looked at me a long time afore she said owt. I felt myself thrown on the scales – and I must have been found wanting, for she did not disclose her true name, but merely continued her narrative. 'We lived, the three of us, in France for four years. And then, this would have been in the year eighteen twenty, Master Siskin became the guardian of his newborn cousin, Elise. He said that he was not expecting this to happen, and that he did not relish the responsibility, but he had no choice but to have Elise come to live with us. He was all the family she had. The great surprise of the news, and then the arrival of the baby, are mixed together in my memory.

'Master Siskin was Elise's guardian, but she was raised by my mother. I thought she was my sister, and I doted on her. She was the great gift of my girlhood, of my life. She was something I could love. Something that could love me. It was hard to love my mother because of how life had dealt with her. She had been made very hard. There was so much fierceness in her care for me, I could hardly recognise it as care at all. But Elise was all gentleness. As she grew to girlhood, we all – Siskin, my mother and I – protected her gentleness, I think, because we had had so little of it in our own lives.'

At this, I murmured that I was in greater sympathy with her than she would have believed, but my words were not acknowledged.

'Elise and I grew up together, close as sisters, secluded from the world. Master Siskin's ways have always been like this. He has always preferred to stay far distant from people. In society, he must wear a mask. A man can wear a mask only so long. But this isolation meant that I was sheltered, and for a long time I did not even know that Elise and I could never have been true sisters, since she was European and I was African.

'Master Siskin raised Elise as his daughter until she was sixteen. And then he married her.' Laguiole said this so quickly that I felt it like a blow – a glancing blow that makes your head spin all the same.

'That . . . that is . . . a terrible thing,' I said, feeling, more than ever afore, the inadequacy of words at the times when they are needed most. I cast about for some fancier phrasing, but in the end only added, 'She would have seen him as her father. It is unnatural. It is incest.'

'I know the word for it. It was done suddenly and secretly. Master Siskin took Elise away one day on a trip to Paris, so that she could see the great city, he said. He had business there, and it would be good for her to see the world. I was to stay at home, of course. I expected nothing else. I was older, by this time, and Master Siskin made sure that I understood the difference between myself and Elise very well. They left as father and daughter, and returned as husband and wife. Elise, who had been our daughter and sister for so long, was now our mistress.

'With this alteration to our household arrangements, a change came over my mother. She grew ever more fearful. I think that, by marrying Elise, Master Siskin had broken a promise that he had made to my mother, or had broken an understanding. She now saw how she stood upon a reed, not a log. The gentleness in Elise, that we had protected so long, now worked against us. We could not begin to make her understand that it was wrong to have married Master Siskin, that he was wicked for compelling her. Soon after this, Master Siskin told us we must prepare to leave France for England, and my mother and I must learn a new language, and he had already changed his name from Tarin to Siskin at the wedding ceremony, and – all was changing, and in ways that were a great surprise to us, but which we could see he had planned with great care.

'As I came to understand my mother's fear, I began to see that, just as I had helped to protect a gentleness in Elise, something had been protected in me – not gentleness, but a kind of innocence. Innocence as to the nature of my mother's duties to Master Siskin. Innocence as to his true nature, though I knew by then that he was an evil man . . .'

Laguiole stopped a moment to poke violently at the fire. I shifted my weight, and my whicker chair squeaked and tutted and groaned as it always did when I moved an inch. It sounded like it was trying to warn me about something on the quiet. The pressure of the atmosphere in the room seemed to intensify as we sat there, Laguiole staring into the fire as though building up the nerve to say what she was about to say.

'And so, one day, when we were alone, my mother told me what I am about to tell you. When she told me, I could not believe her. When I tell you, you will not believe me. I understand this, but I will tell you anyway. I had to see, with my own eyes, the way it was. And, in time, you will see it for yourself as well. And then, at last, you will believe.'

Laguiole sat back and looked at me then, and again I felt

myself being weighed. And then she glanced at the door, and then back at me. And then she began to speak once more, her eyes never leaving mine. She said that Siskin was not a man, but a wolf in the guise of a man. His true form asserted itself for a few days each month. His father had been of the same kind, and his father afore him, and so on. It was a curse, passed down the male line of the family.

Now, Laguiole's words will no doubt strike you as risible, but, after she had spoken to me with such clarity and candour, I can only say that I didn't, at that time, feel able to reject her statement outright. That said, I couldn't accept it, either. So I endeavoured to hold off making a choice about whether I thought the poor woman had lost her mind, and kept the matter in suspension, so to speak. I could not wholeheartedly believe her, but I believed that *she* believed it to be the case, and I reckoned it would be politic to keep my scepticism to myself.

I learned that the change occurred more or less in step with the full moon, though it was not always punctual. (In this, said I, it put me in mind of a woman's menses, being somewhat variable. I enjoyed the sour look Laguiole gave me for that. Our circumstances were dire, but the devil of perversity would not allow me to refrain from facetiousness.) The transformation was not always completed, and sometimes it could be held off entirely – or, more rarely, induced out of season – by a concerted act of will.

The change – though I might call it the 'shift', for that was the word Laguiole liked to use – the shift, then, often took the best part of a night to be effected, but sometimes was accomplished within an hour. Once shifted, Siskin would remain fixed as a wolf – or whatsoever form of chimaerical hybrid, or *loup-garou* as she called it – for some two or three days, afore shifting back. Again, the reversion usually took a full night to be achieved. The older the man became, the bigger the wolf became – it never seemed to stop growing, which made shifting increasingly painful as the years went by. Nowadays, the shift was a debilitating ordeal: immediately afterwards, Master Siskin's health and vitality would be at a low ebb, and sometimes he kept to his bed for days.

I was still avoiding making a decision about whether I should believe what I was hearing, but, when I looked at Absalom, I realised that I didn't now take this to be the creature that had so terrorised me that night on Windy Top. I didn't think it capable of killing the poor souls in the cellar. That Siskin was the culprit, I could well believe. If I could not, then, entirely accept that he had accomplished such tyrannies in the guise of a wolf, well, I was willing myself to do so.

Laguiole explained that her mother had played a complicated and essential role for Master Siskin, and now Laguiole played the role herself: sole confidant of the family secret and, when Siskin was in wolf form, the person entrusted with the running of the house. It was Laguiole who hired the few other staff that were required, and she even knew many details of Siskin's business, for it was sometimes necessary to have her write letters on his behalf. But in other regards, she, like her mother afore her, was a menial helper – fetching and carrying and cleaning – and they could never leave his employ, for how far would a Frenchified, dark-skinned woman get, telling tales about a powerful, rich gentleman who was in fact a wolf in disguise? And he paid them 'in kind', providing them with board, lodging and meals, but no wages, and gave them the merest pittance on top of this for necessities, so they could never hope to save enough money to make a go of it alone. And if they had robbed him and made a run for it, how far would he have pursued them, a man of such means and with such a secret to protect? To the rim of the world.

So it had continued for many a year. But lately, Laguiole explained, Master Siskin was often making an imperfect shift back to humankind. On several occasions, she gave me to understand, his legs had remained covered in a thick pelt of hair for the entire month. So mournfully serious was her expression as she said this, I heard myself presently burst out in a laugh. To think of old Brinsley Siskin, attending his freemasons' meetings, or sitting in his family pew at church, or feasting on roasted swan with good Queen Vic, and all the while under his trousers he's being carried about on a pair of woolly wolf-legs! I laughed until I had to spit.

Laguiole talked on unperturbed, and explained that what had especially put the fear into Master Siskin was the business with his teeth. The fact was, for a full year now Siskin had been forced to live as a man with a set of wolf's teeth clustered in his gob: they had simply failed to retract back into his gums at the end of his shift.

My laughing fit was over now, and the horror of the

situation was apparent once more. 'Hence the extravagant moustaches . . .' says I, and Laguiole nodded grimly. Master Siskin but rarely went out in public these days, and had put the word about that he'd suffered a stroke, since when his speech had been maimed, which explained how it was he shushed and sloshed his esses, and made such a mess of his victuals that he didn't like to be seen at table. But the day would come when he shifted into his wolf form for good, and what would all of his money avail him then?

After this, and with a note in her voice that told me she was coming more nearly to the heart of the matter, at least as far as she was concerned, she told me about Master Siskin's son, Absalom.

'His *son*? Did he name the dog after his son, or his son after the dog?'

Laguiole gave me a straight look, and I began to see how things stood. She explained that the dog, Absalom, was not a dog, after all: it, too, was a *loup-garou*, albeit one whose shifting worked contrariwise – he was a wolf who, once a month, became a man.

I exhaled a long breath, and with it tried to let go of the last of my old, fond hope that the world could be held to account, that reason and actuality could ever belong together. And then, when I could speak once more:

'Back at Windy Top, the lads used to speculate that Master Siskin had a son that he kept locked up in a room in his house, and that the son had inherited a certain affection of the blood from his father . . .'

'How did they know this?'

'They didn't know. They was supposing. And what they was supposing was syphilis.'

'*La grande vérole.*'

'Aye, and the French disease would have been bad enough, but I reckon young Absalom caught something worse yet from his old man.'

And then – though it stranged my mind to consider it – I had to ask Madame Laguiole whether young Absalom had been born a human babe or a wolf cub.

Her face gave me my answer, and then she confirmed it. It was as a wolf cub that Absalom came into this world, and a wolf he remained for more than three years, afore he began to shift briefly human-wise, more or less in tandem with the full moon.

'Poor Elise Siskin. A more terrible childbed is not to be imagined. It must have been the death of her, as I think?'

'There was a lot of blood, and I often thought that Elise must die before the birthing was accomplished. All through her pregnancy there had been bleedings and pains and troubles of every kind, so I had been expecting it to be difficult. And, as my lady had only been with child for four months, I thought at first that this was a miscarriage. And so it was, you may say. Many hours it took, and Master Siskin in the corner of the room all that time, as he oughtn't have been, for it isn't right for a man to be in such a place, though all he did was sit in the corner covering his face or covering his ears or gnawing at his fingertips. But he would be there. I think he half-suspected it would be as, in the end, it was. He wouldn't permit the presence of a doctor, though Elise cried bitterly for need of one, so I was alone with it all. It would move anyone's heart to hear how that good lady screamed, time and again; but how much louder grew the screams once the creatures started being born.'

'*Creatures?* God in Heaven, how many were there?'

Her gaze hardened, if such were possible, and she said, 'Six. There were six in the—'

'In the litter.'

'Five of them were dead already. Only one survived. When I noticed that it moved, when I saw its little chest rising and falling, I reached into the mess of dead cubs and blood and I lifted it out. With its eyes closed tight, and ears pressed flat to its head, it looked as though it wanted to keep as much of the world out for as long as it could. I held it in my hands and . . . it was as though I could block out Elise's shrieking, for she had caught sight of it by now, and you will imagine how she was taking it. But I was gazing at him, at Absalom, a raw scrap of life, and for a moment it seemed I escaped this evil house, and I thought then how abject a creature he was, not having, nor ever like to have, a friend in the world, and being little more than a curse on his mother and father. His only piece of luck, I thought, was that he seemed utterly deaf and oblivious to the way the sounds that accompanied his delivery were not cries of joy but shrieks of anguish and fear and shame. And, there and then, I felt a sort of love for him, in defiance of my instincts.'

I looked at Absalom, where he lay upon the dark oak floor, chin resting on his great paws, and tried to guess at whether he understood what was being said. You never know, with dogs.

'Master Siskin had come to his senses by then, and was staggering towards me, his face filled with hatred for the newborn creature I held. I saw him raise his cane above his head – it is a leaded cane, a weapon – and I knew that he meant to dash its brains out even as I stood there holding it, so I turned my back on him. I mean, I spun around instantly. Master Siskin broke some of the bones in my back, and the mark remains, and shall always remain. But I saved Absalom's life.' As she said these words, Laguiole's face was twisted as though she were crying, but her eyes, I noticed, were dry. Once more, I tried to steer her towards the painful subject.

'What became of Mrs Siskin?'

'Master Siskin had a man come here, and he said he was a doctor, but I do not think he was a doctor in fact. But he wrote that my lady had died of *an affection of the womb* . . . and that is how her death was recorded. I have found that, in this country, if a thing is written down it becomes an accepted fact. If it is not, then it is not.'

I grunted my agreement. 'Much depends on the hand that does the writing, but you are correct.'

I listened to the ticking of the clock, and presently Madame Laguiole arose from her chair and subtly stretched to her considerable height. Absalom watched her attentively. The fire was burning low, so she tended to it. To herself as much as to me, she said, 'Elise knew nothing of Master Siskin's secret until the night Absalom was born . . .' She rose and stood over the fire. 'Now that Elise is dead, and now that my mother is dead – now that it is too late – I allow myself to think things that I kept hidden from myself before. Now I think, Elise was not a cousin of Master Siskin's at all. This was merely another lie. Now I think that Elise was truly his daughter. He had sired her in secret. Who knows what became of her mother. And then he bred with his daughter, thinking perhaps that this would purify his blood, for the curse passes only from father to son, you see? But he did nothing but concentrate the curse that was on the blood.'

It is not often that we are present when another body is occupied, as Laguiole was then, in trying to take the measure of how far she had misled herself hitherto. The sight of the scattered carnage in the cellar, which had shaken me so badly, must have played havoc with her. Part of me wanted to ask if she'd had any inklings as to the Master's activities, but this didn't seem the time. She stood so erect that she trembled, walked to the window, carrying herself like a brimful cup of something bitter and precious, and looked out over the moors. The rain had let up, and the light in the room seemed rinsed clean. I wheeled myself over to join her, and the pair of us gazed over the slowly undulating law that spread before us. We were at the top of the world. Far below, patches of ground mist were gathered hither and yon, and I mused on the difference atween that far-off haziness and the sharp, cold light in which Laguiole and I were presently to be seen. I thought how our fondest, warmest memories lie nestled in such dreamy vagueness, all fuzzed about to the highest degree; and, contrariwise, our worst moments retain all their hard edges. The conversation that she and I had that day has kept all of the stark clarity it had when first she spoke – and I knew that it would be so, even then.

'How did this madness begin?' I asked softly. 'You say that Siskin got the curse from his father, who got it from his, but how did this get started?'

The answer was that once, long ago, one of Master Siskin's wicked forebears had chosen the life of a wolf – so Laguiole said, and she'd heard this from Master Siskin himself, one night many years back, when he'd overdone it with the sherry and was feeling sorry for himself. That first, fatal choice, made by Master Siskin's distant antecedent, had been effected with a ritual conducted some time in the fifth century – with the drawing down of the moon and the infusing of its powers into a balm to be applied to the body, and then with the donning of an enchanted girdle made of wolf-fur and human skin, which proved impossible to remove, growing into the wearer very hideously. The intention was to gain the power to shift into a wolf shape for only seven years, but, as with the enchanted girdle, so with the lycanthropy it induced: having once been chosen by free election, it proved impossible to put off the habit. ('Like being a freemason,' I heard myself say, and thought at once what a foolish and contrary fellow I was.) Worse, it became apparent that it would be passed on down the bloodline. Character is fate. The Siskins would never escape the hubris they showed that day; howsoever long they lived, they would banquet on its consequences. Hard lines for them!

Evidently, Northalbion in those early centuries had been

a site of tremendous supernatural activity, and the Siskins had been able to tap it all too easily; but when it came to undoing their wolfish magic, they found themselves in need of something stronger. So it was the Siskins turned to Mithraism, for what better antidote could there be for an excess of moon-worship, than to exalt the one who stood in victory over the sun itself? Their goal, their only priority, was now to find the Knack, in which so much Mithraic power – and so much of the region's *fors*, to use Siskin's word – was now earthed and locked. We both looked at my bandaged hand, which had presently begun to throb, as though the wound were waking to the sound of its name. I didn't wish to think of my predicament in this light, so I asked Laguiole to please continue her narrative.

Many generations later, I was told, a deviation occurred. Twin boys were born – and if one brother saw his inheritance as a curse, the tother saw it as a licence; and if one was slow to anger, the tother took the April rain personally. When these two came of age, the family tree forked: the good son stayed in Northalbion, and he and his successors forswore human flesh, and searched for the Knack here in Northalbion, believing it to be buried here somewhere; the bad son left England, believing the Knack to have been taken back to Rome, where it had likely been stolen by the Goths. So both branches of the family searched by any and all means for the Knack, in hope that it would provide a cure.

Though these lycanthropes did not *require* human flesh to survive, the bad son and his successors appeared to prefer it, or at least they enjoyed the getting of it, and they hunted mankind freely – so freely, indeed, that their lives became an unending migration. They were barely able to settle anywhere for more than a generation afore the suspicions began to grow, and the tongues began to wag, and the dragging of the tail was no longer enough to cover the tell-tale tracks: all the way from England to Serbia and Herzegovina, where they presented themselves as the Sichkin family, until the peasants began to grow suspicious of their new neighbours and called them *voukodlaks*, which soon enough became *vrykolakas*, as the family, now travelling under the name Flóros, fled to Greece, and then on to Italy, where once again rumours gathered like shadows around this mysterious family, whose name – Lucherino, so they said – began to sound all too exchangeable with *lupo-mannaro*; and so to Spain, where a family calling itself Chamariz settled – but only for the time it took the pattern to repeat, and within a generation they were feared as *lobombre* – and then Portugal, where, it seemed, no sooner had the Verdilhão family arrived, than a cry was taken up against them as *lobisomem*; and then the move to France, where a man who introduced himself as Monsieur Tarin brought his son afore, at last, with whispers of *loup-garou* swirling about him, young Monsieur Tarin became Master Siskin, and, taking his two servants and his young wife with him, he moved back to Northalbion, with his tail atween his legs, so to speak.

Master Siskin's return to the old country was not a joyous occasion. As Laguiole explained, when two wolf packs conjoin perforce, there can be no bloodless union.

'In eighteen thirty-seven, soon after his marriage to Elise, Master Siskin took us to England, and then brought us here, to these hills – the *laws*, as you call them. He took rooms in an inn in Empingham, and there I stayed with my mother and Mrs Siskin. Master Siskin would ensure that all was ready at Brink House for our arrival, he said. We were to wait for his return, and not send for word, though he would be gone several days, nor stray far from the inn. So we waited.

'He was gone for a week. By this time, I was grown used to his monthly disappearances, but on this occasion I found myself wondering whether he would ever return. I hoped and wished that he would not. But he did come back. And when he did, he had changed again. He now spoke with the English accent you hear in his mouth today, and he was dressed in clothes we had not seen before. He said that he had made it to Brink House just in time to hear the dying words of his last living relation in England, an old man who had left the house and estates to him. The house had been let go to wrack and ruin, so our work would be before us in the tidying-up of the place.

'My mother and I knew all of this to be a lie. We were not fools. But we did not know what had truly occurred. When we first came here, to Brink House, it was in a deplorable state, but it had not fallen into disrepair. Rather, it looked like it had been the scene of violence. Furniture was broken; there were lumps gouged out of the walls here and there; doors had panels missing, or else the locks on them had been burst from their sockets.

'What could we do? We knew not a soul in this country, we could barely speak your language. We cleaned the house. We repaired what we could. I never learned the truth about the events of those days when he first came here; I suspected – but I never knew for sure until the day before yesterday, when we saw the cellar beneath the cellar. I think that Master Siskin first came here in the form of a wolf, and he slaughtered his family. They must have fought back. At least some of them must have shifted into wolfish forms, for we saw wolf skulls in the cellar. But the branch of the family that had been living here was no longer accustomed to hunting and killing. For Master Siskin, like his father before him, it was all he knew. When he returned to us, to that inn in Empingham, I think he must have been wearing the clothes of the cousins he'd slain.'

Well, I thought, here was the source of Brink House's strange quality of being breathless as a stoppered bottle. All of its inhabitants murdered in a day. No wonder gloom and silence had stolen into the place and possessed it utterly.

'You will think it incredible that we stayed, that we could ever settle for living here with him. But Master Siskin is as clever as the Devil. He has the power of a lie. Once you have consented to believe one lie, believing a second comes more easily. The third is easier still. Soon, you hardly understand that these are lies, and that you are in compliance with them. My mother stayed, perhaps, because she thought it the safer choice; her concern was me. I stayed for the same reason – my concern was my mother, and Elise. Elise could not even think of leaving. She was a rich man's wife, and was coming to understand freedom only now that she had forever lost it.

'My mother died soon after this, and I inherited her duties, her responsibilities, her secrets. I inherited the great compromise she had had to make. I told myself that I must try to believe the lies that Master Siskin was telling me: that, although he shifted, he did not kill; that he fed as a vulture feeds; that, at most, he took a beast for prey.'

'Did you know that they were lies, though but?' My question was artless, and I regretted asking it as soon as it was uttered. It seemed to fall from the air and lie, inert, on the carpet, where I stared. When I gledged at Laguiole, she had looked away and was silent. The matter was a stew of lies and smothered truths and fond hopes.

'We hired maids from the orphanage . . .' Madame Laguiole paused, and, turning from the window, stared up at the ceiling for a moment. 'And they would work here for a time, until Master Siskin told me that they had taken a position elsewhere, or had been caught stealing and been dismissed. And men came, from time to time, looking for work. Perhaps some of them were sent on to the Sill, but I think, now, that many of them never left Brink House, and their bones are here today.

'The doll that I found in the cellar, it belonged to an orphan. Her name was Sara. She had made the doll herself, when she was living in Master Siskin's orphanage. When she was thirteen years old, she was taken on here as a maid. She brought the doll with her. One day she disappeared. Master Siskin said that she had run away . . .'

In my mind's eye I saw, once again, the heaps of bones and rotting bodies in the cellar. But now, in my recollecting, the skulls that had lain variously scattered all seemed lined up to face me, and into the shadowy pits of their empty eye-sockets was crept an imploring look; and what had been a scene of rank desolation was now an imperative that we avenge these murders, or at least that we remember them, and tell of what we had seen.

'After Elise died, I would have run away, I think, but for Absalom. I do not ask you to approve, Monsieur Malarkey. I do not expect you to understand. But it is the love I have for him that keeps me here. As innocent as he was that day, so he has remained. He has hardly learned human ways, and is the more noble for this deficiency. You see him as a monster. But he is a child of nature, nothing more. In one thing alone is he unnatural: he has neither hunted nor tasted human flesh. I taught him to disavow all such tendencies.'

Laguiole said this with feeling; evidently, this was how she partook of her portion of pride, and I realised that the fear and disgust I'd displayed upon first meeting Absalom must surely have put bitterness in her heart against me. She was confiding in me, but this was a strategy, not an intimacy. She'd never like me. With this in mind, I thought it wise to remind her of the great need for solidarity . . .

Solidarity. The word had slipped into my mind like a thief in the night. It was not a quality I'd given much thought to, until now. But did I really mean solidarity, or was I proposing a more cynical allegiance – mutually beneficial, yes, but resulting not from genuine fellow-feeling, and formed only in reaction against the most recent betrayal? Or is that all there ever is to human politicking? I'd have to ponder this another time. I made my case to Madame Laguiole.

'You asked me, after we got out of that lazar-house cellar, whether I had recognised a body down there. The man sitting beside the door, with his heart ripped out of his chest. Well, I did recognise him. And I won't say I liked him, but I knew him to be a loyal servant of Master Siskin, and one who now has received the reward that awaits all of Siskin's servants.'

The good woman picked up on my drift – that we were in perilous danger; that the quill-driver had been obedient and was nevertheless eaten alive, so we'd face a worse fate, should we move against Siskin and fail. She announced, 'I am ready, now, to act. Master Siskin is planning something. I know his ways: how he grows secretive and quiet and especially pleased with himself when he is planning something. He was like this before he took Elise away and married her. He was like this before he made us all come to England. When you asked me to show you the cellar – when you said that there was something bad in this house – I thought, perhaps here is my chance. Now we are three. We must work together, I think?'

'I think we must, Madame Laguiole. And quickly. The moon waxes, and I assume we'll be better off tackling him while he's still a man . . .'

'Yes, of course. But, you will have noticed, he is stronger than he appears, yes? It will be hard for you to remember that he is not human. He is only a creature that looks human.'

'Looks human three weeks out of four, anyway,' I said.

And then I asked why we didn't just make our move as soon as he returned? The house had guns, knives, poison and the Lord knew what else – and we'd have the element of surprise, so . . . ?

But Laguiole shook her head. Master Siskin would not be returning alone. He would bring with him a full complement of staff, for this was his way when he had to entertain visitors: he hired, for a brief time, all of the staff that any other gentleman would keep as a matter of course. The house was to be full of people and activity for several days.

'*Visitors?*' I repeated, dumbfounded. My imagination had shown great pluck in keeping pace with Laguiole's story of pirates and werewolves and incest, but one thing it could not conceive was a gloomy puzzle-box of oubliettes like Brink House ever becoming a centre for society.

Well, I was to be proven wrong on that score, for Laguiole informed me that none other than His Royal Highness Edward, Prince of Wales would be visiting us. (She said this so blithely, I could only admire her.) Such had been the meat of the telegram that had so excited Master Siskin the day before. Siskin had long been angling to arrange the visit, and now confirmation had finally come. In consequence, Master Siskin had left for Empingham, to oversee a vast purchase of provisions. When I asked whether it was strange that he chose to do this himself, when it was the sort of task that a gentleman might delegate to a housekeeper such as herself, she delivered a 'Ha!' and said that yes, she would usually take care of such a thing, but Master Siskin would be collecting Thomas on his travels, his latest favourite from the orphanage: a youth of seventeen years, who was become Master Siskin's ward. Master Siskin was a jealously protective benefactor, and never permitted anyone to speak to this boy without his being present. Rather than permit the boy to live at Brink House, where he might learn a little too much about his guardian angel, Siskin had given him his own rooms at the orphanage, where he was kept apart, and made much of.

So then I wondered why such a hullabaloo was being occasioned by the visit of a bairn. It would be different, I said, if the Prince of Wales was to be accompanied by his mam and dad, but as that didn't seem to be the case . . .

Laguiole gave me another of her looks, so I explained that a 'bairn' was an infant.

She asked what I meant by 'infant'.

I said I meant a person in the earliest phase of life, and that the French must have a word for this.

'Monsieur le Con makes a joke. He wishes to amuse. But he is in the wrong. Edward, Prince of Wales has now reached eighteen years of age, and if half of what people say about him is true, then he is, on any reasonable assessment, a man of the world.'

I assured her that *she* was in the wrong, as she was a foolish Frenchwoman, and I was an Englishman, and I knew the age – more or less – of the heir to the throne. And he was three, or maybes four years old. Not more than five, certainly.

She looked on me with a kind of pity, and then sat down

so we were eye-to-eye. 'I think that Monsieur worked in the Sill for longer than he knows.'

I felt an old fear awaken and start to uncoil in my brain. 'What are you getting at?'

She took her time in answering. 'Do you know what year this is?'

'It is . . . why, what nonsense is this? Woman, it is eighteen forty-five! Anno Domini!' I tried to sound more certain than I felt about the matter.

'No, Monsieur,' was the reply. Keeping her voice low and steady, that I might more readily accept her words, she said to me, 'That was long ago. See how changed you are. You were a young man, then. This is the year eighteen sixty.'

I did what I do when words fail me.

Laguiole shook her head. 'You laugh, but I think you understand that what I say is true. The Sill is a special and a terrible place. A moment down there is a day aboveground.'

'Eighteen sixty!' I said, and laughed again, but my throat was dry. When I breathed, the air shuddered through me. I didn't want to look at her any more, so I stared down at my knees, which seemed very bony, and my legs very thin, as I sat in my perambulator. I'd grown small in my clothes, like an old man, it was true. Indeed, to look at me, I'd gained – or, rather, lost – a good deal more than fifteen years.

And then she struck on an idea, and disappeared for a moment, and returned with a copy of *The Times*. She handed it to me, and, when I saw the date, I handed it back to her. My brain felt suddenly altogether too full of strange thoughts. I held my head in my hands for a long time, and was glad when she left me in peace.

I kept my own company for the rest of that day, and slept but little that night.

11

The Prince and Poor Thomas

Next morning, Brink House was all astir with preparations for the Prince's visit. The promised flush of new staff had now descended – like a lost flock of migratory birds, I thought, that had made landfall somewhere not entirely to their liking – and, for the first time since I'd awoken, I could hear the sounds of life echoing in Brink House: the scurrying of feet, the instructions and asides, the clang and shunt of furniture being moved about. From my window, I saw two young girls drag a Persian carpet out on to the gravel, hang it over a frame and beat it to death with wickerwork paddles. Still ruminating on my having become so aged so quickly, I considered that I had more in common with the dusty carpet than with the lassies whacking it.

Well, I was feeling right sorry for myself when Madame Laguiole found me. She had but little time, she said, for the house was being turned upside down. Apparently, it was the Prince's habit to descend suddenly on his chosen hosts. His visit had been long expected – Siskin had been angling for it for many months – but the telegram of confirmation had given them scant time to make all ready for what Master Siskin called the great honour.

Now, I asked myself, does honour obtain in the wolf? A nice and important conundrum! On the whole, I thought it unlikely. So I asked her, was there not money involved?

Laguiole pronounced a great 'Ha!' and said, 'The Prince's visit will occasion a demonstration of Master Siskin's prototypes: guns of a new design. For many months he endeavoured to secure a contract with the admiralty for them. The contract would have brought investment. But the admiralty were not convinced, which was a great blow . . .'

'So Siskin is looking elsewhere for the funds.' It was as well, I thought, that our adversary would be thoroughly preoccupied with his inveiglements for the next several days, as it would give us a crack at forming a plan.

I know that a lot of men would thrill to be present at the advent of such novel armaments, but years of setting charges in all sorts of groves, and fleeing from the lit fuses in fear for my life, had left me with no wish to hear the report of the black powder ever again. I said words to this effect to Laguiole.

'That may be so, but Master Siskin asked me to invite you to attend the demonstration as well.'

I was given to understand that this was not an opportunity I'd be allowed to refuse. And so, at noon, Laguiole wrapped me in a woollen cape and helped me into my bath chair, whereupon two sturdy strangers in livery lifted my chariot and me as if we weighed no more than a wedding cake, and carried us bodily down the stairs, out of Brink House and away down the easterly part of the drive, which led not towards the road by which I had arrived in the quill-master's barrow, but beyond the craggy outcrop into which the house was set, and up on to the moorland beyond. This was the extension of Master Siskin's estate, dozens of acres out across the law, and upon this land he could do whatever the hell he liked. And what he liked was discharging ordinance.

Once they had climbed the bridleway and reached the crest of the fell, the two fellows set me down without a word, and without huffing and puffing as any normal person would have done at such exertions. Fit as a lop, the pair of them. There was a snell wind blowing, and I felt skinny and shrunken in my cape, which I pulled closer around my shoulders.

This was as close as I was permitted to get. I'd have to stay put with Madame Laguiole and the other servants, while Master Siskin and a few select others got a closer look at the guns. Siskin and the chosen few were grouped about forty yards away, where the bridleway withered off into heather and stretches of burnt gorse. My eyesight had been good enough for me to look down from the bedroom window and see what transpired in the environs of Brink House, but, now that I was tested with a longer view, I found all appeared fuzzy and dim. Amongst the figures I could make out Siskin, but the other four or five could have been anybody; one of them, I supposed, must have been the Prince, another must have been Siskin's ward. In any case, they were all fussing and cooing around the guns, both of which were a canny size, though one was larger than the tother, and both had long barrels about the thickness of a man's thigh. The barrels, which rested on two great cart wheels, were tilted skyward, and each had a long trail that steadied them at the rear. Both guns shone with a sense of deadly newness, like a nest of baby adders, perhaps, with neither will nor sense.

One of the men, I saw, was crouching behind the guns. By his flat cap I guessed he was an assistant or operator, admitted into the Prince's presence simply to coax the guns to perform. He was attending to the smaller one, busying at the rear, near the trail, seeming to unlatch it and lift something inside – shot, I presumed, or a shell – then close it up again. Then Siskin waved his arm and shouted something, and all but the assistant stepped back, and then a spark was lit and Siskin folded his arms with preemptive satisfaction.

The spark met the metal and vanished. The barrel gave a jolt and coughed a plume of black smoke, and the wheels jounced and rocked back a foot or so. In the windy open space of the moorland, the boom of the cannon was quickly lost, but it startled pockets of grouse, who lifted from the heather with their usual grunting, clapping racket, and I must admit it made me jitter like a proper old gadgie. Then there was a second boom as the shell found its target and, as we'd been led to expect, exploded upon impact. The sound travelled to us like rolling thunder across the law; given the distance it had travelled, it must have made a canny racket. Only then did I realise the mysterious thunder that had punctuated my stay at Brink House was in fact the sound of these guns being tested. Siskin's circle were delighted with the demonstration, and the group of servants around me gave a cheer and those wearing hats took them off and waved them. We all stared off into the distance, where presumably some target had been destroyed. The select group had glasses and scopes, but of course we did not, and the rim of the fell was a blur to me.

Now the group turned their attention to the bigger gun, and once more the assistant knelt behind it and lifted some hatch and packed whatever needed to be packed inside. They all stepped back as before, and the assistant knelt with his flame and touched it to the fuse. The spark travelled – Christ, how well I remembered the sight of that racing sparkle as it chittered along a fuse! – and reached its destination, and again the gun bucked and bounced, but I felt a spook of foreboding at the sight of it, even afore the assistant blew backwards into the gorse in a belch of smoke produced, not from the barrel, but from the rear of the gun. It seemed thuddingly obvious, in that moment, that the outcome of such a demonstration could only ever have been grievous harm.

In the silence that followed, I heard distinctly the exclamation, 'I say, is he *dead*?' But then the unfortunate assistant evidently came to and began to cry out very piteously, and I could imagine how Siskin's moustaches must have tightened at that. He put his hand on the shoulder of one of his companions and steered him swiftly away from the guns and back towards the path on which I sat in my chair, which, I supposed, looked rather like the wheeled chariots on which the guns were mounted. As Siskin approached, his words became audible: he was reassuring his companion that his servant was new to breech-loading and clearly hadn't achieved the correct seal in the chamber, but when done properly he could assure them that breech-loading was very much more efficient than loading from the muzzle, and he had dozens of documented tests to demonstrate this fact. Indeed—

But the two burly servants had reappeared quietly behind me, and my chair was lifted and turned and carried back down the stony bridleway afore I could catch the rest, and so I was wobbled back to Brink House.

Dinner was at eight. The dining room was all a-shimmer with a combination of candlelight and Siskin's newfangled electric sconces flickering about the walls, which buzzed and throbbed and gave off a queer chemical smell. They were powered – I heard Siskin declaiming to the assembled company, who stood about the room with sherry glasses in hand – by a hydroelectric system of his very own devising, engineered on the property over the last several years by getting up enough of a head on the stream to turn some sort of dynamo housed in a shed beside the lake. As he spoke, the light pooled and glimmered on the fluted lines of the marble pillars behind him, which framed the vast mantelpiece, and on the planes and carved reliefs of the mantel itself, which towered to the high ceiling and sank into darkness. It was like a version of the mountainside into which the house itself had been built, I thought, and the open fire blazing behind the grate, though it gave off wafts of heat, surely couldn't touch the coldness of that gigantic mausoleum slab any more than Brink House could warm the whinstone it adorned.

At last, noticing that I and Madame Laguiole had arrived, and that all of his guests were now present and correct, Siskin clapped his hands with conspicuous geniality and gestured to the table, which was laid with many glittering glasses and carafes and ornately folded napkins and a centrepiece of waxen fruits.

Once we were settled in our seats, Master Siskin introduced everyone by name.

'First and foremost,' said Siskin, 'may I present His Royal Highness, Edward, Prince of Wales.'

'Call me Bertie,' murmured the Prince – indeed, he frequently encouraged us to do this during the course of the dinner, but no one ever took up the invitation.

Next was the Prince's governor, comptroller and treasurer: a rather dour gentleman by the title of Admiral Bruce, who seemed a little forlorn, a little uncomfortable. At first, I imagined it was because he'd rather be bellowing orders on a poop deck than sitting at table with twenty pieces of cutlery before him, but I soon learned that his life was an endless humiliation, as you shall see.

Next to Admiral Truce (which is, of course, what I'd immediately decided to call him) sat I, Mr Caleb Malarkey.

Siskin said little about my talents or occupation, save that I was assisting him with his mining speculations.

On my other side sat a plump, sweaty, persnickety-looking fellow who turned out to be Dean Dudley, a minister of the Church of England, who was clearly delighted to be in such illustrious company, and with such an array of dainties ahead of him.

Beside Dean Deadly sat the boy I kept hearing about: Thomas, Master Siskin's ward, and – I realised with a shock when Siskin announced him by his full name – the orphaned child of Mr Playfair, for this was none other than Thomas Plover. Poor Thomas, as was. I looked at him while Siskin introduced him with a fatherly fondness. The ward's manners appeared very nice, and he seemed not in the least discountenanced to be in such illustrious company, so much so that, throughout the meal, I'd keek at him to see which knife or fork or spoon I was meant to be using for any given dish.

'I don't suppose the name Alfred Russell Wallace means aught to you?' asked Dean Dead-end, accosting me alone, for Siskin and the Prince had begun a separate conversation that he couldn't quite join. 'I should hope not. He is a scoundrel, Mr Malarkey, a scoundrel utterly, and not the only one, not by any means. You cannot imagine what some of these young fellows are saying. They would have you believe that the globe is little more than a great flying haggis, yes, a lava pudding hurtling through a godless cosmos, and we who live on it hardly to be distinguished from the animals . . .'

I kept one eye on Master Siskin during this discussion of

the human and the animal, but I took pains to be wily as I did so, for if Laguiole and I were caught making eyebrows at each other, then he'd jealous our intentions, sure as fate.

'Master Siskin has established an orphanage,' explained Dean Deadened, though I already knew this. 'Upon the lintel, the words are carved very beautifully in the stone: *Pure religion and undefiled before God and the Father is this, To visit the fatherless and widows in their affliction, and to keep himself unspotted from the world.*'

'Ah yes,' said I, 'James, chapter one, verse twenty-seven.'

I thought he'd be pleased to hear that I knew the book; but he frowned, as if my knowing were a sort of rudeness, and said, 'So. You have already seen this inscription.'

I caught his drift, and observed that James also said *If ye have respect to persons, ye commit sin.* I told him that I knew the book of James canny well, it being a favoured text of the Primitive Methodists.

'And what do you know of the Primitives?' he cried, and, afore I could answer, he added, 'I consider them to be a pack of notorious pickers and choosers!'

'Well, I didn't pick and choose to be raised by one. But she did at least instil a certain reverence for the Good Book. And, yes, such learning ought not to be a purchase but rather a natural inheritance – and yet, the world is as we have made it.'

'The world, sir, is as God ordained it!' he spluttered, pretending to be insulted by my words, when, really, he was offended by a low-born fellow such as me having the ability to find them.

'That that is, is, Dean Diddley' said I, quoting a fool to the fool.

The Dean did not even correct my mangling of his name, choosing instead the high road of forbearance, though he looked at me as if I'd just farted. (As a matter of fact, I *had* just farted, but he had no way of knowing this.)

The dinner, at any road, was very fine. It began with whitings and prawns (the first I ever tasted), followed by lamb, and then a smoking pudding, and then cheeses (an Ecklesrowe sheep's cheese and a Northalbion nettle cheese: very delectable), and then a sumptuous dessert of grapes, pine-cakes, French plums and brandy cherries.

That last was said to be the Prince's favourite, though he browsed on them without visible enthusiasm, as he did all of his food. Only at a glimpse of the serving-maid, who entered to deposit these various dishes upon the table before him, did his eyes betray something like interest.

Now that I was close, I could see Prince Call-me-Bertie well enough. His hair was longer than a gentleman's should be, and had wax in it; it was clamped down across the top of his head and then defied gravity in womanish curls on either side. His lips were protuberant and voluptuous; his eyes heavy-lidded; his cheeks, in the words of the song, too red and rosy to face a cannonball – though this might in part have been caused by the brandy he was drinking. His nose was indecently long, and his chin receded apologetically beneath it. His speech was slow and careless, with many 'oh's and 'er's and 'um's, all of which Admiral Truce seemed to find very disagreeable, and made him squirm as though he were sitting on a cushion stuffed with peach-stones. The Prince was supposed to be eighteen years of age at that time, but I wouldn't have guessed that, had I been asked: in some ways he seemed too childish – untried and untested – but in other ways he had the bitterness of a more advanced age.

Laguiole had schooled me in how to address a prince: you must say 'Your Royal Highness' the first time you say owt to him, and then 'Sir' after that. It did not seem likely that I would be called on to speak to him, however, as he showed no inclination to talk to anyone; that is, he *said* a fair amount, but addressed the words, as it were, to everyone and to no one, or to a body he could see but who remained invisible to our sight. He was a very strange fellow.

'My parents . . . have conspired to ensure that almost nothing interesting has ever happened to me. When I was, oh, fourteen years old or so, I visited the King of Sardinia. Great, big, burly, athletic sort of chap. *Veh* impressive to a young boy. He showed me a sword so big, he said, it could cut off an ox's head at a single blow.'

Admiral Truce grimaced at this, and urged the Prince to talk of something more edifying.

Without raising his eyes from his glass, and without raising his voice above its customary murmur, Prince Call-me-Bertie told Admiral Truce to shut up. This done, he continued. 'So I told him . . . I told the King of Sardinia . . . that I would personally give him *one hundred pounds* if he could demonstrate it. The great ox-slaying sword. Just wanted to see the head come off, you know. A single blow. But it was no go. Really, just imagining the head being sliced off was a great thing. Imagining all the blood and what-have-you shooting out. Spurting in great jets, and ladies fainting, and chaps trying to catch them and slipping in the blood and falling over. Almost as good as seeing it happen, you know, imagining it. Tried crying for it, too. But it was no go. Would've been the most amazing thing I'd seen. On that tour, anyway.'

His murmur was so indistinct, I found that I was holding my breath, so as to maximise my chances of catching his words. A glance around the table told me that others had hit upon the same idea. There was now a lull in the chitter-chatter as everyone tried to frame a response to what the Prince had just said, but this didn't seem practicable, so Admiral Truce opted to change the subject by main force, and praised the demonstration of the new Siskin guns we had witnessed earlier that day.

'Fifty-seven times as accurate as our common artillery, according to the tests,' said Admiral Truce. 'Indeed, I think the Siskin gun can do everything but speak!'

There was a polite titter from the assembly at this witticism, if that is what it was, and Master Siskin was clearly gratified by such a compliment from such a fellow. At this moment, I happened to catch the eye of the Dean, who was nodding very vigorously at the direction the conversation had taken, and suddenly the devil of perversity was speaking with my mouth.

'But, Dean Doodley, if I might ask, how do you square your being a man of the cloth with your approval of armaments capable of the most efficient form of slaughter yet conceived? I'd have thought there was a certain incongruity—'

'Incongruity!' he spluttered. 'I can assure you, sir, my faith, my profession and my approvals are most congruous indeed.'

Now, I must admit, it's entirely possible that I hadn't hedged and fudged my words enough for the company I was in. Fortunately, Master Siskin was in a permissive humour, and mock-covered his mouth to mock-hide his mock-smile, and said, 'Ah, Dean Dudley, I'm afraid we have all had to accommodate ourselves to Mr Malarkey's curious little questions. But, speaking as the inventor of these guns, let me say this: if I thought that war would be fomented, or the interests of humanity suffer, because of what I have done, I would greatly regret it; but I have no such apprehensions. The power which science gives us, whether as applied to peace or war, is always on the side of civilisation, and the spread of civilisation must tend necessarily to diminish war and to make it less barbarous . . .' At this moment I glanced over to Laguiole, who happened to be in the room at that time, overseeing the collection of our plates and cutlery, and I noticed that at her bosom sparkled an impressive jet brooch that I fancied must, once upon a time, have belonged to poor old Elise Siskin. The look in her eyes matched the jewel, for it was an expression of pure, cold fury at what Siskin was saying. 'We deplore the suffering that war entails, but we must not regard it as destitute of all admixture of good. The conquests of ancient Rome scattered the germs of civilisation over the whole of the then-known world, and similar effects have attended many of the conquests of more recent times . . .' Here, Master Siskin twinkled an indulgent smile in my direction, remembering our talk of the Romans and their ways, concluding, 'Courage, patriotism, self-devotion and honour have found their brightest examples among those who have followed the profession of arms.'

'Hear, hear!' cried Admiral Truce with such earnest enthusiasm that I think it diminished him in all our eyes.

'Hear, hear!' drawled the Prince, belatedly. '*Veh* excellent demonstration. Didn't have to offer the fellow a hundred pounds, either.'

The Prince was looking at me when he spoke, so it seemed reasonable to assume he was talking to me. I ventured to reply. 'Well—'

'Call me Bertie,' said the Prince.

'Well . . . a hundred pounds sounds like a deal of money to have offered the King of Sardinia, and I reckon if he had in actuality possessed such a terrific ox-lopper of a sword, then he'd certainly have used it as described for such a sum. A hundred pounds! He must've been fibbing. You see, you cannot believe a tenth of what rich folk say . . .'

'Couldn't offer more than a hundred,' slurred the Prince. 'My entire annual allowance. But I'd have given it all to see the head come off the ox. At a single blow, he said.'

'Your allowance?' said I, in all innocence, though I'd noticed Master Siskin flinch when the Prince used the word. For a moment, I thought that Bertie must be in receipt of lent money, like a miner, and I pictured Vic and Albert totting up his spenditure at year's-end in a fancy royal ledger.

'Yes,' he sighed. 'My pocket-money. All that they – my parents, I mean – will allow. These days it's *five* hundred pounds. Back then it was *one* hundred . . .'

I noticed Master Siskin now sat hunched in his chair, keeping very still, as if at the mercy of a pain that was beginning to overmaster him. His features had assumed a rigid, mask-like quality.

'You really ought to try some of this kirschwasser. Delicious. Double distilled, you know. Sour cherries. *Veh* good . . .' murmured the Prince.

It dawned on me that Master Siskin was angry, and that this was the change that had come over him. I felt foolish for not having understood it sooner, but the anger of another person can be like that. I should know, for in my time I believe I have enraged many a fellow. Intrigued as I was at how mysteriously incensed Master Siskin was becoming, I was also aware that I was conversing with a prince, and that I wouldn't be likely to get another crack at doing so, so I kept him talking, and said that five hundred pounds was so much more money than I'd make in my lifetime, I'd hardly know how to spend it.

'Oh, it's a piffling amount to *them*,' said the Prince, with some venom. 'It's a bloody trifle! Five hundred pounds. Five hundred pounds of bloody trifle. And I'll tell you what you'd spend it on. If you were me, I mean. In my position. You'd spend it on what *I* spend it on, which is to say: rare experiences. Yes. You'd make the best of your embarrassed affairs by travelling around the world hunting up remarkable spectacles. Like this chap,' – here, the Prince gestured vaguely towards Master Siskin, who had turned red as a plum by this point – 'with his famous big guns. You'd hear tell of them, and then you'd decide you had to clap eyes on them for yourself. Famous big guns. Even the nine-pounder: the old chap said he could use the nine-pounder to fire a shell eight feet deep into a solid butt of elm. And he could. Proved it, this morning. His built-up gun makes the shell spin, you see. Conical shells. Studs in them. That's the trick. Innovative design. Conical shells with studs in them. Say, old chap, how's about tomorrow we see what your famous spinning shells would do to a bevy of deer? That would be something. Big gun blasting away. Bits of deer flying in all directions. You'd make short work of them. Turn them into . . .'

'Bloody trifle?' I suggested, but the Prince had seemingly dozed off, and no one else seemed to appreciate how deftly I'd picked up on his former figure.

Master Siskin pushed himself up from his chair, nearly dipping his face into his dinner to do so, grasped his cane, and very uncertainly made his way out of the room. As I watched him go, I noticed that I wasn't the only one observing his withdrawal: Poor Thomas had noticed it too, and I found an expression of concern on his pale face. He had an open countenance. I do not mean that he'd an air of simpleness. It was more like a sort of gracefulness. Still, whether he was worried for Siskin's wellness or for the ramifications of his Master's anger, I had no way of knowing.

At this point, the dishes of pine-cake were presented to us, and I spied Thomas reaching for a very small golden fork, and so I reached for the corresponding fork in my own place setting, and felt as I did so a pricking sensation beneath my bandage, almost a fizzing, as of shaken cider, that resolved into pain. I dropped my hand into my lap and nursed it there, the pine-cake forgotten, and was so preoccupied that it took me a moment to realise I'd been addressed.

'I said, you are knowledgeable of the lead-mines hereabouts, Mister Malarkey, I believe?' This was Admiral Truce, and he spoke with polite lack of interest. 'Are they still a good yield?'

I replied, still clutching my hand under the table, and forgetting that my information on such matters was fifteen years obsolete, that the seams hadn't let us down yet. But Dean Dead-loss shook his head.

'Whoever has a share of patriotic feeling about his heart cannot but hope and pray that the produce of our native mines may with all speed obtain once more a remunerating price, so as to relieve the mining districts from that distress which now, like a glowering cloud without rain, hangs so heavily upon them.'

This startled me, for I'd heard nowt of falling prices or further impoverishment – but then, how could I have, having been either buried alive at the Sill or locked up here in Siskin's bastion of luxury, where his workers never merited a mention? I pushed away an image of Mop on her knees on the dressing floor, scrabbling to scrub up ore worth next to nowt; and, as I mentally pushed it away, I felt my hand, under its bandage, clench and throb, as if to aid me in banishing the vision.

Now Thomas Plover finally spoke, in a voice sober with regret. 'If all prices but one will climb, and that the most important, little wonder there are children in the street.'

I looked more closely at him. Although he was the same age as Call-me-Bertie, the two fellows were worlds apart. Where the Prince was all artificially ruddy and waxed and perfumed and liberally bespangled with frills, curls and ruffs, Thomas's person was short and neat, and either clean shaven or never yet shaven, giving an impression of cleanliness that somehow extended to the slant of his shoulders and the set of his mouth. He was tidy and open and plain. The worst thing you could say about him was that he was Master Siskin's ward. He had been parted from his dad, Mr Playfair, for most of his life – and, of course, I'd been parted from mine, so I might have harboured a bias in his favour for this reason – and yet I felt there was a sense of Mr Playfair about him: a gravity, a solidity. It gave me pause. I wondered what he knew of Master Siskin. I wondered if he jealoused the danger he was in, or if his plainness were a sort of ignorance, in which case he was maybes not that dissimilar to the Prince after all.

Before I could enquire further of Thomas, however, Master Siskin reappeared. Slowly, leaning heavily on his cane, he made it back to his chair. He picked up his napkin and scrunched it into a ball. He put it down again. He turned to the Prince, who had now slid down in his chair a little and was quietly but perceptibly snoring.

'Your Royal Highness,' proclaimed Master Siskin, at a volume nicely judged, so as to awaken but not startle the royal sot. 'Are you giving me to understand that you are not, after all, in a position to invest in my guns?'

Master Siskin was doing well to keep his countenance as he said these words, but the Prince, newly awoken from his slumber, ignored him, and spoke as if picking up a thread he'd put down but a moment afore. 'And then, last summer, when I was in Turin, they – my parents, I mean – they wouldn't let me visit King Victor Emmanuel. Vulgar Victor, they called him. All because he'd been rather *naughty* when he visited us at Windsor. Apparently, someone caught the old boy giving one of the scullery maids some *fun*. So they thought he was bound to be even more dissolute when at home, you know. So it was no go. Wasn't allowed to visit him in case something *interesting* happened. Would've like to see Vulgar Victor. And his pretty maids, all in a row. Got dragged off to see the Pope, instead, who insisted on talking to me in French. Of all things. Didn't see that coming. Finally got the old boy talking about something interesting – Roman Catholic hierarchy in England – when this one, here,' – at this, the Prince jabbed his finger directly at Admiral Truce and looked him in the eye, which I'd noticed was not his usual habit, afore continuing – 'this soft Johnny declares the visit over, and fairly drags me from the Curia, before there's an *incident*, he says!'

In the silence that followed, Master Siskin, keeping his features very still, said that he was sorry to repeat his question, but, as the Prince's five-hundred-pound annual allowance would fall short of the required investment by a factor of one hundred, would he nonetheless be investing in his guns, as he'd been led to believe, by some other means?

Call-me-Bertie heaved a sigh and said, 'Well, yes, I gather that that was your little scheme, old chap. But as you see, they – my parents, I mean – they have me at their mercy with this allowance business. They keep a tight grip on the old purse strings, you see. So I'm afraid it's no go. Came here to have a gander at your guns. And *veh* impressive they are, too. But . . . shan't be investing. Sorry, old chap.'

At this news, Master Siskin's face fairly closed altogether, and after that he hardly said three words until it was time to repair to the library for brandy and cigars. I know not what transpired there, for by this time I was exhausted from the day's excursions, and so made my excuses to the company, in particular to Dean Dawdler.

By the time I got back to my room, the bandage felt as though it had grown tighter, and it pinched and bit me in a dozen places so that my hand felt ablaze with twitches and unpleasant sensations of every kind. My blood was all for dancing, like a water droplet on a hot skillet. I raised my hand above my head, hoping that this might relieve some pressure, but it was no help; I swung it low, and that made everything worse. I gripped my forearm, as if to strangle the sensations that were racing down it from my broken hand, and still it buzzed with sensation – and as I stood there, braced tight and breathing in little sighs and gasps, I looked and saw the bandage bulge, though I'd felt no corresponding sensation of movement in my hand.

If you have seen, as I have, a dead man lying under a blanket, and then you have seen the blanket move – why, what do you think of? You think of rats. And that's the direction in which my thoughts leapt. It was impossible that a rat could fit in there, but I had an image in my mind's eye of a baby rat swaddled in the bandages, and I couldn't get it out of my thoughts. In any case, nowt, I thought, could be worse than this abominable feeling and supposing. Sickened, I could bear it no longer: I began to tear at the bandages, which smelt of rancid butter and were matted with sweat and some sort of pinkish syrup that made them cloy together and stick to my finger-ends. And then, as I finally peeled them loose, you can imagine my horror when I saw, sprouting in a terrible fork of flesh from the end of my right arm, *not one hand but two*. Above, the lumped remains of my old hand, with its familiar scars and missing fingers and all; below, where I'd thought I held the Knack, a copy of its elder brother, only smaller, curled and perfect, like an infant's hand, or a doll's, quite smooth and hairless and unscarred, except it was somewhat thinner and more bony than an infant's hand should be. Pale and wet, it looked like it had been carved from unseasoned wood. And then, of its own accord, the new, diminutive hand flexed back, as though it were abashed at the attention I was giving it, until it lay all but nestled in the palm of the old, like an egg-spoon nested in a teaspoon. Everything felt suddenly warm and quiet, there was a rushing sound in my ears, and I – copiously, noiselessly – bowked, giving me the opportunity to reacquaint myself with the prawns and the lamb and the cherries I'd so recently consumed, a salmon-coloured slurry, the sight of which at once persuaded me to bowk again.

12

an extract: *op. cit.*

[...] Let us return to our Mithraic initiates. It was prophesied that, among those who took the final trial and survived it, a chosen one would be rewarded with the growing of a new right hand in place of the old, a gift of Mithras that would confer the greatest powers upon him. In the earliest extant reference, this appendage is called *Dei manus*: 'God's hand'. The nomenclature subsequently changed, however, either by textual corruption or intentional substitution, to the rather more secular *donum manus*: 'given hand'. In the last of the surviving Latin texts, this has changed again to *daemonium manus*: 'demon's hand'. In English, it came to be known as the Knack.

For decades, the prophesy went unfulfilled. And then, in the fourth century AD, an imperial slave was born close by the Mithraic temple on Trajan's Wall. As expected, when he came of age, he joined the army and took a Roman name, Claudius Marcellus. His original name has been lost. Even in his youth, Marcellus' commitment to Mithras seems to have been fervent, though hindsight may have coloured the few accounts we have of this. In any case, his devotions were repaid in the form of a series of promotions, from *contrascriptor* (a clerk) to *scrutator* (inspector) and so on through the ranks of the Roman army until he was made *beneficiarius*, a privileged soldier. By this point, he had already joined the cult, and he rose through its ranks just as he had those of the army, at last becoming a Pater – at which point he made good on his long-held promise to Mithras, and cut off his right hand. The records tell us that he cut it off himself, and even, it is said, cauterised the wound himself. As this was not a requirement of the sacrifice, we may wonder whether his fellow initiates saw the embellishment as prideful. They would have been wise to do so, in the light of what came after.

Many a Pater before Marcellus had had his right hand lopped off, and in each case the survivor claimed to have been subsequently visited by Mithras in their dreams. We who live in a more cynical age might well respond, 'Well, he would say that, wouldn't he?' But, as in all walks of life, many are called but few are chosen. And not a one of these Paters *was* chosen to receive Mithras' most precious gift – until Marcellus. For now the prophecy came round, and, as foretold, Marcellus grew a new hand in place of the old: the Knack.

The records tell us that, as expected, the Knack conferred

great powers upon Marcellus – and they also say that these powers, or else the malefic influence of the Knack itself, poisoned the man's brain, and that with every day that passed there was less and less of Claudius Marcellus, and more and more of Mithras Sol Invictus. Now, ladies and gentlemen, I wonder about this. We know so little about the man, it is hard to be sure that his course changed significantly at this point. Was he not always turbulent? How else could a pagan have risen so high in the Roman ranks? In any case, Marcellus is said to have become increasingly quarrelsome and flighty; ever more easy to anger, ever more difficult to restrain. He swore many oaths, but he could not be trusted. St Aidan, whose account of this early history I have drawn upon for this lecture, says that an angel knows not whether it is the living or the dead that he moves among, and that, in a somewhat similar manner, Marcellus knew not whether it was a friend or a foe he had met. He was good for nothing but conflict, bloodletting, battle and slaughter. Marcellus had been born a pagan but became a Roman; now he was sliding back into his former category: the Latin sources that Aidan depended on begin by describing Marcellus as *inimicus* – that is, 'not-a-friend', which is to say an enemy who was a fellow Roman – but they end by describing him as *hostis* – that is, 'alien', which is to say a subhuman enemy. The scribes can barely find the language with which to describe the man.

Eventually, after leading an insurrection against the Roman army to which he had dedicated his life, after causing chaos throughout the region, and after many deaths, the man who was now Sol Invictus Mithras incarnate was tricked and trapped. The Knack was cut from him, and he was slain. The Knack could not be destroyed, so it was hidden deep underground. All remaining members of the Mithraic cult were buried alive in their Ordeal Pits. With only a few exceptions, all written records of the cult were expunged. Throughout the empire, the Mithraic temples – all four hundred of them – were destroyed, and Christian churches built on the sites where they had once stood.

Christianity was, of course, the latest, and the last, religion to have been adopted by the Romans. They borrowed Mithras' birthday at the winter solstice and gave it to Christ; though, to speak fair, it had been Zeus' birthday before that. And the idea that they may also have adapted that queer business of tearing and eating the flesh of their god, and calling it Communion – well, that was, in the eyes of the early church councils, the most diabolical heresy. Still, I would not recommend, at Christmastide, raising a glass of port to *Dies Natali Invictus Solis*. It seems to me that Mithras' power lies in unlocking that which is imperfect in us, that which we have left unaddressed and unheeded, the means by which we defeat ourselves. In Marcellus, it was his prideful hubris. Who among us would ever want to be confronted by such a shadow? [. . .]

13

The Knack and the Shift

I spent the entire night staring in horrible fascination at my two right hands. Impossible as it sounds, my new one – the Knack, as was – seemed to grow during this vigil, and, though it was but a few scant hours afore the light of day started to keek between the curtains, already my new hand appeared a little less withered and bony, and a little more like a healthy hand, though still appreciably smaller than my old, mutilated right hand, which – and, again, this surely must have been an effect of my having stared at it fixedly so many hours – seemed to have waned as its younger sibling waxed. It was a knotty, decrepit thing.

I found that my new hand would sometimes move of its own accord, though by making a great effort I was able to control it . . . but then I'd wonder, had I truly made it move, or did it move of its own volition and then instantly convince me that its motion had been my idea? I could think of no perfect way to test this. Contrariwise, my old claw had grown very sluggard in obeying my commands.

As the dawn came on, sleep finally overcame me, and I drowsed and dreamt, and then jumped awake – a moment later, it seemed – to discover that Master Siskin had entered my room, opened the curtains, and was now bending over me, examining my monstrous new appendage, which I had very foolishly neglected to wrap once more in the bandages afore I dozed.

I made a rather belated move to hide my deformity.

Master Siskin finally looked up at me, and said, 'So you couldn't resist taking a peek inside the bandages, eh?' His tone was more confidential than reproachful, but that might merely have been the effect of his hushing and shushing lisp, which seemed especially pronounced. 'How long have you known it was thus?'

'Only since last night,' said I, while trying to waken myself as quickly as possible. It is a horrible thing, to know that you must be on alert when your thoughts are slow and foolish. 'Did you know that this would happen to me?'

Master Siskin shook his head and returned his attention to the Knack. 'There was no way to anticipate how the Knack would behave once fusion had taken place. When you first came here, your hand appeared to be burned beyond recognition. It was not clear whether it could be saved, or if you would survive. I'm afraid you ought never to have touched the Knack . . .'

I don't suppose I've ever taken to a fellow who used the word 'ought'. For me, it belongs in the same category as 'ghastly'. I felt my contempt rise up on command at the sound of it, which helped me to come fully to my senses. I said that, as regards the *noli me tangere* Knack stipulation, this crucial part of the procedure had been very imperfectly communicated to me.

'Ah, yes,' said Siskin. 'You were not properly prepared. Most unfortunate. You're not to blame, of course. The fault lies with the chap who hired you. I'm afraid I rather *read the riot act* with him after he'd delivered you here . . .'

Siskin looked at me as he said this, and I am pleased to report that I met his gaze and kept my countenance. He was testing and probing – if he outright knew that I'd seen inside his killing-bottle of a cellar, I thought, then we wouldn't be having this conversation.

Once this difficult moment had been overcome, I asked, 'Why do you suppose the Knack has taken this hideous form?'

Master Siskin shrugged. 'Perhaps it is trying to hide again. Such is its nature. It found itself attached to a man's wrist; what better shape could it have assumed than a hand? Perhaps it is remembering a shape it assumed long ago . . . But it is idle to speculate. It is time, Caleb. It is time that we unburdened you of this responsibility once and for all.'

A great lurching wave of panic seemed to lift me up. 'Now? That is, today?'

'It must be today. My laboratory is ready. The stars are aligned.'

I had no idea whether his reference to sidereal propitiousness was literal or figurative, so I asked why it had to be done that day, especially.

'I can't quote the Good Book as expertly as you and Dean Dudley, but I believe it says, somewhere or other, that *to every thing there is a season, and a time to every purpose under the heaven* . . .'

'Ecclesiastes, chapter three. *A time to plant, and a time to pluck up that which is planted* . . .' I looked at my weird new hand, which had, without my knowing it, formed itself into a diminutive, blue-veined fist. It looked like a bulb of summer garlic. 'But . . . isn't Call-me-Bertie still visiting?'

Master Siskin smiled indulgently, which, I thought, boded ill for me: ordinarily, my disrespectful epithet would have angered him, but he was willing to allow it today. It felt like a concession to a condemned man. 'His Royal Highness has had to curtail his visit. I'm afraid he was discovered – well, as he might phrase the matter, he was discovered trying to *give some fun* to one of the maids. For her part, to her credit, she was doing her utmost to repel him. But the Prince would not be gainsaid . . .'

'Who discovered them?'

'Absalom! Yes, the faithful hound chased off the amorous prince!'

'The great image of authority: a dog's obeyed in office.'

'Quite so, quite so,' said Master Siskin absently, and I wondered again whether he recognised the quotation. Really, how a fellow could have such a fancy library but not twig to a bit of Bill Shakespeare was beyond me, utterly. 'Yes, it's a curious thing,' he continued, lightly, 'Absalom happened upon them just in time. Almost as though he'd been sent there expressly to protect the maid . . .'

I couldn't think how to frame a response. Master Siskin

was grinning at me now, which was altogether disconcerting, for I knew of his disgusting fangs, though they were hidden – almost entirely – by his moustaches.

At last he said, as though to dismiss the subject, 'Well, I think our dear Madame Laguiole may have had something to do with it, don't you?'

'*Noli me tangere*,' I said again.

'Anyway, no harm done. Well, no harm done to the maid, anyway.'

'There was harm done to the *Prince*?'

Master Siskin made a vague, expansive gesture. 'I'd say he learned a valuable lesson. *Thou shalt not give a maid some fun if fun is not wanted, or else thou might get bit!*'

I gasped out a laugh, or laughed out a gasp. 'Absalom *bit* Call-me-Bertie?'

'The merest scratch, really. In any case, His Royal Highness, and his entourage, has left the premises in high dudgeon. I'm surprised the noise of it all didn't wake you. You must sleep the sleep of the just! Good riddance to him, in any case. An allowance of a mere five hundred pounds! And the nerve to imply that he might be in a position to invest, that we might form a combination! Well, well. His leaving has allowed me to dismiss the hired staff ahead of schedule, so . . .' – and here he drew up the hated wicker bath chair – 'we will not be disturbed, Caleb. It is time.' He threw back the blankets, leaned over me and swung me from my bed as easily as if I were a basket of chestnuts. He deposited me in the bath chair, and beamed encouragingly at me. I did my best to return the smile.

It is a hard thing to recall the terror I felt as I was wheeled from my room and along the gloomy hallways of Brink House, where silence once more reigned. I neither saw nor heard a sign of Madame Laguiole or Absalom or any other soul in the house, and so, of course, I was weighing up the likelihood of her betrayal having been guessed, and of my comrade having been killed already, and all our nascent plans thwarted.

We fairly rattled along, and Master Siskin seemed to be taking progressively less care to avoid jostling me in my rickety carriage. He was eager to get to work. My hands rested in my lap, but the Knack was spasming and grasping at the blanket with which I had covered it.

At last, we reached Master Siskin's laboratory, and he wheeled me inside. It was a room of modest proportions, the walls of which were lined with maps, charts and annotated designs for what I assumed were armaments. It was not a room to inspire fear, in and of itself. Desperate as I was, I clutched at this meagre reassurance. Perhaps all would be well. Perhaps the knot of horror might yet be untangled.

I tried once more, and rather hopelessly, to cajole my host – my captor! – out of performing the amputation.

'Surely it isn't necessary to do this here and now. Surely we might send for a doctor to assist with the surgery? You know, I once had a very interesting conversation with a doctor about performing just this sort of operation. I paid him for a bit of his know-how . . .'

Siskin didn't reply, merely removed his jacket and hung it upon a hat stand.

'Well, I'm sure you'll've done the same already, but let me just remind you that the great principle of such an operation is disarticulation of the joint, meaning separation, as far as possible, of the two bones, so as to avoid cutting through a bone, which is a great faff.'

Still Siskin said nowt. He unbuttoned his cuffs and rolled up his sleeves. His forearms were disconcertingly hairy.

'And – I'm sure you probably know this already! – with the wrist, this means severing the radiocarpal ligament, and then sawing atween the scaphoid and the radius. Do you follow me, Master Siskin?'

Siskin ignored these desperate sallies utterly, and wheeled me in front of a bookcase that stretched from floor to ceiling. Stationed thus, I couldn't do owt but scan the titles on the books' spines . . . but they were illegible. And then, as I looked closer, I saw that the titles were not in English. And then, as I looked closer still, I saw that they were not in any alphabet I recognised. And then, with a sinking heart, I saw that this was not a shelf of books at all, but only a thin wooden panel made up to pass at a distance for a row of spines. Siskin reached into the bookcase and threw a hidden lever, and with a soft *clunk* the bookcase, which was of course not a bookcase at all, swung away from me into the next room.

I squirmed in my bath chair, but a heavy hand clamped down upon my shoulder, and Siskin wheeled me into his real laboratory, still not saying a word. The first, modestly appointed room had merely been a front. All of my instincts about Brink House had been well founded. All of my instincts about the savagery of existence, the brutalised reality of godless creation, had been well founded, and I'd been a fool ever to doubt them. But doubt them I had. And now – the secret door clapped shut behind us – I was doomed to die in this chamber of torture. I was become, by this point, somewhat hysterical, I will admit.

I was stationed in the centre of the room, and Siskin was busying at something behind me. I scanned my surroundings, looking for owt I might make use of, but seeing nowt. This room was much bigger than the last, and it was filled with an array of bottles, demijohns and tubes of various dimensions, some of which were connected to a metal framework to hold them in place. The walls were hung with the stuffed heads of big game, and there were glass cases that held stuffed animals – monkeys of various kinds, none of which were familiar to me – and one held what looked like a golden pheasant, though, when I looked more closely, I saw was in fact a rarer bird – a Lady Amherst's pheasant. And here and there were bottles of greenish fluid in which, very horrible, bobbed such things as the foetuses of conjoined twins.

I remembered having read about the Lady Amherst's pheasant, and suddenly my frenzied brain made a connection. 'You're collecting hybrids.'

'Precisely!' said Siskin, in something like his old, convivial manner. 'Hybrids, chimera and other mutations. Those heads on the wall belong to big cats, but they aren't lions and tigers: they're rarer and queerer beasts altogether. Ligers and tigons! The liger is the offspring of a male lion and a female tiger . . . now, did you know that the liger actually grows to be more massive than either of its parents? A most unusual hybrid . . .'

I had reached the nadir of my existence. Or perhaps I had reached the zenith of the loathing I felt for myself and for all who suffered in this defiled world with me. Either way, I was now beyond all shame. 'Are you going to kill me, Master Siskin?' I asked. My voice was steady, and devoid of emotional appeal. Circumstances had now been carried far past any such foolery. But if my head was destined to be stuffed with sawdust, and to spend the next century staring out through eyes of glass, then I deserved to be forewarned.

'Certainly not,' said Siskin. 'I'm going to keep you alive – for the present, in any case. You see, it's devilishly difficult to create a hybrid, but it's nigh-on impossible to split one that has already been made. The human hand was shaped to muddy, not to purify, the waters of this world.'

He said this with such complacent melancholy that I hated him the more, and found myself possessed of pluck enough to say, 'You are not, nor have you ever been, human, Master Siskin. You must know this, surely.'

The monster stalled but for a moment. We looked into each other's eyes, mammal to mammal. 'Well,' says he, 'if it comes to that, Caleb, you aren't human, either. Not any more. This is what I'm trying to tell you. You're a hybrid now, too, chum. But I'm going to do something about that. I'm going to split you from the Knack. I want to know whether you can survive it. I want to find out all I can about the Knack. And if you do survive, why, so much the better!

Who knows the uses you may yet have? In return, you will get to see something very special!'

Siskin spun my chair around, and I saw, laid out on a table, the body of young Thomas Plover. I couldn't make out if he was breathing.

'Is he dead?' I asked. My voice sounding strangely nerveless again.

'Your imagination is rather morbid these days, Caleb. I think you've been spending too much time in your room. Has Madame Laguiole been filling your head with gloomy stories? Hmmm? Sad stories about pirates bobbing about in the sea like bits of cork in a glass of sherry? Something of that? No, no. Young Tom isn't dead. He has merely taken a sleeping draught. It will make the transfusion easier. Now, let's get you prepared!'

Siskin lifted me again – and as easily as before; he might have looked like a frail old gadgie, doddering about with his cane, but all of that was an act: he was preternaturally strong – and deposited me in a roughly hewn wooden chair, fitted with leather straps for my wrists and ankles. At the last moment, I showed some pluck and struggled against him, but to no avail. He was able to hold me down and still manage the straps with ease, as if he were practised in such manoeuvres. I was soon secured, with my right arm strapped in place in such a way that he could get at the two hands.

Next, he drew back a cloth from the table beside me, and uncovered a silver tray of knives, saws and callipers. He selected what looked to me like a common dovetail saw, and the image of Dr Braistick and his chisel flashed through my mind; but the tears were flowing, and I could hardly see. The Knack clawed at the air, as if trying to tug itself free of my wrist. I ransacked my brain for any hint or scrap of knowledge that I might use to buy myself some time. There was nowt. I cried out for laudanum, but no, Siskin said, he didn't want me to miss the show:

'Mr Malarkey, you are about to become a living document, a record of the first and only Mithraic transfusion to be conducted in fourteen centuries. We want you awake, that you may catch the precious details. Let me tell you in broad strokes how it shall be. First, an opening salvo: I shall separate you from the Knack, taking especial care not to touch it, of course. Next, with battle met, I shall so contrive it that young Thomas and I grasp the Knack at precisely the same moment. And last, the division of the spoils: the transfusion. This is the most mysterious part of the operation. As mine is the stronger personality, it will be my mind and memory, my very essence, that enters into combination with the Knack's Mithraic power, not the boy's. Young Tom's head is already so stuffed with my thoughts and my business that the process should be the easier.'

'And what of young Tom? Where will he go when you have infested him?'

'Why, he will be deposited into my old vessel. I shall have no further use for it!'

He placed the saw-blade upon the root of the Knack, where it joined with the veins of my wrist and pressed down. As the beads of blood welled up beneath the teeth of the saw, my head rang, and I heard a world of rage and pain suddenly find a voice: I screamed.

There was a clatter as the dovetail saw hit the stone flags of the floor, followed by an undignified *whumpf* as Master Siskin collapsed in a heap on top of it.

I stopped screaming and shook the tears from my eyes to stare at the prone figure of Siskin, and wondered, somewhat madly, if my terrific scream had somehow killed him. Was I now possessed with the power to kill with only my voice? Was I become a banshee? No, they were ladies, were they not? In any case, Siskin wasn't moving. Was he breathing? I couldn't tell, but I prayed that he was dead. It was a hateful prayer, but, in the moment, it seemed worth a shot.

I tried to focus on my hand, to see how far he had cut me. The news was good: he'd only managed to draw back the blade, having dropped to the floor afore making his first true stroke.

My breathing steadied, and the flare of elation I'd felt at not having the monster carve me up gradually faded away. I began to take stock of my changed situation. If Siskin was dead, then I was reliant on Poor Thomas waking up and saving me, otherwise I'd die here, strapped to this chair. If Madame Laguiole were still alive, would she ever find me here? Did she even know that this room existed? Siskin had said that Thomas was merely sleeping – that he'd been drugged. If that were true, how many hours would he be unconscious? And what if Siskin was still alive? To be forced to sit there for untold hours, strapped in my chair, watching the two bodies, waiting to see which of them would wake up first, would be a miserable fate ... My brain shuffled through such questions, time and again.

And then I saw Master Siskin twitch and jerk. I held my breath; I didn't blink. Surely he would not wake so soon? His eyes fluttered open. He clambered to his feet. By now, my heart was churning in my chest, as you can imagine, but something told me to remain silent. Siskin stood, swayed drunkenly and then centred himself. Now he began to walk in a slow circle in front of me. He seemed unaware of my presence, and began pulling at his clothes as though he'd never afore been so encumbered, moving absently and distractedly, more like a baby kicking at its blankets than a gentleman undressing. His eyes, when I glimpsed them, were rolling back in his skull; whatever state he was in, it was not true wakefulness. Now and then, his jaw would loll open to reveal the clusters of wolfish teeth I'd heard tell of.

In desperation, I looked back at Thomas, and my heart leapt when I discerned that his eyes were now open; but I quickly surmised that, though he could see – and he was in deep anguish and shock at what he saw – he could not yet move and, apart from his eyes, the rest of his body remained asleep. So he often appears in my recollections, even now: his living eyes, beseeching me.

In any case, Master Siskin was oblivious to the pair of us, and kept undressing, quite shamelessly, until he was naked as a newborn baby. His body, I saw, was twisted, and his limbs oddly distended – and it was only at this moment that I twigged that this was the beginning of the shift. It had commenced just in time to save me. Or, rather, it had commenced just in time to save the Knack; I suspected that my personal welfare was incidental to the mythic, geological gears that were grinding all around me. Siskin's misshapen body either meant that the shift was already well underway, or else this was simply the form that he'd assumed when last he reverted from wolfish to mannish.

Either way, once he was naked, he began to look here and there. He stared all about him – but, I thought, he stared without properly seeing; certainly, he did not see me, though I was placed conveniently before him like a plate of food – and then he kicked his clothes into a heap, with a series of little scuffing motions, never looking at the clothes themselves but all about him, as if keeping toot for observers. And then, once his clothes were all in a heap, he did an extraordinary thing, and pissed in a circle around them. I was astounded to see the old man aiming his pizzle as though he were quite alone. Very serious was his manner in so doing, frowning like a doctor lancing a boil on a magistrate's arse.

After making his watery circle around his clothes, he took himself off a few yards, and then crouched down until presently he was lying on one side, curled up like a child asleep, making no movement except that one foot was jiggling side to side in a series of spasms. His feet, I noticed, already seemed to have narrowed and lengthened.

He was breathing in quick gasps and shudders now, and when he exhaled his stomach collapsed as though it had been sucked up under his ribs in the most alarming way. Now his shoulders began to squirm, and he writhed as if he were being tickled by invisible hands, every twitch accompanied by a crack or pop. I looked on from my chair and did not utter a word. Remaining silent had been working very well for me thus far, and I intended to keep at it, though I willed Thomas to fully awaken soon, and I kept looking back to him to see if he'd budged. But he was yet unable to move, and only looked on in horror.

At about this time, I noticed the hair that had been sprouting so rapidly over Siskin's body all this while. Much of it was silver in colour, and in the candlelight it blended into his pale flesh too perfectly to be discerned, only glistering somewhat in the dancing light as though he were bathed in sweat or some sort of wax, but here and there the fur – I should say fur, after all, rather than hair – ran in darker-grey lines, and where it was thicker it appeared swart.

Suddenly, he jerked about, as at a summons, making me jump again and strain at my straps, and I gasped when I saw his face, for already its brute-like shape could not have been mistaken for human: the nose and mouth were now pushed out very horribly, as if Siskin's head had been squashed and warped in a vice. Despite this, my mind could not refrain from trying to interpret his distorted features as though they indicated some thought or emotion that he was feeling. I suppose it was just my mind trying to make rational sense of what I was seeing, as if such were yet possible. In any case, I found myself thinking that Siskin looked as though he had something of great moment to impart, but that it must be said with discretion, and I even found myself wanting to lean toward him to hear him better – but all of this was an illusion. He was no longer capable of speech, nor sensible of my being there, though all manner of grunts and moans and rasps and squeals came from him – but as it were incidentally, as though his lungs and throat were no more alive than a set of Northalbion small-pipes, and the air was being forced through them by an accidental mechanical process.

There seemed to be a sort of lull in the shift at about this time, as Master Siskin simply lay there, half man and half wolf, frozen absolutely immobile for what seemed like several minutes together. His breathing was now very irregular and laboured, and more than once I thought he might have expired outright, but this was wishful thinking.

After a brief hiatus, the shift resumed: his movements were smoother now, and more controlled. His fur was thickening, engulfing his body, and every time I looked at one part of him, it seemed hairier than afore. His legs and feet had been – I want to say 'tortured' – into crooked new shapes. His face was now unrecognisable. Again and again, he shook his head violently from side to side, whereupon his body would shudder; each time this happened, I thought that it must surely be the last of the shift, but, no, it would happen again after a brief interval. The sounds he made were now identifiably those of a wolf, albeit one being subjected to a great deal of pain.

My situation was growing more dire by the minute. The shift, which Laguiole had said might ordinarily take the best part of a night, had already been all but completed, as far as I could judge. Surely this meant that Siskin would soon wake up to find two meals before him. I felt the panic rising in me once again – and then I heard the *clunk* of the secret door's mechanism turning, and then the door swung open and a familiar voice called, 'Monsieur . . . ?'

I laughed with blessed relief, and felt the tears threaten to resume once again, but I overmastered them – and then, as Madame Laguiole stepped in front of me, I felt suddenly furious.

'Where the devil were you?' I demanded. 'The slaughterous bastard var-nigh chopped me up! And that's nowt compared to what he had planned for young Tom, there. Free me, you tardy French baggage!'

'I was with Absalom,' said the unabashed Laguiole. 'He has shifted; he needs me at such times.'

'I reckon *my* need was probably the greater!' I cried, nodding my head vigorously and very foolishly at the table of saws and knives beside me, and at the creature at my feet.

Laguiole shrugged and, as she unbuckled my straps and helped me into the bath chair, said, 'It is as well. You would not have believed unless you saw the shift for yourself. I told you this. I could not truly believe the word of my own mother until I saw.' She wheeled me over to the slab upon which Poor Tom lay, and began to undo the straps that held him. Seeing that I could not tear my gaze from the prone beast, she tried, against the grain of her nature, to reassure me. 'We are safe. Master Siskin will lie still like this an hour or more.'

No sooner had these words left her lips, but the beast heaved a sort of great sigh and rolled over, so that I found myself confronted once more by the repulsive character of its face. Laguiole and I held our breaths for several seconds, waiting to see if the thing was about to make a liar of her. But no, it stayed asleep.

I indicated that I did not share the confidence she had reposed in her timekeeping. And then, once I had found a more normal voice – it required several attempts – I asked Laguiole, very quietly, 'When he shifts, does he always piss around his clothes?'

She looked at me as if to say, *You witness a man become a wolf, and this is what you ask me?*

And then I shook my head and said that it was all very strange – an entirely extraneous remark that I saw fit to repeat several times.

Laguiole gave young Thomas some gentle slaps to the face in hope of waking him properly, but without success: only his eyes were awake, though they were doing their best to speak. She lugged him off the table and sat him on my lap, though he was easily the same size as me. I held onto him as she got the bath chair turned about and began to wheel us from the room. But then she paused and turned to look at the wolf, and I saw her lips pinch together in a contemptuous sneer.

'Madame Laguiole . . .' I said in a low voice.

'We have him now, Monsieur. We will never have a better chance. Why should we wait?'

Truly, I had become a frightened old man, for in my heart all I wanted to do then was flee. I shook my head and whined something unintelligible, as Laguiole snatched a scalpel from the tray. She crouched over the body of the wolf, gripping the scalpel in her fist as though it were a dagger. We looked at each other for a moment, and, though I don't know what I'd hoped to communicate, it seemed that she took something from my expression, for she raised the scalpel high in the air, and then, as I shook my head, she plunged it of a sudden, deep into the wolf's left eye.

The beast convulsed and let fly a deafening howl. It swiped Madame Laguiole across the room with a gesture, and started to scramble to its feet, but its legs betrayed it, and it still moved as if it were drugged. To my horror, it now seemed about to fix its attention on Tom and I sitting before it, as if it could sense our complete helplessness. But after taking a lurching step our way, it became aware once more of the blade Laguiole had left jammed in its skull, and shook its head furiously for several seconds. This was just long enough for the redoubtable Laguiole to pick herself up, and for the three of us to slip from the room and close the bookcase-door behind us.

'There is no lock on the door!' I cried.

'And we cannot barricade it: it opens the wrong way. But we can lock *that* one—' and so we pressed on out of the false laboratory and back into the hallway beyond it. Laguiole secured the door behind us, and turned the key. The door was good, thick oak, but—

'How long do you suppose . . . ?'

'I think we will find out, yes?' answered Madame Laguiole, whose commitment to honesty at the expense of consolation never faltered.

14

The Plan

We were soon in Absalom's bedroom. On our way there, whenever we'd passed through a door, Laguiole would lock it behind us. Brink House was likely too much of a warren for this to form a particularly dependable barrier, and of course the wolf would eventually break each door down, but the policy might buy us a little time.

We hurried into the room and lay Thomas on the floor as gently as we could manage. Strange how, in such a group, folk will naturally gather about the youngest when danger looms. I think we all felt the impulse prick us, that we must protect Thomas above all, though the lad was scarcely known to any of us.

Absalom's room was a bare, monastical cell, with painted white walls and no furniture except for the French bed and a washstand. Absalom, in his human form, lay upon the bed, slowly awakening from his shift, naked as the terrible day he was born and with no more sense of shame about this than any wolf would feel. In the guise of a man, Absalom was a tall fellow with long, lustrous black hair, an aquiline nose and blue eyes that seemed altogether artless and depthless. Many of his features, seen in isolation, should have passed for beautiful, but, taken for all in all, he was ill made, and was sombre faced in a way that seemed odd and unintelligent.

It was only then that I recognised him as the mysterious man whom I had taken for the personification of Death when I was recuperating. Looking at him now, with my health somewhat restored, I could see why I'd misidentified him. The quality of his sadness indicated a heaviness of soul that must have been inherent. He looked as though, given the chance, he'd have gladly taken up anyone else's burden of real griefs, howsoever wretched, rather than labour on alone under his own metaphysical miseries.

Laguiole judged that Absalom's shift had now been fully effected, and from a shelf on the washstand she brought a great jar of white unguent smelling strongly of herbs, which she commenced to apply to the man, rubbing it all over his body. Very familiar she was, having evidently performed this duty many times afore, which made me the more uncomfortable to be witnessing the ritual. Not a sound made Absalom while Laguiole was about her matronly offices; nor did he move, but only lay there, quite still, watching me the while, as though I was merely an interesting new addition to the furniture.

'When he properly wakens, will he know me?' I asked Laguiole.

'You will appear to him as an old acquaintance, all but forgotten, but now met with unexpectedly,' she said. 'He may give you to understand that he knows you, or remembers meeting you long ago, but this is not so.' She kept on applying the smelly unguent as she said this, like a baker kneading her dough, not deigning to look up, and then added, with a shake of the head, 'In this country, even the *loup-garou* feel embarrassment.'

Within a few minutes, Thomas at last began to revive, regaining the power of motion and latterly of speech, and, as soon as was practicable, the four of us put our heads together to form a plan. I tried to summarise what we knew so far.

'As Siskin described it, the Knack has the power of a kind of induced metempsychosis. I think he was going to use it to shift his personality into a new vessel . . .' And here I inadvertently met the gaze of the vessel in question.

Thomas breathed deeply, letting the implication of my words settle, and then said, 'He would often tell me, "When you come of age, you will be master of Brink House." He phrased this in many different ways. "One day, you will fall asleep as young Thomas Plover, and awaken as master of Brink House . . ."'

'That was not an altogether false promise,' I said. 'When you woke though but, you'd no longer be yourself. Fellows such as Siskin amuse themselves like this, by finding ways to imbue a partial truth with more deceit than an outright lie can possess.'

'"We shall seal it with a handshake," he would say . . .'

'Aye, even so you would: you would both grasp the Knack – and, after that, there'd be no letting go until it was finished with you.'

'Let me get my hands on him,' said Tom quietly, 'and there'll be no letting go until I'm finished with him.'

It gladdened my heart to hear him say that. I drank in his words like a cordial, and clapped him on the shoulder. That all-day bastard Siskin had thought he could buy young Tom, but the youth already had his inheritance: he was Mr Playfair's son. 'Siskin's plan,' I continued, 'was, I think, to remain in his current body, that is, as an old man, only for as long as it took to secure investment for his guns. People knew Siskin; they knew his face and his reputation as a businessman. He'd lose that advantage once he slid himself over into young Tom here. So he kept me alive, and the Knack secure, until the Prince's visit, and he tried to land one last deal. But when his plans came to nowt, as they did last night, then he saw no need to further delay making use of the Knack,' I said. Well, this was my best guess at what Siskin's plan could be. But it was only a guess, as I freely admitted. 'Or maybe he did it out of sheer bloody petulance! Maybe he was incensed because his financial plans had failed, so he cheered himself up with the thought that he could still chop off a fellow's hand and rob a boy of his allotted lifetime . . .'

'Maybe,' said Tom, 'and I also think that the timing of the – what did he call it, a Mithraic transfusion? – the timing might have been under a constraint. He often made reference to my waking up on my eighteenth birthday as master of Brink House. It is my birthday in two days' time.'

'And the moon is full,' I added. 'His time was under a constraint and all.'

I looked at Absalom, whose pitiful melancholy had deepened yet further. Laguiole had, at least, got him dressed, that he might have some degree of dignity. I felt sorry for the big lump. I was also experiencing a certain amount of trepidation as to whether his misery might give way to rage, and how we'd ever control him should this happen. He'd sat up, and was staring into the fireplace. Laguiole was gently stroking his back.

'I'm sorry, Absalom,' I said to him. 'Your unworthy father planned to disinherit you. Forgive my bluntness. In time, it will help if you can face this frankly.'

'I have often felt that a rival was near . . .' Absalom said at last. His voice was softer than I expected, and deeper than I'd have believed possible. 'When I met Thomas, I thought that he must be the rival. But now I understand. My father is the rival.'

What a poor father Master Siskin had turned out to be, I thought, to have underestimated both his adopted and his blood-born son. Truly, he was neither a lover of books nor a reader of men.

Thomas wanted to know what our next move should be. He supposed poison should be our first recourse, as it was the safest bet. A piece of meat laced with arsenic should do it.

'I fear he will not take the bait,' I said. 'His mind is too fixed on the Knack.'

Laguiole said that she felt I might be right, and if Master

Siskin's brain was now hot for hunting, then he would not be likely to stop to eat dead meat, but that we should try poison nonetheless, for if it should work, then it would save us from having to approach the beast more nearly.

'Try it, by all means,' I said, but I was filled with a new idea, and I asked Tom if he knew where Siskin kept the black powder for his guns, and if he knew where there might be a bit-and-brace for me to do some drilling.

Tom could help with the black powder – for some time, Siskin had been educating him in all such details of Brink House and the family business, including the demonstration of the guns – but he was less sure about the whereabouts of a bit-and-brace. Laguiole piped up, however, and said that if one was to be found, it would be in the workshop outbuilding in the old stable block.

'What is it you're planning, Mr Malarkey?' asked Tom.

'I've the bones of an idea. It'll come to nowt if your scheme with the poison works, so I won't waste time explaining it to you. But I'll be cavilled in the library, and if my guess is right, the wolf will be headed that way. The Knack will draw him, like it drew the automata down in the Sill. Slow the wolf down any way you can. Lock the doors, strew poison – owt you can think of. But that's where he'll be ganging: to the library, to find the Knack.'

This was really little more than an intuition, but I found grounds for it in my observations of the wolf's behaviour back in the laboratory. For instance, the way it had, despite Laguiole saying it would lie fast asleep for an hour, rolled over to face me; and also the way it had, after Laguiole woke it with the scalpel, fixated on me rather than on avenging itself. My suspicion was that his wolfish form simplified Siskin's character down to its fundamentals. Rather than invite comment on my flimsy evidence, however, I simply asked Tom to bring the powder and the bit-and-brace to me while Laguiole prepared the poisoned meat.

It might surprise you to hear that I delegated this mission to Tom, but seeing as a body would have to venture out to the workshop, I reasoned it might as well be the lad: he was young and able, quick on his feet, he knew guns, knew where the powder was, and it seemed to me that if anyone was likely to be safe from attack, it would be Tom. While I couldn't know for sure, I reckoned that Siskin would have gladly killed me, or Laguiole, or Absalom, but he would surely want to keep Tom alive, so as to pick up his plan where he'd been forced to break it off.

I said as much, but Absalom had a different view, and insisted that he accompany Tom 'for protection', he said. He wouldn't be reasoned with, and we needed to keep Absalom's spirits up, so it was agreed. The two of them went on their way.

I got Laguiole to wheel me to the library, and, once there, I surveyed what I had to work with. First, and most important, the doors to both the antechamber and the library itself could both be locked: this was as I remembered, and would be essential to my plan. Once inside the library, I looked at the state of the ceiling, and at the twelve massive oak pillars that ran down the room in two rows of six. I looked at the vast quantity of books that I now planned to destroy, and thought what a strange career I'd had, I who had started out as a worshipper of the written word!

Tom was a bright lad, and he'd try everything that would occur to such a fellow to stop the wolf, but something was telling me that all he could think of would not be enough. A short time later, he found me in the library, and gave me the bit-and-brace I'd asked for, and even then, even when I saw that he had a rifle slung over his shoulder – a double-barrel Purdey Express, he informed me – still something was telling me that poison and a rifle wouldn't do.

When I took the bit-and-brace from Tom, I noticed – only once I'd done it, and with a slight shock – that I'd instinctively reached out and grasped it not with my old, original hand, but with the Knack. It was the first time that this had happened. The first time, as far as I knew. I didn't dwell on the thought, but got to work drilling, asking Tom if he'd seen owt amiss outside, but no, Tom says,

'All's still except for Jenny Howlet, making her nocturnal to-do . . .'

I said I reckoned my predilection for verbal ornament was rubbing off on him, and he grinned.

'Where do you find your words, Mr Malarkey?'

'I mint them from a bountiful fund of thought.'

'I cannot believe they are made up.'

'If a thing isn't born, then a body'll have to can make it.'

I was still struggling to drill the first hole in the first of the wooden pillars. The wood was dense and tough, and it was slow going; I needed a good deep hole and all.

Tom was loitering, I realised.

'I'm excavating dust from fluff,' I said. 'What a tchew. I think this bit is blunt . . .'

Tom cleared his throat and announced, 'I've been thinking that, given your age and line of work, there's a chance you might, at one time—'

'It's blunt, all right . . .'

'A chance you might have known my father, John Plover?'

'Blunt as a Methodist brother-in-law . . .'

'You see, I know so little about him. I've no memory of the man . . .'

I looked at Tom helplessly. I suppose I should have been expecting him to ask after his dad, and yet the question had taken me unawares. 'Yes, I knew him,' I said. 'We're just so short of time now, Tom . . . Maybes after we've . . .' But my words died on the air. It was foolish to talk of 'after' when there was no guarantee that either of us would still be here then. 'Well, the fact is, I worked with your dad,' I admitted. 'Aye, we dug for sugar at Windy Top. That's to say: we mined lead.'

Tom's evident delight at this news only made me feel the more awkward. He'd be expecting a close-painted portrait now, but my calling was of another kind.

'He'd forgive you anything, like he had no side. I couldn't get to the bottom of it. And *the quality of mercy is not strained*, oh aye, I can speechify! But twasn't mercy anyways, it was something smaller – or that's what I thought at the time. You can't just go around forgiving the world for being as it is, like you're Jesus Christ Almighty.'

'Is that what Jesus did?' asked Tom politely.

'No. Oh, Tom, this isn't what I meant to say. I suppose I just think that it's no good, in the long run, to be so . . . paternalistic. Like with his pigeons. I mean, a fellow keeps pigeons so's he can race them. That's the whole bit. But not your dad: oh no, he makes them all his pets, and won't risk them in competition. Named them and everything. I'd say to him, John, you're the most ineffectual pigeon-fancier in Northalbion! You're soft as clarts, utterly, I'd say . . .'

I was still riving at the pillar all this while, and making nowt but a mess. I gledged at Tom, and caught his desolate expression before he could hide it. What was I saying? Criticising a fellow's paternalism to the son he never got a chance to know? I was and am a devil of a fellow! So I caught myself, and said, 'Look, if we're to talk about this now, you'll have to can help me with this drilling,' and we switched positions.

Tom commenced work with the bit-and-brace, soon making better progress than I had been, and I sat back in my bath chair, already feeling exhausted and we'd hardly got started yet.

'He was a good fellow. He was the best of fellows, in fact. I called him Mr Playfair. We disagreed on many matters, but he was in the right. He was able to look at a thing and see right down to the root. And when he looked at a problem, he wanted to pull it up by the root, and had the courage to try. And I hated that, because I was inclined to make no end of accommodations with the problem, you see? The more you thought about his ideas, the clearer they got; whereas, with most of us, the longer we cogitate on our positions, the muddier and dafter it all seems. Your dad wanted us miners to enter into combination, and to act with the one will. He was a leader in that regard, or he would have been, anyways.' This was the best I could manage, and I let Tom enjoy hearing this praise for a moment or two, before I added a necessarily grim epilogue. 'He would have been a leader, I say, but he was killed.'

Tom said that he'd been told only that his father died in a mining accident.

So I had to break the news that he'd been told a lie. His father hadn't died in any accident; he was murdered by Siskin. I heard him stop his drilling. When I looked up at him, his eyes were closed and his hands were fists. I said I was sorry, and that we were going to make Siskin pay for it.

I gave him as long as we could spare, but he was badly needed in the here and now, so I said, 'Are you a canny shot, then, young Tom?' and gestured towards the rifle strapped across his shoulder.

Tom didn't say anything, so I mithered him a bit, saying I bet he was a dead shot and that he was bound to sink a few bullets in the foul wolf's carcass before the night was out, and things like that.

He caught my drift, and smiled sadly and composed himself. 'Mr Malarkey, I am an abysmally bad shot. Siskin but lately introduced me to shooting. He himself does not care for the sport, and told me that he only attends hunts and shoots for business reasons. I marvelled when he said that, for I thought all rich men enjoyed killing birds and animals. But Siskin does his hunting in another way, doesn't he? Once you've hunted as a wolf, firing a gun must seem a poor substitute.'

'I reckon. Guns were his business, not his pleasure. But if you're so bad a shot, why . . . ?'

'Because it makes me *feel* safer to have a gun, even if I know that I'm not!' said Tom with a shrug. 'How are you with a rifle?'

'A deal worse than you, I reckon,' I said. 'I never so much as held a gun.'

Absalom rejoined us then, carrying an enormous quantity of black powder in hessian bags. My stomach turned over when I saw him carrying enough explosive to blow the hat off the house. Was this, I wondered, a fellow in which to place so large a trust? And then he let on that one of the bags contained a patented nine-pound Siskin conical exploding shell! What a bloody fool, I thought, to have brought a shell into the house when we had no gun with which to fire it; but I didn't say this to him.

Absalom placed the bags of powder beside me, with Tom and me imploring him to be as careful as his muckle gangly frame would allow, and then he loped off to the kitchen.

'I don't suppose we'll need any more black powder than is loose in these bags, but if we do require more, do you reckon we can get this shell opened safely and use what's in there?'

Tom looked aghast, and ceased drilling so that he could clearly explain. 'That would be a very bad idea, Mr Malarkey. Siskin's shells are not loaded with black powder, but with a blend – a patented blend! – of ingredients that he developed: two-thirds potassium chlorate and one-third red phosphorus, with a dash of sulphur and calcium carbonate thrown in. It's what they call unstable. Deliberately so. Transporting the shells is passing difficult, and firing them from a gun is work to suit the Devil, as Mr Kinrade, God rest his soul, discovered on the moors yesterday. Poor Joseph. Well, we mustn't risk carrying the shell back outside, so let's just put it somewhere out of the way. And, I would say, not too close to the fireplace, eh?'

It had been decided that Absalom and Laguiole would leave the poisoned meat in the Great Hall, for, howsoever the wolf made its way through the house, it would have to pass that way. And if, while doing this, Absalom should happen upon the beast then of course he'd have what I believe was his wish, to engage in combat with it, one-on-one. But – and this was the tenderest I ever saw the woman behave – Madame Laguiole had begged him to avoid this chance if at all possible. Siskin was an old wolf now, she'd reminded us, and much bigger than his son, for their wolf-forms never stopped growing, no matter how old they got.

Soon enough, the two of them would be setting off on their part of the mission, with their arsenic-salted meat. Laguiole knew the labyrinthine layout of the house better than anyone. Absalom knew it only when he was a wolf; as a man, he still lost his way chancetimes. But he would accompany her – 'for protection' he said again, very seriously – and, indeed, she'd accompany him for his protection, though I didn't say this in so many words. Madame Laguiole had been raised by pirates, had personally delivered a litter of wolf cubs, and had later instructed one of them to bite the Prince of Wales. The woman had led a textured life.

Once Absalom was gone, Tom resumed drilling, and asked again what my scheme with the black powder was.

'I'm hoping to lure the wolf into a trap.'

'A trap? I can't conceive of a snare or a gin strong enough to hold him . . .'

'I'm going to rig the library with black powder. The Knack will lure the beast: he will come to the bait. And, when he comes, we will light the fuses that I'm going to set, and then – somehow or other – we'll get ourselves out of the room and lock the beast inside. We might need to lock the first door to keep Siskin out until we're ready, but then, as soon as he comes crashing through, we light the fuses, then get ourselves past him into the antechamber, and then lock the library door behind us. There are but two windows here, and they look out onto a dead drop of two hundred feet down the brink onto the crag. Siskin is welcome to take his chances that way should he wish, but otherwise he's trapped in here—'

'Until he batters the door down,' cautioned Tom.

'We won't need to hold him for long. Just the length of a fuse. A minute or less.'

'Then we blow him up!' said Tom, brightening. 'We'll turn him into raspberry jam – ah, this is an excellent plan, Mr Malarkey. Though, I notice, you are a little vague on how the lighter of the fuses is to get around the wolf and back into the antechamber afore the roof comes down . . .'

Tom had identified a certain thinness, a certain softness

in my strategising, so I ignored this, and said, 'I'm not sure the blasts will kill the wolf, but they will certainly injure him. More to the purpose, in this higgledy-piggledy house the library is immediately below the dining room. If we can take out these pillars, or even some of them, then we'll have sufficiently undermined that enormous marble folly in the dining room above us. Even as 'tis, the structure cannot be sound. That mantelpiece must weigh in excess of ten ton. If we can bring down, say, eight or nine of these pillars, then that, I reckon, will do it. The structure is too femmor. The marble edifice will simply come crashing through the ceiling. *That* is how we'll make our raspberry jam.'

My plan was to bore two holes in each of the twelve wooden pillars that supported the ceiling. While Tom was doing this, I measured out portions of the black powder onto lengths of paper torn from the books all around us. I then rolled up the papers into tight cigarillos, poking one into each of the holes Tom had made. I reckoned that two such cigarillos should be enough to split a pillar, and either bring it down altogether or render it ineffectual. It was, of course, an improvised version of the blasting we used to do at Windy Top, and I was fighting to keep off thoughts of the Iron Devil and the last stand we made against the automata, lest sorrow distract me and I wound up killing my companions in the blast, as had happened at the Sill.

We had all but finished rigging up the fourth pillar, when we heard the sound of running and scrambling drawing near, accompanied by a heavy, rhythmic tattoo. Laguiole and Absalom came belting into the library and told us the news: the wolf had rejected the poisoned meat, having taken but a cursory sniff of it. Well, I'd jealoused that would happen, I thought. The two of them had barely escaped with their lives, and had put a number of locked doors between themselves and the wolf, only to hear them crack and splinter as the locks were burst out of each one in turn.

We got the first door shut and locked, so as to keep the wolf out for as long as we could. It wouldn't hold for long. I saw that we'd fall short of our target to rig at least eight or nine pillars, but there was nothing for it.

'He is possessed with a rage to hunt us down,' Laguiole said.

'It is the Knack he is hunting,' I said. 'We've come atween him and his quarry. I reckon he'll still relish the killing of us though but, if we give him the chance . . .'

And now the wolf reached the door we had just locked against him. He must have been butting it like a ram: he made it judder on its hinges with every blow. We had seconds now – no time to drill or set any more charge; we'd just have to see if bringing down four of the twelve would be enough. My thoughts flipped back and forth from a despairing hope that my plan would work to a triumphal pessimism that nothing would.

I'd one last idea – 'Belt and braces,' I said to myself – and hastily began pulling armfuls of books down from the shelves and piling them up in a heap in the middle of the floor. Tom was occupied checking and rechecking his rifle with trembling fingers, so I called on Absalom to help me, and we soon had the makings of a puritan bonfire. I asked

Laguiole to see if she could coax the hearth back to life, and she began to ask what my scheme was, but then she understood and knelt by the smouldering grate to see what she could do.

The door was holding, but we could hear it splintering each time the wolf thudded against it. I was sweating and panting with fear. You forget how physically unpleasant and painful an emotion fear is, until you're right there feeling it. In a moment, I knew, we'd hear the rattle and skitter of claws on the floor tiles, and then our nemesis would be through the antechamber and in the library with us, and, ready or not, our fates would be decided.

Laguiole had the fire in at last, and, after tossing another armful of books on our heap, I looked up – only to be confronted by the sight of the wolf stepping into the library. Its obscene size made my mind spin uncomprehendingly. It was staring at Tom, who was staring right back at it from where he stood in the centre of the room, his rifle trembling in his hands. The blood surged around my heart. The beast was bigger even than I remembered it being at Windy Top, and of a different and somehow more threatening shape and dimension than Absalom's wolf form had ever been. Had I been able to compare the two dispassionately, without being wrong of my mind with fear, I'd have found them to be quite distinct. Its legs were long, yet stouter and thicklier muscled than a wolf's ought to be, and when it swung its great head left to right, surveying us where we stood frozen in our attitudes about the heap of books, I thought it must surely have had the power to leap the length of the room at a bound. Its fur, which had grown longer since last I'd seen it in the laboratory, was of a whitish grey complexion. But I think, though I could itemise the wolf's appearance now, to do so would avail me little, for I would merely be describing a very massive and ugly dog. And the thing I saw in the library that day was not a dog. When a dog looks at you, even if it is an ill-favoured or a vicious specimen, there will be something imploring or else something noble in its gaze. Indeed, many dogs are able, as humans are not, to convey implorement and nobility at one and the same time. And the defining feature of this beast was an utter absence of either quality.

This was our chance. We would not get a second. I saw Tom slowly raise the rifle. The wolf tilted its head and sniffed at something, and I could see its destroyed left eye, the socket sunken and caked in blood. Now it sniffed the ground. Christ, I thought, could it smell the black powder? If so, would it remember what it was, or guess at what we were up to? Would it run off and escape? Would all our efforts come to nowt?

Tom cocked the rifle, and the wolf snapped its head up in a snarl that set its black lips shivering. Tom made a clucking sound with his tongue, whether out of nerves or to distract the beast I don't know, but it set the wolf's ears on the twitch. All this while, Laguiole, Absalom and me stood there, hovering like three lost ghosts. My senses seemed to be twangling along nerve-strings tuned too tight. And then Tom pulled the trigger.

We all jumped at the report – it is piercingly loud, to hear a rifle discharged indoors – and the shock of it seemed to set time ticking once more. What happened next came in a panicky rush, and it marched to the beat of the pulse that I felt in my chest and my throat and my ears. The wolf took the bullet, and yelped as it was knocked back – like it had been hoofed by a horse. But it rallied at once, and made a snarling leap at Tom. Tom got a second shot off, but it was wide, and the wolf was on him in the same instant. We scarce had time to breathe afore it had leapt upon him – and, without a sound, he fell.

Now Absalom took a run at the beast and, as Madame Laguiole cried out in anguish at the sight, he threw himself into a wrestle with it.

Our plan was falling apart from one moment to the next, but I had to press on nonetheless. Begging for Laguiole to help me, I started to light the fuses, and together we did it, pillar to pillar, one after another, as fast as we could. Soon they were fizzling and frittering. The fuses we'd had at Windy Top used to burn at all sorts of speeds: you never knew whether you had a fast-burning one or a slow-burning one until after you'd lit it, which added to the fearfulness of the operation. Well, if I'd imagined that the fuses made by Siskin, the great armaments manufacturer, would be more reliable, I was wrong. Some were slow and desultory, while others were sparkling away at an alarming rate.

'They're lit! They're lit! We must get out of here!' I roared, and the wolf, whether or no it was cognisant of our plan, instantly leapt away from Absalom and got atween us and the door. It stood there snarling, with thick strings of drool flying from its maw as its whirled its head about, so as to see us with its one remaining eye. 'We have seconds, now!' I screamed, looking at Poor Tom where he lay, face down. I think I was hoping to rouse him with my words, but he paid me no mind; nor did anyone else.

Absalom shook his head to clear it, and then once more hurled himself at his wolfish father. His face, I saw, was already masked with blood, but whether it was his, or his father's, or Poor Tom's, I couldn't tell.

There was an almighty crack as the first of the charges ignited, spewing out a jet of dust and splinters into the room. I'd never been so close to a blast, and I leapt at the sound with the force of a lifetime's habit, thinking my ears had burst and feeling a multitude of pricks and stings from the spelks and splinters that were flying through the air. I grabbed Laguiole's arm and tried, with all of my puny strength, to drag her from the room. She easily resisted me, and wouldn't tear her eyes from Absalom's struggles.

The second charge ignited with the same crack – the noise seemed to detonate inside your skull, making motion, speech or even thought impossible for a space of time. And then, with even louder reports, the third and fourth followed in swift succession; these were closer, coming from a nearer post, and, with them, the windows in the room blew out, either through the pressure of the air or due to flying debris. Their shattering made an almighty racket. If the noise was alarming to us, it seemed to affect the wolf even more: it convulsed at the sound of each of the charges, and, when the windows blew out, it jumped and, though it had Absalom's arm in its mouth at the time, released him and backed away, snarling and barking indiscriminately.

The first of the pillars now began to fall, moving, it seemed, impossibly slowly through the air. It crashed into a bookcase, and the books splashed out of the wall. The second pillar began to sway, and we heard two further charges ignite. I bellowed again that we had to get out of there afore the ceiling came down on us all, and Laguiole seemed to understand at last. She made for the door. Like me, she was trying to watch the progress of the tumbling pillars – the third one had come smashing to the floor at my side, missing me by the margin of an inch – and also trying to keep the beast in view, where it jumped and snarled at the sounds. I had not expected it to be so shaken, but was very glad of the chance. The noise bamboozled its brains.

Laguiole was helping Absalom, who was bleeding heavily. Together, they were at the door to the antechamber. I staggered toward the fireplace. My legs were giving way beneath me. My heart was in my throat. Laguiole shot me a look as if to ask what I was playing at, but I yelled at her to get Tom out of there, and then, when she merely looked at me in bafflement, I bellowed 'Go! Go!' – which she duly did.

Now a new sound was filling the room: an incredible groan, as of some great dragon awakening. It was the sound of many timbers being brought under an unbearable strain, as Brink House shifted its weight . . .

I reached directly into the fire – or, rather, the Knack reached into the fire: I saw its fingers amid the dancing flames as it grasped a burning log to lift it out, easy as if it were pinching a pear drop from a sweetie jar. Feeling no pain, I saw myself hoy the log onto the heap of books I'd piled up earlier. Then I hobbled towards Poor Tom, to see if I could drag him out of the room somehow, for all my feebleness.

And then many things happened very rapidly. As the great pyre of books took the flame, the wolf shook itself once more, to clear its head for the next round of combat. As I recollect it now, I can see the uppermost book's leather cover curl, much as the lips of the beast were curling as it growled afore making its final lunge at me. At this moment, I found myself hoisted up in the air; Absalom had charged back into the room to rescue me, and was now carrying me over his shoulder like a sack of spuds. But who, then, would save Poor Tom, who still lay prone and unmoving on the floor? I tried to cry out and ask this, but could not be heard above the roarings of the wind and the wolf.

Absalom crossed the room in a few mighty strides, scarcely an inch ahead of the wolf. Laguiole was holding the door to the antechamber open for us, and Absalom leapt through before Laguiole slammed it shut and shot the bolt home. We heard the wolf crash against the other side of it a moment later. I pictured the books' pages fluttering, as if being hastily read by a demon of fire, as Laguiole scrambled to lock the door. I pictured the books gathering into scrunched-up fire-roses, and I tried to tell my companions that we had to run, but couldn't find my voice. Within seconds, the heat of the book-pyre would intensify, and reach a certain nine-pound shell of an innovative, conical design, which was filled right up with Siskin's own patented blend of potassium chlorate, red phosphorus, sulphur and calcium carbonate – and then, as the Good Book has it, *Behold, how great a matter a little fire kindleth!*

Madame Laguiole shouted an instruction to Absalom, and, next thing I knew, I was hoisted back up on his shoulder and being carried at speed down hallways and through the broken doorframes the wolf had left in the wake of its progress. We'd reached the Great Hall when the explosion ripped through Brink House. We all went tumbling like skittles as the floor trembled beneath us, but Absalom picked me up as soon as he had his feet under him, and the three of us went scrambling on, as the house threw out many groans and cracks and sighs and rumbles, and spurted out dust from the cracks opening up in the ceiling, and generally gave every sign that it was about to collapse around our ears.

Laguiole bounding along on her great long legs, and Absalom keeping pace, we whistled down into the servants' quarters, past a row of a dozen bells that each had the name of a room printed beneath it – I remember, the bells were all ringing, for the whole house was shaking now, demanding its nonexistent servants look sharp – and then we burst through the servants' doorway and went scudding out onto the gravel courtyard just in time to see the great undoing begin.

It was a slower process than I'd expected. I'd thought the mass of marble would simply clap down in a single wallop onto the library below; but this was a gradual folding-in of the eastern half of the building, as if Brink House were some mortally wounded animal, gathering in a broken limb with its bones too shattered for mending. The roof ridge on that side, with all its treatments, crumpled and dropped, the spires of the gables disappearing – and then, from out of the goaf that was opening up, there came a sudden eruption, a great flourishing belch of red flame that must have been trapped in the structure, and it shot brandishing up to join the sunset. It seemed, as I gawped at it, that this flame resembled – just for a moment, you understand – another kind of bird, or some other creature of the air, the soul or *genius loci* of the house, ascending on vast, dissolving wings of sulphur, red phosphorus and the devil only knew what other combustibles.

We watched in awestruck silence, until at last it was over. The eastern side of the building was now entirely caved in, reduced to a heap of rubble: the highest points left standing were the diagonal jags of various half-forgotten staircases that had lurked in many a nook. The rubble smouldered here and there, but there were no flames; I suppose the fire had been smothered by the collapse of the structure. The other half of the building, the one nestled most deeply into the crag, still held together, for the moment anyway.

I looked again at the debris, and thought of Poor Tom Playfair – Thomas Plover, esquire – who lay buried somewhere under all of that rock. 'We must try to find Tom,' I announced, somewhat madly. 'We must rescue him.'

'But,' said Absalom wonderingly, 'I saw the wolf fall upon Tom, back in the library . . .'

I protested that I hadn't seen this happen, as if that was the decisive factor.

Absalom was puzzled by this, as any bairn is apt to be when they see a body suddenly depart from the path of logic and reason, so Madame Laguiole took over, and tried to make me see sense. 'You may not have seen it, Monsieur Malarkey, but Absalom did, and that is enough for me.'

I merely shook my head and repeated that we must try to find him, that there might yet be hope.

'No one could have survived this, monsieur. There can be nothing left of him to find . . .' said Laguiole gently.

'We must try. I've lost one marra to such a blast, and I left him where he fell, and if I do so again, I'll not can forgive myself. We must try.'

This was the very folly of grief, and I think Laguiole and even Absalom knew it, but when they saw that I was set on digging alone if they didn't join me, they tagged along to help me, for it is a difficult thing to negotiate with the shock and mourning of another person, and even so flinty a body as Madame Laguiole might try to placate a soul in such a state.

So we set to work. We found a pair of pickaxes and a shovel in the outbuilding – it seemed almost comical that it should yet be standing, when its vastly bigger neighbour was in so ruinous a state – and we plouted up the hill of rubble to where we thought the library would be, buried under the dining room with its vast marble edifice, and the whole other storey of servants' rooms and the like, and also the remains of the roof.

It was a hopeless cause, but our brains were jangled from our near escape, and we hardly knew what we were doing. So we began howking up rubble. I did so very ineffectually, as I had to stop and lean upon my pickaxe so frequently, but I found the labour reassuring in its familiarity. I'd been asking these motions of my muscles all of my life, and, though I was grown feeble now, there's benefit to be felt in doing the work you know best. Madame Laguiole made her way here and there, rolling some of the debris away without enthusiasm. Only Absalom took to the task very well, being possessed of an uncanny strength; he made swifter progress than Laguiole and I put together and timesed by ten. It seemed no time till he was tossing books as well as bricks aside, so we could tell he was now excavating what remained of the library. Burnt bits of paper hung in the air and drifted like black snow. At length, Absalom struck upon a great slab of marble, a chunk of the massive mantlepiece that had brought the house down, and which now looked very like a sarcophagus. Perhaps that was why we all felt it likely to contain Tom's body. In any case, Laguiole and I came over to help Absalom excavate it.

We cleared it of debris. I think there was an unspoken agreement between the three of us that, if this tomb were empty, so to speak, then we would call off our digging and searching, and let the dead stay buried. There was a large piece of masonry at one end of it – the rock that must be rolled away, indeed. Laguiole and I used our pickaxes to paze it away, and watched it tumble off down into a crater in the debris. I peered into the gloomy interior, looking for

I knew not what . . .

The wolf's head surged out of the darkness, its maw opening ever wider as it took a great lunging bite of air where my head had been the moment afore. I shrieked and stumbled back, nearly overbalancing and rolling down after the piece of masonry we'd just shifted. Now the wolf pulled itself out of its marble sarcophagus. Its fur had been burnt off, exposing blackened limbs corded with muscle; one of its back legs was broken and trailed behind it, and it was moving more slowly than afore. Its remaining eye was wild, dying, livid.

I raised the pickaxe above my head, and – drawing on a lifetime's experience with the tool, and on every ounce of memory I had stored in my muscles for how best to aim and angle the thing – I brought it down on the wolf's head, looking to split it clean through the crown.

And I missed. The beast simply shunted its huge head aside like swinging a lantern on a pike, and I saw my pick fall shy of its mark by inches.

I had a moment in which to register an extremity of frustration and rage at my inadequacies and infirmities – and then I realised that, although I'd missed the wolf's head, my pick had found its paw, and had staked it to the timber beam on which it stood.

With an almost human sense of outrage, the wolf howled in my face: a noise so piercingly loud that I dropped the pick and covered my ears – and that was when the wolf saw its chance. It made one final, savage lunge, aiming for the Knack, looking to bite it off and gulp it down, and thus be joined with it, once and for all. I felt its teeth sink into my flesh.

In that moment, time stopped, and I momentarily fell into one of my fits. I'd a vision of a world in which Siskin won. I saw the wolf rip the Knack free of my flesh, and swallow it, becoming one with it, becoming one with Mithras Sol Invictus. I saw the beast stand over me and throw back its head. I heard its howl of victory. I saw my death, lacking all dignity or mercy. I saw the deaths of Laguiole and Absalom, likewise. I saw our unburied corpses atop a hill of smouldering rubble, the corbies circling high above us as the terrible new day dawned.

But, by whatsoever fluke of fate, the wolf's jaws had closed not on the Knack, but on my old, crabbed, half-withered hand. The bones snapped quick as dry twigs, and I screamed. I'd spent my life, it seemed, having this hand tortured, and I don't know how it was that I could yet feel such pain in it, but somehow I could. Pain never tires. Most steadfast of companions, it will hold out with you, nor ever stop for breath, until the end. Without releasing its grip, the wolf shook its great head, wrenching me off my feet. I felt the sinews at my wrist giving way, as my old, long-suffering hand began to be uprooted.

My saviour arose: Absalom, wielding a shovel. Standing there, high up on the ruinous remains of human and nonhuman vanity, his feet planted wide apart, swinging his shovel like a scythe, he was become Death indeed: the great leveller, who makes all odds even. He swung the shovel in a great arc and brought it down like an axe on the wolf's neck. The jolt when the shovel connected entirely severed my hand, and I roared in pain.

I thought Absalom must surely have sliced the wolf's head clean from its damned carcass, but no, he was only Absalom, not Death indeed; and he was armed only with a shovel, not with the King of Sardinia's ox-lopping sword. The wolf was yet standing – frozen in place, it seemed, but yet alive . . .

Absalom swung the shovel again and again. The wolf's head remained stubbornly attached to its body, but, at last, the monster's legs buckled and it folded into a heap of guts at my feet, its neck broken. Its burnt, blistered flesh, scorched of fur, looked humanoid – or, at least, as close to human as it had any right to look – and my old, maimed hand was still clamped, dripping, atween its teeth. The Whindale Wolf was dead, but it had died with a mouth full of meat and blood, which is surely how the beast would have wanted to go.

15
an extract: *op. cit.*

[...] We are nearing the end of our tale, ladies and gentlemen. The Mithraic cult has been obliterated, and, soon, the Roman Empire itself will fall, and all trace of the cult fade from memory ... So we have been told. But my new working hypothesis is this: to name a thing is a powerful magic. Perhaps, after naming a demon, we can never entirely exorcise it. Perhaps, in naming it, we help to create it out of the inchoate forces that would otherwise flow through and around our world without ever crossing the horizon of the perceptible. Perhaps the entity that learned to answer to the name of Mithras, though it could not be destroyed outright, grew weak without a human host and without worshippers and believers. Perhaps, by degrees, it slunk back into the earth to become once more a *genius loci* of Northalbion, so that the land remained latent with its weird power.

The Knack lay undiscovered for fifteen centuries: a talismanic distillation of the Mithraic rituals, and the device by which the entity could manifest once again. It was the philosopher's stone, able to transmute one thing into another, one form of energy into another. But I think the Romans did well to bury it. They realised their mistake, in conceiving of an otherworldly force in worldly terms. One wishes to know, when entering into any combination, what the other party stands to get out of the bargain; but it would be hubris to think you understood the point of view of a demon. And hubris is how a demon will undo you.

Despite this, Mithraic worship did not die out at the end of the fourth century after all. The case of one family in particular has recently come to my attention, a family that continued to worship the old god, hoping – across many generations – to 'change the bargain' they had long ago made with another power altogether, and free themselves from one of its conditions. This family honoured Mithras in a way they thought he'd understand: by manufacturing engines of war. My investigation is underway, and I hope to have publishable findings soon, but it is true that, at present, I am relying on anecdotal evidence, and from a source that some would consider dubious . . . certainly, he is one of the strangest and most trying old fellows I ever met, and if his name shares its initials with Claudius Marcellus, I would like to assure you that this is mere coincidence. But then – who knows? – coincidence may be Mithras' way of remaining anonymous [. . .]

16

The Prodigal

I don't remember exactly what happened next, but I must have been carried back inside the rickety workshop, which was still intact, and Laguiole must have given me laudanum: I think she kept a bottle on her at all times, either for the shifting-pains of Absalom or Master Siskin, or perhaps so that she herself had ready access to oblivion. Night had fallen. I drifted in and out of consciousness, as Laguiole dressed my hand – again! – by candlelight. Absalom talked to me. He didn't seem to mind whether I was fully awake or no. Having so little time to have his say, but three days a month at most, he couldn't be fussy about whether his audience was sufficiently attentive.

When he was a wolf, I gathered, he remembered being a man as you or I might remember a dream; and then, when he became a man, he was as a fellow who wakes to a coolness, to a silence, to a clarity like that of a blank canvas, upon which the most guilty remembrance is suddenly painted. How painful it is to think remorsefully of our most low and bestial behaviour, to see it again with human eyes when the blood is cool – but such was his wretched life, month in, month out, under his mistress moon, mute arbitress of more than tides!

He had met his father – met, that is, when both parties were on two legs – only rarely, when the shift had come especially early for the one or especially late for the tother. Then indeed they were brought face to face, like accuser and accused under the old Roman law. His father thought him a pure idiot. Now, it's true that Absalom was childlike, but Siskin was being unfair in this regard, as in every other. Like any motherless child, Absalom understood more of this miserable world than he was credited with; like any child with an evil father, he'd learned that concealment was a good policy.

Now he had disowned the name Absalom and wished to be known henceforth as Adam. Very good, thought I, for his namesake, the first man, was another such who never had an infancy, being brought into the world full-grown with his manly limbs unused, his strength untested; and he, too, came into his own through an act of disobedience against his father. From Absalom – *Adam*, I should say – from Adam's point of view, his father had been his gaoler. In itself, this wasn't so offensive to his sensibility, but his father's plan to divert his line into a new vessel, eliminating the need for him to keep his true-born dog-son alive at all, was unforgivable. Apart from owt else, this would have complicated their relationship, since, in executing his plan, the father would in a sense become the younger man. This is not fitting behaviour for a creature as invested in pack hierarchy as a wolf.

I listened to him, and talked to him of the Lord knows what, all through the night, as Adam slowly shifted back into the guise of a wolf. His voice grew less and less distinct as his neck lengthened, and his lips slowly darkened, and a muzzle rose out of his human face – slowly, imperceptibly, but surely as a lump of dough will prove. While all of this was happening, he lost more and more of his powers of speech, but Laguiole sat with us and, like the doting mother of an infant, she was able to translate his words for my ears long after they'd passed beyond my ken. At last, there was nothing of him that was not wolf, and everything of him that was, and, as he lay there with his head in Laguiole's lap, I could but guess at whether he yet knew me.

Dawn had given way to morning proper. I walked over and opened the workshop door, and surveyed – not the apocalyptic frescos painted on the walls of the Great Hall, but the world itself: first, the great heap of rubble in jagged silhouette, and then, beyond it, the vastness of the moors that would outlive all of our structures and strategies. What prideful folly could ever persuade us otherwise? I thought of Poor Tom, and how I was looking out on a day he hadn't lived to see. The last thing he heard would have been Laguiole and I screaming our curses. The last thing he saw would have been a mutant, one-eyed wolf. The last thing he smelt would have been his own blood. I thought these grim thoughts even as I looked out at the beauty of the morning, and I thought how all of our trials and miseries must take their place in this world, with all its unexpected sweetnesses. A world of feelings fought inside me.

'Monsieur,' said Laguiole, 'I see that you walk now, quite easily, without the stick. How is this possible?'

I looked at her wondering face, and then looked down at my feet where they were planted on the floor, and then had an uncertain moment where I thought I'd topple, but no, I stayed upright. I took another few steps, and all was well. 'I don't know,' I said. 'I feel strangely refreshed. Rejuvenated, almost. As though I've shook off a long illness.' I stood on one leg, and smiled at Laguiole as if expecting her to say 'Well done, Monsieur!' – which, of course, she did not say.

'We have killed the wolf,' said Laguiole. 'We are free of it – perhaps, as a curse may be lifted, this is why . . . ?'

'Aye, maybes. Or maybes it's the Knack. I had my old hand bit off, so now I'll be keeping the Knack. And I suppose it'll be keeping me. I'll can walk home, now, anyway. I'll can walk back to Whindale.' It was just as well, I thought, for the alternative was not attractive: it might have been that a French-Algerian woman, accompanied by a wolf and pushing an old scab in a bath chair, would not have received the warmest of welcomes. Whindale folk were a narrow-minded bunch. If they haven't changed, they still are.

Since I was up and walking, the three of us took ourselves outside. With our backs to the ruins of Brink House and the law spread before us, the air tasted of possibility, as it can do on a summer morning when you're up with the larks. I thought how strange it was that I now thought only of returning to Whindale. I had longed to leave it for so long, and I could not expect a friendly welcome from a soul who lived there, so why return now, when I scarce had a reason to do so? Well, as Mr Montaigne said, 'Where I seek myself, I find not myself; and I find myself more by chance than by the search of mine own judgement.'

I asked Laguiole if she knew where she and Adam would go next, and she shook her head. Truth to tell, I think she had an idea or two, some long-held dreams of where she'd go if she ever escaped Siskin's vile influence, but she wanted to keep those plans to herself. I felt our alliance loosening: it had been forced upon us, and it had served its purpose, and now, although the old mistrust would not entirely return, the union would not survive. I could not resent this then, nor can I now, but I wished to salute it somehow or other.

'Together, we have seen the strangest days I ever hope to live through. You have my deepest admiration, Madame Laguiole.'

The good woman thought for a moment afore replying. 'You asked, some time ago, for my true given name. I did not tell you then, but I will tell you now: it is Safia Saifi.'

'Safia Saifi,' I repeated carefully, with a nod. 'It is an honour.'

'It is *not* an honour,' said Safia Saifi smartly. 'I no longer wish to be known – by anyone, and even in their memory – as Madame Laguiole.'

I said that was fair enough, and she gave a token of

having something further to say, but in fact her only words were 'Good-bye, Caleb Malarkey.'

And so they went their way together, Safia Saifi and Adam. I watched them go, the last of the morning mist creeping daintily about their feet as they walked out across the gravel towards the bridleway, with no possessions and all the world before them. Where they would settle, and what the nature of their accommodations were or would be, was for themselves alone to decide. There are mysteries in this life that I pray God it never falls to me to violate.

After some searching, I found a wheelbarrow in the stable block, and wondered if it might have been the very one in which I'd been brought to Brink House, and this set me to remembering my old marra the quill-driver, who was now another soul buried under the remains of Brink House, and there he'd have to stay, alas. I wheeled the barrow to where the wolf lay dead, and then I had the devil of a time trying to heave the sack of guts in. It was going to more than fill the barrow. I eventually decided to adapt my plans, and found a tenon saw in the outbuilding. Holding the wolf's head steady atween my knees, I managed to saw through the beast's neck where Absalom had been whacking it with the shovel. Once I'd sawn the head off, I lobbed it in the barrow and threw a rug over it to keep it from prying eyes on the road, for I didn't know how long my journey was going to take me. The barrow seemed manageable enough when I first tested it, but of course the wound where the wolf had bitten off my old hand soon began to bleed afresh, and soak right through my bandage. Even apart from the wound, I was still in a weakened way, and my arms and shoulders began to ache, and afore long my entire back joined in the complaining. It was a terrible long trek to Whindale, and that's where I was headed. I needed to transport evidence of the wolf, for I'd a scheme in mind.

After half a mile, I had to stop. I had knewed it would be difficult, but this was too much for me. I left the barrow by the roadside, and walked all the way back up the hill to Brink House. In the workshop, I found Absalom's collar and leash hanging on a hook, and I took them back with me to the barrow. Now, it shames me to say this, but at that point I slipped the collar around my neck and tied the leash to the right-side handle of the barrow. This meant I could take the weight of it with a combination of my left hand and the collar around my neck. Unbecoming for a fellow to yoke his own neck! But I'd never have managed my load otherwise, and so I continued on my wobbly way.

It was a day of days. The sun was bright and the air was warm, and there was a single vaporous vestige of cloud in the sky, like a flaw in a sapphire. The heather was in flower, and the law was all a-shimmer with varieties of purple, along with the yellow flowers of the whin flackering in the breeze; seeing that colour again, I thought back on the ugly encrustations that had adorned the walls of the Sill, and it seemed to me that this flower was in fact quite a different shade, and so I tried to unhinge the association. The whin flowers had enriched the air with a smell like honey.

Like a pair of black gloves tied together, a peewit fluttered up and tumbled hither and yon on the breeze, as though it had learned how to fly by watching cabbage whites – as, for owt I know, it had. It kept a few hundred yards abreast of me, rolling over in the air like a dusty-foot, thinking all the while that it was leading me away from its nest – and no doubt it esteemed itself very wise for doing so. And no less wise do all our schemes appear to us, I thought. My adventures had turned me into a philosopher, evidently.

As I tramped the old road home, I seemed to be lured on continually by my shadow that loomed hugely afore me, and I got to thinking that perhaps it was not merely my shade that I saw, but the very spirit of contradiction that had held such a sway over my life – but I knew not whether I was then hunting it down in defiance or following on still in thrall to its contrary counsel. I was so practised at making things difficult for myself that to do so now would be the easiest option. There was nowt for me to do but keep to the road, and trust that it would lead me home.

By the time I arrived in Whindale Town, flies in enormous numbers had gathered over my barrowload and were buzzing in my sweating face, fit to send me demented. Indeed, I nearly felt the old anger picking up inside me, but no, I kept it at bay, for I'd had enough of such foolishness. The collar had bitten into the nape of my neck and I knew there would be blood trickling down my back amongst the sweat.

The town was deserted, and I had the eerie sensation of being the only man left alive in the world, for it had been highly unusual not to have seen a soul upon the road all this way. But presently, it occurred to me that maybes this was a

Sunday, and everyone in their various churches, so I headed for Reverend Wrather's old preaching box that Mam and Mop had favoured. I was staggering along very slowly now, feeling weak and coggly.

Here was the familiar church, staring out with its sleepy-eye windows, unadorned with any bonny coloured glass; and here was the lintel with the old line:

> *Ye are a chosen generation, a royal priesthood,*
> *a holy nation, a peculiar people.*
> 1 Peter, 2:9

I parked the barrow at the door, but the knot where I had tied the leash to the handle was now pulled too tight to unpick, so I was stood there a minute, bent over my barrowload, gnawing at it with my teeth until I could loosen the damned thing, hoping that nobody would come out and find me in such a predicament.

Inside, a service was underway, and I could hear a voice I knew, albeit grown a little reedy now, preaching familiar hellfire. Given all I'd seen since I last visited this preaching box, I found the Reverend Wrather's words to be closer to horseradish than hellfire. But, as I've said, I'd a scheme in mind. I approached the church door, hearing his words boom out, '*Here* is the valley of *Gehenna*! Here is the *Topheth*, where the heathen sacrifice their children unto *Moloch*! *Here* is the cloud without rain!—'

The church door had always used to require a hefty shove to get it moving, and I put my shoulder to it without thinking twice, but evidently it had been filed down at some point during my wanderings, as it now burst open, so that I entered the church with something of a crash, and all heads turned at once to see me. There was a collective gawp and gasp, and my frightful appearance drew shrieks from a number of the womenfolk. My hair had only just begun to grow back, in odd patches here and there – and it was coming in white as snow, as you see it now – and I was skin and bone, trembling with exhaustion and heat, with about a thousand flies about my head, and a red right hand, and a bloody collar around my neck. I'd have been an alarming sight, even if you weren't a Primitive Methodist.

'Is Mr Caleb Malarkey still a pariah here?' I asked, having found a voice from somewhere, and I was pleased to see that even Reverend Wrather was at a loss for words by way of an answer to my question. He had been old when I left Whindale; he was ancient now. 'It has been fifteen years, brethren – long as Jacob toiled for Leah, long as then he toiled once more for Rachel, and then some – but I have returned!' I let them cogitate upon that for a moment while I took an uncertain step into the church, which felt splendidly cool to me; in truth, I lacked the energy to speak and walk at the same time, but every face appeared very amazed, and I was in no danger of being interrupted. I let them get a look at me, and then I said, 'Yes, I have returned, and am come to tell you that I have seen the cloud without rain, and it is no more and no less than a mass of nasty bluebottles, and I have followed it for many a mile. Now, come and see, for I have brought you a thing that I would not besmirch this house by dragging indoors. I am like the prodigal son, am I not? Long lost in the wilderness of the world, but now returned. And I've brung you a peace offering, in hopes of your forgiveness and that. It was an evil thing in life, but now it's good and dead. Come and see: I've brought you the head of the Whindale Wolf!'

My bringing home of the loathed beast was accepted as a fitting sign of repentance – they took me back in, anyway – and the whole town turned out to build a bonfire and burn it. To this very day, they mark the anniversary by burning a vast wooden replica of a wolf, and they tell stories about it to scare the bairns, who grow up to think it all a nonsense. Once they'd took me back, I recommenced going to church, and even held the collection box, doing so for quite a while, until the Reverend Wrather finally burnt himself out and died. They found a replacement for him, but by then the lead-mines was all worked out, and a lot of folk had gone off to find a living elsewhere, and many of the Primitive Methodist preaching boxes was closing and all, so I gave it up.

Whindale had changed during my long absence. All of my old marras had long since left to seek Spanish silver or California gold, or for some such far-flung place. They'd had little choice but to leave, because they'd been blacklisted by Siskin for striking. All the mine owners had clubbed together in a combination, though they would not have used this word, and they had agreed to turf out any strikers and disallow them employment at any other mine. They reckon it had been Siskin's initiative. It smacks of him, all right. As soon as I knew that my marras were gone, never to return, I began to miss them, despite all that had occurred. A very foolish feeling, but there it is.

I learned that Mam had given up the ghost soon after I left. She'd always said that her side of the family didn't make old bones. Well, my hope then and now is that she was permitted entry to that Heaven she was so looking forward to. I wouldn't begrudge her it, for, truly, she believed in eternity more than she ever believed in life. And Mop, they said, was yet alive, as far as anyone knew, but had gone a-wandering: she'd contracted the preaching fever after Mam died and had made a great success of it, by all accounts, finding her way onto the Oldshield circuit, and thence further north to Lenterencleugh, Carrickshield and beyond. She never came back to Whindale, and is surely dead and gone by now; for all I know, she never got wise to the fate of her brother.

As for me, once I'd given up the churchgoing, I found myself ever more attracted to the idea of having a go at painting. That might sound strange, but it's what happened. Maybe it was seeing all them frescos at Brink House put the notion into my head. I don't know how else it got there. Anyways, I gave it a try, and found I'd a turn for it. Really, I'd never been happier than I was just painting the wildflowers and birds. It has become my life's fascination, and I've made hundreds of paintings now, and I dedicate each one to Coventina, the old goddess of the waterways and forces here in Northalbion. Long ago, she was evicted by Mithras, the lord-god-king of bum-bailiffs, and Coventina's Well, which had been a holy place once upon a time, wound up getting a Mithraic temple and then a bloody great church built on top of it – so her and me have two old adversaries in common anyway.

I suppose you'll be wanting to know what happened next, and how I ended up here at the Wintergreen clinic of all places, but that's another story. The long and the short of it is, I kept bachelor's hall. I never cared to marry. I did nowt but paint and paint for years and years on end, and stayed chaste as a fish. Dr Wintergreen reckons my paintings 'celebrate the female principle', and says that this is something I'd a proclivity to skip hitherto. Well, maybes they do and maybes they don't, but even if I celebrate it, I never felt inclined to partake of it. An uplands woman isn't worth house-room: if she's spent her life out in the fields all day picking stones, she'll know nowt of housework and have no conversation. Besides that, men and women live disagreeable; maybes it was ever thus, but there's nowt like poverty to make them quarrel, and I didn't want to bring a woman into misery. And much less a gaggle of bairns, for what if one of them turned out like me, and found it var-nigh impossible to adjust to the simple realities of human nature? What would I have said when this dawned on them, and they first tasted the horror that belongs to their lot? Would I have told them not to fret, that the savour would sweeten in time? Or would I have been honest, though they would hate me for it? No, no: no bairns for me!

Anyways, Dr Wintergreen reckons I've got to keep up the painting for the benefit of my health. I'll never know whether I'd have become a painter by my own hand, so to speak, or if it's entirely the doing of the Knack, for that's what's holding the brush, after all. But I don't worry about such things. All in all, my new hand worked out canny well, and soon grew to be much the same size as its older brother, and within a year or three it was nearly as battered and blistered, for when I wasn't painting, I'd be topping beets or catching moles or what-have-you to make a sort of living. To look at it now, you'd never guess its strange history. The scar from where the wolf bit off my old hand has faded, and only this glib mark on the back of my wrist remains, see? If you didn't know better, you might think that I'd once been manacled. You might even think that I was just another convict shipped in chains to Australia to labour under the sun, and that's how I lost those fifteen years!

Mr Montaigne reckons we are not born for our particular, but for the public good, and when I see such a sentiment written down I feel myself the better half of half-persuaded; but then I remember that Mr Montaigne never had the opportunity to meet me. And when Erasmus says that all blokes forge their fortune, I wonder did Erasmus ever see inside a forge? Did he ever so much as singe his eyebrows working the bellows on his own hearthside? And if not, what's it to me what such a fellow thinks?

Today though but, having reached such an extremity of age – and after looking and talking like an old gadgie for so much of my life; indeed, ever since getting out of the Sill I've been like a winter spuggy that chirps on incessantly of things he saw a lifetime ago in the spring – I'm being looked after very well. Dr Wintergreen has been very kind, and very attentive in listening to my story. It's he who encouraged me to write it all down, and says he's going to have it published by and by. As a wise woman once said, it can make all the difference in the world to get a thing written down.

We've spent a good while in each other's company, now, haven't we, you and I? And I've made my story part of yours. Like newlyweds holding hands in the dark, I reckon we're all but united, so. And that's all the Knack ever was, as I see it: the power of union. A combination, as Mr Playfair would surely have said. It's time I let you go. But you'll remember Caleb Malarkey, and I reckon from time to time you'll think of Safia Saifi and Adam, and Poor Tom Playfair and the Iron Devil and all. Certainly, you'll never forget the Wolf of Whindale. Even now though but, there are some who say no, there was never any such thing.

Glossary

bait: food, especially a packed lunch
blowsabella: an unkempt woman
Bore da, ffrind, sut wyt ti: 'Good morning, friend, how are you?' (Welsh)
bowk: vomit
buddle: apparatus for washing ore
bum-bailiff: a bound bailiff, i.e. one empowered to collect debts and/or arrest debtors
burn: a stream
can: often used as a double modal verb
canny: a marvellously elastic word; the three primary meanings in the present text are 'considerable', 'pleasant' and 'quite'
cavilled: to be allotted a place to work in a mine (pron. *kyeh-*vild, emphasis on first syllable)
cawk: sulphate of baryta (heavy spar)
cenfigenus: 'jealous' (Welsh)
chancetimes: occasionally
chats: galena and rock that has been broken up on the *knockstone* ready for the *hotching* tubs

chokedamp: air containing an excess of carbon dioxide or carbon monoxide; also called *stithe*
church bell: an excessively talkative woman
cobbing: using a hammer to separate spar from lead ore
coggly: sick, faint
dead work: the rate of pay for excavating in search of a lead seam, determined by the distance dug
deek: look
Dies Natali Invictus Solis: the Birthday of Mithras Sol Invictus; lit. 'the birthday of the unconquered sun' (Latin)
dowk: part of the waste contents of a vein: a brown, friable, soft soil
dunch: to bump into something or someone
dusty-foot: acrobat
ex homine commutatus nuper in lupus: 'he was lately changed from a man into a wolf' (Latin)
fathom-tale: another term for *dead work*
femmor: frail
fiddle-duffers: swindlers who impersonate drunk musicians
firedamp: methane, the most combustible of the gases produced by coal mining
flackering: flickering, shimmering
flannel: exaggeration, bluff
fopdoodle: a fool
Fy duw: 'My God' (Welsh)
gadgie: a man, usually an old man
galloway: a breed of pit pony, but also used generally of any pony

get: git
ghee: huff
gizened: parched
gledge: glance
gliff: fright
grundy: granulated pig iron
gubbin: ironstone
hacky: dirty (usually combined as 'hacky-dirty')
higgle: to fatten up
hirpling: stumbling, limping
hockering: laughing in an unpleasant way
hotch: separating ores by using a sieve agitated up and down in water
hoy: throw
impittent: impudent, rude (emphasis on the second syllable)
jailcrop: shaved hair (with an implication that this is because of head lice)
Jenny Howlet: an owl
jowling: tapping the wall with a stick, either to check its condition or to send a signal
keek: peek
keep toot: keep a lookout
knockstone: a stone bench upon which lead ore is broken up ready for the *hotching* tubs
laidly: loathsome
law: uplands
lop: a lop is a flea, and to be as fit as one is proverbial
lowse: the end of a shift of work
lucifer: a match that could be struck on any rough surface

lupus non timet canem latrantem: 'a wolf is unafraid of a barking dog' (Latin)
magsmen: small-time swindlers
marra: friend, workmate
mither: to coax
the morn: tomorrow (but not necessarily tomorrow morning)
the morn-morn: tomorrow morning
mounging: complaining
muckle: very, huge
noli me tangere: 'touch me not' (Latin); see John, 20:17
nithered: very cold
paze: to lever something up
plouting: walking with difficulty
ragging: the process of separating ores by washing on an inclined plane
rattlescawp: a naughty child
shaddering: the process of breaking ore with hammer, so that it can be put through a crushing mill
shieling: originally a small drystone hut, a temporary shelter for shepherds; later used figuratively
shofulmen: dealers in forged coins
smiddum: the small particles that pass through the sieve during *hotching*
solve et coagula: 'dissolve and coagulate' (Latin), a saying associated with the processes of alchemical purification, and the words tattooed on the arms of Baphomet in Eliphas Levi's 1856 illustration
soss: to lap at water
spalling: breaking up ore with a five-pound sledgehammer

sparty: marshy

spuggy: sparrow

stithe: air containing an excess of carbon dioxide or carbon monoxide; also called *chokedamp*

swins: swings or curves

tchew: an awkward, difficult experience: 'I've had a tchew of a day'

thill: clay

trahor fatis: 'I am driven by fate' (Latin)

turn-bat: a wooden stick used in turning the tongs that hold a steel bar under a hammer

twisty/twisting: peevish, complaining

var-nigh: very nearly

wyrm: a dragon in the form of a great worm

yark: to punch, or to push or pull violently

yon time o' night: a very late hour of the night

Acknowledgements

Love and thanks above all to Cat. I would also like to thank Leonora Craig Cohen and Alba Ziegler-Bailey for their invaluable editorial advice and support, and Jessica Bullock at the Wylie agency.

Dr Wintergreen's lecture on Mithraic worship is a mixture of historical record and fiction. Everything concerning the Knack is fiction. Wintergreen's theory that images of the Mithraic tauroctony form a star map, found on pages 68-70, is indebted to David Ulansey's *The Origins of the Mithraic Mysteries* (Oxford University Press, 1989).

Master Siskin's claims for the moral benefits of war, found on pages 230–231, are closely modelled on the arguments put forward by Sir William Armstrong. Some of the details of Siskin's guns are drawn from Armstrong's innovations, and Brink House is partly modelled on Armstrong's house Cragside.

Some of the rhetoric in Reverend Wrather's sermon against scabs and blacklegs is based on an actual speech delivered in Swinhope Chapel during the Great Strike of March 1849 by the Chairman of the lead miners, as detailed in George Dickinson's *Allendale and Whitfield: historical and descriptive notices of the two parishes* (1884).

Dean Dudley's opinion that the best way to relieve the poverty of the lead miners is to hope for a more buoyant market echoes a sentiment expressed by the engineer and later mining agent Thomas Sopwith in *An Account of the Mining Districts of Alston Moor, Weardale and Teesdale in Cumberland and Durham* (1833).